Merlin's Charge
Peter Joseph Swanson

Stonegarden.net Publishing
http://www.stonegarden.net

Reading from a different angle.
California, USA

Merlin's Charge Copyright © 2009 Peter Joseph Swanson

ISBN: 1-60076-142-9

This is a work of fiction. Names, characters, places and incidents are products of the author's imagination or are used fictitiously and are not to be construed as real. Any resemblance to actual events, locales, organizations or persons, living or dead, is entirely coincidental.

StoneGarden.net Publishing
3851 Cottonwood Dr.
Danville, CA 94506

All rights reserved. Printed in the United States of America. No part of this book may be used or reproduced in any manner whatsoever without written permission, except in the case of brief quotations embodied in critical articles and reviews. For information address StoneGarden.net Publishing.

First StoneGarden.net Publishing paperback printing:
August 2009

Visit StoneGarden.net Publishing on the web at
http://www.stonegarden.net.

Cover art and design by Peter Joseph Swanson

Many thanks to my editor,
Shirley Ann Howard
~PJS~

Chapter One

Nimm woke up to the sound of a faraway bell. "*Come!*" it ordered her. "*The tree will sup your blood. Come!*"

She shuffled out of her wattle and daub roundhouse. "Aye. I come. Are you a banshee? Am I to die?"

"*Nay. You're not worth forewarning. Stop thinking. Come.*"

Nimm noticed the images of sad children in the trees. They were like limp Yuletide donations. "Rafe?" she called to her son. "Rafe! Oh no! I'm going to die! You'll soon be an orphan!"

"*Stop thinking of him. Come this way... to the Demon Bell!*"

"I won't come! If I do, soon this village will be empty! We'll have *all* wandered off, every last one of us!"

"*Stop thinking about it. Come!*"

With the next peal of the bell Nimm marched for hours through the lands of the fearsome knights until she was at a seashore. Past its strait was an island lit by glowing emerald mists.

The bell coaxed from it.

"Aye. I come." Then Nimm's foot crunched clumsily down into a small hawthorn bush twisted above clover and pungent burning mint. She screamed while her foot clamped as if in a bear's jaw.

The island started calling more urgently. But Nimm only stared, unable to obey the bell until the entire night passed and pink light sluggishly poked through the branches. At the warble of a wren the spell broke. She fell out of the bush into the salty sand, snoring wildly as her lungs fought desperately for the morning air.

* * * * *

In the communal barn, Mother Hubbard awoke early as always. She gingerly put dozens of goose eggs in her apron, and then she started a small fire in the greensward for them to cook.

Priest Owen greeted her. "Look at the eggs for our orphans! But where are the geese? Where do these eggs come from?"

Mother Hubbard shrugged.

Priest Owen raised an eyebrow. "How odd that this should happen every day, day in and day out, that they only leave us their eggs. Do you have any idea where the geese hide all day long?"

Mother Hubbard quickly slipped her feet into her worn wooden clogs. "Eee-*ucht!* And you'll only get *one* egg today. You won't eat all the children's food."

"I need food… to keep up my strength… to work for God."

"Rotten eggs!" Mother Hubbard looked back and forth at the empty crumbling huts around the greensward. Some had no thatch left at all. "It's all rot!"

"Your neck has fallen," Priest Owen observed. "Every morning you seem older. You look older every time you have the eggs. If I was a silly pagan I would think that bringing us eggs is making you old."

She ignored him. As her fire settled into glowing coals, she carefully placed each egg onto them. "I miss our cauldron, and sorely."

He looked at the sky. "How can something so big just fly up and away? It was such a big blessing from Heaven to have a cauldron. It fed every last one of us, as if it were bottomless."

Her eyebrows pinched together in irritation. "You religion mongers will always have us mistaking blessings from Heaven with the fruits of our own industry!"

He touched his small wood cross that he had carved himself. "Whoever bargained our cauldron away to a devil will be burned at the stake for it, I hope."

"Be glad eggs come in their own fragile cauldrons, a precious holy grail unto themselves of the most perfect and holy design, or I don't know what I'd do to feed the children. Especially now that we've eaten up the frog pond."

He touched his belly. "Can't I even have the shells? Where do all the shells go? I've never seen a single scrap of eggshell."

"They go to the birds."

"I haven't seen a single bird in weeks. The drought's chased even them away since they won't eat stones. Where *do* the shells go?"

Mother Hubbard said, "You're asking too many questions and it'll someday make you lose your own head with a *chop chop*." She loudly clapped twice.

Priest Owen huffed, then went to the barn to wake the children. Alone again, Mother Hubbard quickly peeled the cooked eggs and ate the shells. "May the oak, ash and thorn bless us all."

"*Mum! Mum!*" Rafe, a skinny boy of fifteen, ran up to the barn, shouting, "Have you seen Mum?"

"Nay!" Mother Hubbard answered.

"Mum's been taken! She's nowhere around!"

"Nimm?" Priest Owen ran out of the barn. "Nimm's gone?"

"Mum!" Rafe called out again.

Mother Hubbard forced herself to smile. "Maybe she's off with the brownies."

"Are you daft, woman? How can you say something so fanciful at a time like this!" Priest Owen asked the boy, "She isn't out gathering roots?"

"Mum's nowhere! *Nowhere!* Wandered off like everybody else!"

"Don't say that!" Priest Owen warned him. "You'll invite bad luck!"

Rafe clenched his fist. "You're stupid!"

"We now have another orphan." Mother Hubbard said to Priest Owen, "*You* aren't eating today. Not from me, anyway. Unless God wants to feed you."

"I'll go see if she's out gathering roots." Priest Owen's eyes flooded with tears. "I'm sure that's all she's up to as Mother Hubbard suggested, doing chores with the brownies."

"You're all stupid!" Rafe wept. "The sound of the evil bell took her away! Like all the others! And you know it!"

Mother Hubbard wheeled around in surprise to see four men on horseback clopping through the gate and entering the greensward. "Rotten eggs!"

Priest Owen wiped his eyes while cautiously approaching them. "Are you knights?"

"Nay."

He was relieved. They were always raping and stealing. "Oh good! And blessings on you as on me. What fine horses! What powerful men you must be to have them! What brings you to us in this humble village? We've not a drop of food, not any provisions, not many folk, not much humor, but you're welcome."

A man with a distinctive potbelly declared, "I'm the constable of Abbey Town where justice is levied. I have the authority of the Pope of Rome for the inquisition."

"How wonderful!" Priest Owen smiled. "Blessings!"

"Where's your witch."

"W… what? Who?" He looked around in alarm. "But this is a town of Christendom."

The potbellied constable said, "They say the village is an enchanted spot and it's surely causing the drought. Where's your woman named Hubbard?"

"Mother Hubbard? Nay!" Priest Owen pointed right at her. "But she's like… like a *saint*!"

The constable did not look impressed with the glowing testimonial. "Which one of you is Hubbard? Is it *you*?" He pointed to Priest Owen.

"Nay I said it was her!"

The constable said, "In the last town, a witch hid herself as a bald monk and slipped from our fingers."

"Nay! I'm really a man. And I really am a priest of Christendom!"

The constable turned to Mother Hubbard. "And what's your name, repulsive woman?"

She could only reply in disgust, "Eee-*ucht!*"

Chapter Two

Arthur skipped ahead. "I hope there's a bridge for us to cross wherever we please at Salisbury."

Merlin shrugged. "The whole river may have dried away by now."

He stopped. "You think so?"

Merlin looked at Arthur in irritation. "That's what happens in a drought. Anyway, we have more important things to ponder. How to rid you of that sword. A boy your age looks ridiculous with something so grand. You're too young for it." He regarded Arthur's threadbare tunic that had been fashioned from a scrap of old sailcloth.

"Does not! I want to keep it. I need it for when I am the King! Someday." Arthur shifted the clumsy weight of two pale wool blankets, his sword, and a small tinderbox.

Merlin pointed. "Ahead over that ridge is the lake I told you about yesterday, a lake deep and fed by a spring. You will now go and learn a great lesson there."

Arthur looked at the hilltops. "A lesson, now? Here? Like what."

"A lesson you'll master and use a few times in your life, a lesson that'll be especially important on your last dying day of when blood foams out of your breath."

"Must you put it that way?"

Merlin smiled. "But now that we're on the topic of when you will be slaughtered, the lesson needs taught. Dying is so much work. As the King, even if your nose has been chopped clean away from your face, and your innards are outside on the grass about you in disarray, and a few beloved fingers are sorely missing, you must be polite when you die and accept all the rigmarole, accolades, insipid songs, tears and kisses with great dignity and humility… and a simply phrased *thank you*."

Arthur winced. "Because I'm so… brave?"

"Nay! It's not about you; you are but one husk of a person."

"I'll grow some more. I'm sure of it. All boys grow into men."

Merlin pounded his staff. "It's not about being a man. How common. The *King* is dead. The King is the land itself... at least to all the small peasants. And so you must be very careful to be kind so as not to scare them too much. When the banshee calls your name, don't even let anybody else know you heard it, or else they'll all worry about their own name being next. In short, people only think about themselves."

Arthur looked at his hand. "I have to care about peasants, even in death? Wouldn't I rather care about my poor stray fingers?"

"It's *reverence* to be the King and have honor towards peasants. Even in your own sorry passing from earth you'll still be the King. And they'll still be beneath you needing your strength, even as they run about the battlefield to collect your pieces to reassemble and enshroud you... if the ravens haven't already run off with the tinier pieces of you."

Arthur shuddered. "And the lake will teach me how to die? But can't you teach me that later? First cast a spell to make me a fully-grown up man. First things first, please."

Merlin ordered him, "Go throw your sword deep into the lake."

Arthur was shocked. "Do *what?* Why?"

"To teach you now how to dispose of your sword at your death."

Arthur said, "But then it'll sink and be gone! I'll need it when I'm a man!"

"When you need it again, it'll come back and find you."

"How can it do that?"

Merlin said, "We must leave the Lady of the Lake with something to worry about, and that's her worry—not yours, not mine."

Arthur frowned. "That's no great comfort. It'll just sink and be laughed at by the fishes."

"If you must know, when the time comes and you need to save your hide and shire, the Lady of the Lake's servant, a big hawk named

Gwy, will swoop down upon the water and fish out your sword. To only *you* will the hawk deliver it."

Arthur asked, "Do I yell out that I'm in need of it? Do I yell *Excalibur*!"

"*Nay*, how uncouth! You don't have to do anything. The Goddess Summer or the Horned God of Winter will say a prayer for you. Not that you in particular are so important to them, as a person, but they have a vague interest in arming any ole king of their land." Merlin pointed his staff to the ridge. "Hurry before another middling earthly lifetime slips me by."

Arthur trudged away to the lake. Merlin waited. Arthur finally returned, eyes low, the wool blankets now rolled in a manner that was long enough to conceal a full sword. As Merlin looked at Arthur in anger, Arthur regarded Merlin's attire and gasped. "Merlin! Look! Your robe just moved funny again! Are you sure it's not still alive?"

Merlin gave his long black squirrel fur robe, with all of its many squirrel tails still attached, a pert tug. "Don't be bothersome. At the lake, what did you see?"

"All the critters of your robe just came alive for a moment!"

"Nay! What did you see when you threw the sword into the lake?"

Arthur tried to look innocent. "*Aaaaah.*"

"What did you see?"

Arthur admitted, "I couldn't throw the sword away. It's too fine a sword… and I've no scruples, I suppose."

Merlin said. "And why didn't you try to be clever and lie about it. Why be so good?"

"I want to be good." They stared at each other for a while without expression until Arthur added, "Don't I?"

"Come, come. Goodness is for common serfs who must be kept in line. You'll be the King so you must learn to be clever and at least fib a wizard into momentary confusion. You must do that—unless you just want two minutes on a brownie throne—and they live inside a very hot hearth, at that."

"I don't like to lie. I want the world to be what it is. Is that how I'll succeed? Lying? I don't like that."

Merlin knocked Arthur on the head with his staff, harder than he meant. "*If* you succeed. A man's success is usually from being in the company of fools. That's rare when you're a king. Most will be clever in tearing you down. Go. Try again. Take that sword out of your blanket and toss it in the lake. If you don't do it, or can't even lie about it in a clever performance, I'll box your ears until you hear a Roman Hades!"

Arthur shuffled off again. When he raced back without the sword, Merlin knew something had happened. Arthur shook. "Merlin! I can't believe my eyes! I threw the sword into the lake with all my might! And the entire stretch of water rose to it, boiled and turned blood red, all of it from shore to shore… and I could feel heat! And it was a terrible smell like hot vinegar! I thought all of a Roman Hades would devour me!"

"I'm glad you're terrified."

"What?"

Merlin restated, as he began to walk on again. "I'm gladdened that the sword is in a proper hand, for the time being, and out of my hands. That gives me one less thing to concern myself with. But I was hoping to have the opportunity to box your ears, first."

"Why do you act like you dislike me so much?"

"Because I dislike you so much."

Arthur grew angry. "But I'll be the King."

"Kings are the most expensive on a wizard's nerves. Toad on you… in advance."

"*I* won't be so horrible… if I can help it."

"Every king says that. And then life happens. The battles don't go as planned. The heart yearns for more than it can have. At some point family always makes troublesome demands."

"And what did any of this at the lake have to do with when I die? And why must we think of that today? I don't like it and I don't like your constant tricks with my imagination."

"Young man, to die with the manners of a king takes a lot of work and a lifetime of preparation. How to dispose of Excalibur at your death is one of the details you must attend to. A snake never trusts itself to one hole. Anyone can steer a ship when the water is calm. Your life is like an onion, the more you peel, the more it stinks, the more you cry, and then it's tiny and then you get to nothing."

"Stop that braying. You always tell me such horrible things. Why don't you try to pretend you like me."

Merlin paused to lean his beard into Arthur's face. He made a few spiders crawl out. "I can't abide by children, even older children like you. And then when children become as men they're usually worse creatures, beasts to be survived. And men who are kings are especially tiresome."

Arthur ran ahead and spotted a bone yard with the latest plots marked in the new grave fashion. Crosses. "Why are we here? Am I to be buried here? Am to be tormented by you some more about my own death?"

"Don't be morbid." Merlin pointed out a road beyond the bone yard that led to grand buildings of massive dark stones. "We are going to that manor estate."

Arthur smiled. "It must be one of the grandest of villas that Rome left behind!"

Merlin played with his beard. "It may contain a monster, maybe a werewolf! Only monsters are brave enough to seize such goods to live in such splendor. Beware."

Arthur ignored him. "I like how I live when I'm visiting the rich. I finally feel as though I were soon to be the King."

Merlin nodded. "Aye, a king is only a king at the expense of the rich." A raven flew down and tried to take off with Merlin's red feather cap. There was a scream from the cap. Merlin angrily poked his finger in the air and the raven flew off.

Arthur stared. "Your hat is alive."

"Is it?"

At the tall gate flanked by old Roman style pillars, six bonded servants hurried down to intercept them. "Blessed be. Why are you here?" an elderly but robust manservant asked, eyeing Merlin's grand robe in awe. "Where are you and your child from?"

"Blessed be. I'm a wizard. *He* is a not my child. He will soon be the King to rule his grandfather Vortigern's lands of Gwynedd, Dyfed and Powys. All three, he will be so mighty." He gave the boy a dubious glare.

Arthur clenched his jaw and tried to appear manly. He wished he at least had a fine set of pant legs and diadem to look the part, as the servants fell to their faces.

"Get up!" Merlin said to them all. "We require hospitality, not your close view of pebbles and ants. This is Prince Arthur."

The old manservant said, "My master, the great Baron Bearloin, and his son Parsifal, will be so pleased to have you. Our master was a celebrated warrior for Rome who led armies higher and higher up into the northern clans, even against the savage Picts!"

Arthur smiled. "He must be the grandest, then!"

The manservant nodded in excitement. "Do you know how to read?" They nodded, so the manservant continued, "He's so grand now, he's been collecting a library! But the master doesn't know how to read or scribe; he's just collecting it to be grand."

Merlin gently pulled his beard in thought. "Baron *Brrrlyn*? He fought in the north? Is he very old?"

The manservant said, "Bear loin. But say it like *Baaaah*lin, for he's trying to be noble in these nowtimes. As a great Roman general everyone got an animal nickname. For some reason he just got an animal part, but he'd like to sound noble."

"Bahlin," Arthur spoke.

"Nay. Roll the *l* a bit, like a northern brogue."

Arthur asked, "But why speak in the accent of the enemy?"

The old manservant said, "It's just something a warrior picks up. It's odd how much of the enemy comes off on you when you fight them."

Merlin calculated, "If your lord fought those wars back then, then today he must be many hundreds of years old."

The old manservant nodded. "His son, Parsifal is only sixteen until the next Samhain, but the master is far older than even I. He'll never die. He says it's a miracle of a pagan God when he made a pact with Him not to slay him. But I didn't tell you that; I shouldn't have." He put his finger to his lips.

They were led up the grand path to the main buildings of the manor compound. At the door, the manservant added, "Have the house servant show you into the library. We'll have the master meet you there. He may be there before you, so speak quietly when you enter."

"Sound hurts his ears?" Arthur asked. "He's sensitive?"

"Nay, he's just taken on the opinion that loud talking is vulgar." The servant chuckled. "He's very nervous about manners. He doesn't want to be seen as the warrior he once was. Not any longer at all costs. And now he'd have you think he was always courteous and gentle."

Arthur asked, "Isn't he proud of all his brave highland slaughter? Isn't that something everybody wants to do all the time?"

Merlin explained to Arthur. "War is like a romance of the flesh."

"What? How!"

"So easy to begin but very hard to stop. Old men like me get so weary of both."

"And that's sad?" Arthur asked. "Or exciting."

"A season is needed to grow the crops to maturity but they're stomped dead in minutes in one battle, all the while, of course, God is usually on the side that has the most arrows."

"So war is bad?" Arthur asked.

"I didn't say that," Merlin corrected him, "but maybe I did. War is always the gutless escape from the thwarting problems of peace. War is neither to be fearfully shunned nor unfairly provoked."

"So which is it?" Arthur asked, growing impatient. "Good or bad?"

"I'm your tutor, not some crystal on a stick."

Arthur spotted the raven high up on the manor house roof watching them.

Chapter Three

A house servant led Merlin and Arthur to a vast central area where drapes of a variety of colors divided the room into smaller spaces. "Here's the Baron's valued and beloved library. He's not here yet. Sit and wait. If he's long, you may fall asleep where you sit." The servant left.

"Fall asleep where we sit?" Arthur questioned. "I'd fear what I may wake up to."

Merlin felt the thickness of the drapes. "Are you afraid of such a nice room? Someday you'll own your own grand room where you'll sit and ponder and fear. And you'll wish for eternal life though you won't be able to pass the tedious hours of a rainy afternoon."

"Will I be so alone, someday?" Arthur asked.

"Every man is alone. It's not good for man to be alone, but it's often a great relief."

"*Oh* you babble at me!"

Merlin glanced about. "Toad. Where's the parchments? This is to be a library?"

"Don't get us into trouble," Arthur warned him. "Don't poke where we aren't invited."

"But this room is a library, or so someone once said it is. So, toads, where's the library part of it?"

Arthur admitted, "I've never been in a place called a library. You only had me learning the craft of words scratching in dirt."

"An entire Book of Shadows."

Arthur said, "That washed away with the first rain. Have we even ever seen a real scroll?"

"Maybe it's all in that trunk. Isn't that where things of any value are usually kept? I'd have hoped for a much larger trunk. *Hmmm.*"

"Stop! Merlin! What are you doing? Don't touch it. Just because it doesn't have a lock doesn't mean you can... Merlin! Don't be so rude! Don't open it! You'll get us shunned! Get your fingers out of there! Don't reach inside! Oh toad."

Merlin chuckled. "There *are* parchments in here!"

"Careful! Don't touch them! Put that back! They may be old and falling apart. They may crumble into dust!"

"They're reused parchments, sure, but not old. And they won't fall apart. They're all made of sheepskin. Oh look at this one, Arthur. Here's a messy page that declares it's the Psalms of King David, the Jewish hero who killed a giant as tall as the Stones of Stennes." He read from it. "*The wicked will be cut off but those who wait for the Lord will possess the land.*"

"Who'll possess my land?" a great burly old man asked, stepping from behind a curtain. Merlin stood while Arthur froze in embarrassment. "Nay, go on, I'm the Baron of this estate. Baron Bearloin. Blessed be."

"Blessed be," Arthur greeted him. "My tutor meant no thievery."

Baron Bearloin said, "I know that and I was spying on you to see if you both really indeed knew how to read. And I was pleased to hear you read what was really there and not what you'd have me want you to read."

Merlin said, "This parchment says only a few things and then the rest looks like counting marks, or something just to quickly fill the page."

"*What?*" Baron Bearloin took the page. "The cursed monks at the abbey said this was the Holy Scriptures and took my Roman coin for it! A gold coin! Read this one! This parchment is the one I've been waiting a year to hear! Read me that one that's supposed to be *The Path to the Holy Grail*. I'm desperate to understand." Baron Bearloin handed it to Merlin, who passed it to Arthur.

Arthur scanned the parchment and wrinkled up his nose. "What's the holy grail?"

"Read," Merlin ordered, "and maybe you'll learn something."

"It's just that it only reads, *A Prayer to Keep One From The Demon Bell.*" Arthur asked Merlin, "What's a demon bell?"

"*Nay,*" Baron Bearloin said, "this is supposed to be the one to the holy grail."

"You're mistaken to the utmost!" Arthur insisted as Merlin started to pull a few other parchments from the trunk.

"This one, maybe. Nay." Merlin saw that it was only a seed list.

Baron Bearloin said, "That one is Greek Mythology told by Poseidon. It was *very* expensive."

"Nay," Merlin corrected him. "It looks like an inventory list of a monastery storeroom."

Baron Bearloin sat wearily on a pillowed bench. "Have I been so deceived?"

Merlin asked himself, "What's that prayer from a demon bell? It sounds most peculiar. It stirs a memory."

Arthur asked, "Don't you know what it is?"

Merlin thought about it. "It must be something new."

Arthur asked, "A spell can be from nowtimes?"

"Aye. Spells can be as newborn as a baby. Bad witches can always come up with new forms of mischief. Time doesn't stop for them, just as it doesn't stop for us."

"But if it's not for the holy grail," Baron Bearloin said, "who cares what it says? I bought a parchment for finding the holy grail and I've been waiting a year in impatience to hear it!"

"What's a holy grail?" Arthur asked.

Baron Bearloin answered, "Nobody knows for sure what it is, and that's why it hasn't been found. But it cures the land of all its illness, brings back the green and rain and apples, and aye, mostly apples aplenty. And rain."

Arthur smiled. "The holy grail is a luckier find than a demon bell. Merlin, do you really believe there's such a thing as a demon bell or is it merely a monk's fancy to keep children full of fear, to keep them all inside throughout the night?"

Merlin said to Arthur, "Something about the idea of a demon bell struck out at me. I remember one once from such a bygone time before this one."

"The Web of…" Prince Arthur asked, nervously glancing over at Baron Bearloin and not wanting to alarm the man's niminy-piminy sensibilities of Christendom.

"Magic… possibly," Merlin said without care for sensibilities. "The web makes strings that go between all past and future. They have no concern at how odd that may seem to men on piddling earth."

Arthur read more of the parchment, "*A Prayer to Keep One From the Demon Bell. Save us O' Virgin from the peel and the toll at the noon of night that cries out to sap strength and men's blood. Tell the giant trees that they are all a part of a man's bygone times. Save us till morning when the bell will return to nothing and life is in your Christendom*. Well, this was certainly written out in full. And look," Arthur showed both men the page. "The opening letter, the *A*, is so very nicely decorated with branches and leaves. It's a very proper and splendid parchment, indeed."

"But was it? That's it?" Merlin scoffed. "That says nothing. Unless it's really a poem, but I was led to believe that poems are written for great seductions and arousals."

Baron Bearloin agreed, "It's most certainly *not* how to find the holy grail. What did I buy? Oh, I wasted a gold coin!"

Arthur asked, "Who scribed these parchments out for you?"

"Abbot Babble Blaise."

"I know of him." Merlin chuckled. "I now see why he isn't known to the world as Abbot *Pencraft* Blaise." He chuckled louder.

"How do you know him?" Arthur asked. "Why would you know an abbot?"

Merlin explained, "I've used him as my secretary. He put down stories of my life but I had to make sure he did it proper; his hands became so tired. He's had no oversight since then, I see, for some of these look like they've been penned with his feet."

Baron Bearloin made a fist. "I'd like very much to go and punch him soundly in his babble!"

Arthur went to the window. "Is his monastery far? Can we find him and ask him about this? If he knows anything about the holy grail then *I'm* certainly interested. We could cure the wasteland."

Baron Bearloin explained, "It's between the Dubglas Bogs. Most of the monks in that place aren't men at all but still lads the age of Prince Arthur, orphans all of them since the parents ran away."

"Ran away?" Arthur asked, doubting.

"Aye, ran away," Baron Bearloin repeated. "The drought has put such stress on our towns and the parents are always wandering coast to coast looking for food."

"But… but… without their children?"

Clopping footsteps startled them as a handsome tall young man in a fine set of yellow clothes entered. His eyes widened in interest at the sight of Merlin, but then they quickly clouded in distress at the sight of Arthur in rags. "Blessed be."

"Blessed be," Merlin and Arthur both greeted him.

Baron Bearloin announced, "My dear son, Parsifal the Inheritor, blessed be. Bow to the prince. That one. *That* one is the prince."

"Though I'm really a great hunter!" the son quickly said, bowing to everybody.

His father countered, "But he'll be bequeathed greatly. And the land should know to honor him. So only the act of a man greater than I, a king, can rename him."

"Aw!" Parsifal complained. "But it's as a great hunter that I'll be known someday."

"And a proud inheritor," Baron Bearloin argued, "since he has such a famous father. Me. Look how wonderfully he is clothed in the latest fashion to show his father's success."

Parsifal asked his father, "*These* are the men who'll tell us where the holy grail is?"

"Son, it seems the parchment doesn't say what it was promised to say."

"What? What does it say?"

"It says nothing but a prayer to save one from some evil bell."

"But, you thought that you'd bought a text to explain the holy grail! Were you cheated?"

Baron Bearloin nodded. "I've been fleeced!"

Parsifal declared, "If they weren't monks, I'd lop off their heads."

Merlin said, "Abbot Babble Blaise is the only monk at the monastery who can scribe, so we well know that this is all his doing."

Then he nudged Arthur to break him from his spell. Arthur had not been able to take his eyes off Parsifal's matching vest, sleeves and pants, badly wanting them for himself.

Arthur asked Baron Bearloin, "What do all the other monks do if they're not scribing?"

"They're supposed to be flattulating!"

"Flagellating," Parsifal quickly corrected his father. "Those monks should be spending all their days whipping each other with birches until they're holy. That's the fate of a monk."

Merlin said, "Let's go to the abbey now and learn what we can about the grail."

They went back outside, leaving Baron Bearloin behind. The heels of Parsifal's boots clicked grandly on the flagstone courtyard as they walked.

Merlin asked Parsifal, "What are you going to do when we see the abbot who sold your father such nonsense?"

"Punch him in the nose." Then Parsifal excitedly pointed up to the roof of the barn. "Look! It's Opie!"

Arthur asked, "Who's Opie?"

"The raven. He loves me. He follows me wherever I travel. Come Opie!" Parsifal called out. "Come to my hand and travel with us!" The raven merely stared down at him, then decided to groom its wings.

Merlin greeted the bird, "Oh hello, you adorable little banshee."

"Banshee!" Parsifal made a sour face.

"Adorable?" Arthur reminded Merlin. "That might be the same raven that attacked us earlier."

Merlin winked at the bird. "And a lovely banshee for such a bright day. Has she shrieked out my name, I do pray? I do pray I get to go next. I would love to die and get out of here."

"That is *not* a banshee," Parsifal corrected Merlin. "That's a bird and *he* is a raven!"

"*She* is adorable," Merlin corrected Parsifal, and then with the power in his staff, began to walk faster.

Arthur said, "Slow down."

"It looks like rain."

Arthur and Parsifal followed Merlin toward the abbey, first skirting the lands of the violent knight Balinban so they would not lose their heads. Arthur asked, "How does a king deal with men as mean as knights?"

"String them all up," Parsifal said. "The land will be safer for it."

Arthur asked, "How does anybody do that?"

Merlin recommended, "Or you could choose to stay close to your enemy."

"How does one do that?" Arthur asked.

"By making them think they're not your enemy, by making them believe you both have some other common enemy."

"What?"

Merlin restated, "The enemy of your enemy is your friend."

Parsifal repeated, "I say just string them all up."

Arthur thought about that a moment. "Merlin, that sounds like a dangerous idea."

Merlin smiled. "If it's dangerous then that's why it's called an idea."

Parsifal turned and took one last look at his lands before they were over a far hill. "I must say goodbye to a patch of Christendom." He waved it off.

Arthur asked Merlin, "Can an entire nation be Christian? Will that be a fate of my kingdom?"

Merlin shook his head. "That's impossible. By definition. The Christ spoke of turning the other cheek. A nation can't do that if it wants to be around for more than a day. A nation needs to be able to defend itself. The Golden Rule does not work. Always use the Iron Rule."

Arthur picked his nose. "What's that?'

Merlin hit his elbow to stop him. "Do unto others as they do unto you, and you find people learn to treat you nicer."

Parsifal said, "My father said the whole of Britannia would be a part of Christendom someday, and fight for glory."

"Perhaps." Merlin granted him that. "But would it be at the cost of having to ignore all the Christ's mandates? Can men live in a communal brotherhood and share all?"

"That sounds kind," Arthur said. "And kind is bad? For a Nation?"

Merlin added, "The meek shall inherit the earth? And if they did, how long would they hold it."

Arthur grinned. "Maybe the Saxons can all convert from their worship of Odin and then not wish to fight me."

"Men are ready for peace on earth," Merlin stated, "only after all the wars have been won to the satisfaction of all."

Parsifal accused Merlin, "You don't like Christendom much, do you?"

"I'm a Druid wizard. What can you expect? But I'm here to teach Arthur and he'll rule a land of many faiths: old Roman Mithraism, new Roman Christendom, Saxon Odinism, and our own old Druid ways. I'll try to speak about them all in just enough detail so we won't have a King someday who is utterly daft."

Arthur scowled. "Merlin! Of course I won't be daft. *You* taught me!"

Merlin laughed.

Chapter Four

At the noon of day, Nimm stumbled back to her village. Her son Rafe yelled, "Mum! Blessed be!"

Priest Owen and all the orphan children of the barn came running to her. Priest Owen asked her, "Blessings on me, where have you been?"

"Blessed be!" Nimm wept, grabbing her son.

"Have you been molested?" Priest Owen saw that the skin of her foot and leg had scratches on it from a thorn bush.

"The bell." Nimm put her hands over her ears and moaned.

Priest Owen asked, "The bell? Where! To what land did it lead you? Can you take us to it so we can slay it?"

"Slay a bell?" Rafe questioned.

Priest Owen asked Nimm, "Nay! Slay the dragon or fairy devil who rings it! Where is it?"

"I've no memory. I was in an awful spell that filled me with emptiness and pain and great sadness, sadness for my own embarrassing defeat."

"Defeat?" Rafe asked.

Nimm wiped a tear. "I didn't want to go away to die. I want to be with my son. But the horrible sound of a bell made me walk away."

Priest Owen clenched his wood cross. "Blessings on me, the only bell that should be around here will someday be at the abbey."

Nimm moaned. "It was a horrible bell… the sound was… *thirsty*! It wanted to drink me down!"

"Doesn't the ring of a bell drive out all evil?" Rafe asked the priest. "Isn't that how it works? What would the Devil want with a bell? Why would the Devil want to scare himself away?"

"If I had such answers," Priest Owen said, "I wouldn't be in such a sorry destitute village with no blessings on me at all."

Nimm looked off as if in a trance. "I slipped into a half-life of magic. Or a fuller life of magic. I heard otherworldly sounds. My feet felt the quivering of some great world beneath me. Dogs or wolves raced topsy-turvy beneath my feet in a reflected world. I was afraid of it. But I want it back. I want more. I'm hungry. To walk the earth with these feet I have now is dreary—too dreary for me—now I'm ready to fly to the moon to see if there are dragons, there, too."

"Mum, please, don't babble so. Come back to us." Rafe waved his hand before her face. "Mum!"

"I see you," Nimm assured her son. She kissed his forehead. "It's just that I want more. I have tasted something. I want more. More!"

"More of what?" Priest Owen asked her.

Nimm grabbed the chain at Priest Owen's neck and slid her hand down to his cross. She looked at it oddly. "More!"

"You can't become a nun," he protested, as she pulled on him. "You have a child!"

"I wasn't thinking about becoming a nun." She looked deep into his eyes and her expression darkened. He pried her fingers off his cross.

* * * * *

After Parsifal and Arthur made camp in a dry patch of the bog, they gathered kindling. Merlin pointed his staff at the pile of branches and asked Arthur, "Are you ready for some amusement?" Arthur smiled, took the flint and steel from his tinderbox and at Merlin's cue, struck it together. Merlin invoked, "Fire from rock, sky and water, hit the dead fairyless tree. By oak, ash and thorn, so mote it be." With the sudden bright smell of a blackening candlewick and the crackling popping sounds of large bright sparks, the pile of branches vibrated and stirred and then exploded into fire.

"How'd you do that?" Parsifal marveled.

Merlin ignored him.

"I would like to know that trick. What did you do?"

Merlin finally explained, "Just a bit of charged ether. That's all."

Parsifal looked confused. "What's that?"

Merlin glared at the boy as if he were irritating.

Chuckling, Arthur retrieved a few sticks that had scattered from the explosion.

"Children are always so easily amused," Merlin remarked to the rushes about him.

After the fire had burned down sensibly, Merlin placed three prize turnips carefully near the coals to begin cooking. Then he grabbed his belly and moaned. Arthur jumped up in alarm. "What!"

"*Aag!*"

"What's wrong?" Arthur grew worried.

"Am I poisoned?"

"What's wrong?"

"What's this displeasure? *Ooooh*! Toads and warts!"

"What do you feel?" Arthur asked.

"I feel horrible! A horse is kicking inside of me!"

"How?"

Merlin lay on his side. "Methinks I'll be torn to shreds!"

Arthur said, "Perhaps it's your time to pass your bowels. Haven't you been mortal long enough, this time around, to know all your body and its stirrings?"

Merlin didn't answer, but cursed and hurried out into the dark woods, mumbling, "Toads and warts on dung goblin faces!" He was gone.

Parsifal asked Arthur, "He doesn't even know his own body?"

"Nope. I guess not."

"But he's a great wizard. They say he's as old as time and was once the land."

Arthur shook his head. "He spends too much time in the Realm of Dragons. I'm not sure what that is. I just know that it's not this world. He hates this world. He said it was a vile world of rot and dung. But he was called out by the Gods to tutor me to be King."

"Are you sure?"

"That's what he said." Arthur looked off to where Merlin had disappeared. "And then he always finds an excuse to dart away, anyway. I wish he didn't have to leave me like this in the night. It unsettles me to be in such an unhallowed place."

"Unhallowed?"

Arthur nodded. "Aye."

"This place?" Parsifal asked, looking about at the scattered clumps of rushes.

"They say the Romans killed Druids, bards, witches and ovates in great numbers, here, in this very bog."

Parsifal huffed out his slim chest. "Oh, the dead can rot. I can protect any prince. Don't be such a bobblelink."

"When you were my age," Arthur asked, "Were you as small as I am now?"

"You're not small."

"Aye, I am." Arthur frowned, rubbing his thin arms.

Parsifal said, "Then you grow up. It happens to you whether you like it or not."

Arthur wasn't convinced. "Have you ever heard of the magic of manhood missing anybody? Has it ever been reported that somebody wanted it to happen very badly but it didn't happen at all? And then they were forever left small and thin and very sad?"

Parsifal chuckled, "Is the Prince growing hornier with every new moon? Are you at that terrible age?"

"Nay, that's not it! Not like that. I need to be big and strong! I need to be a great warrior! And soon! My grandfather King Vortigern will die any day! He's very old! And then I'll need to be mighty enough to slice off at least two-dozen Saxon heads a day, or I'll be a joke. I have to show I'm a real king."

Parsifal said, "I've never heard of such a thing as not growing up all the way. In a few years you won't look so much like a lass, like you do now. It just happens. And when it happens, you'll find you'll have to take a moment to get used to it, no matter how much you'd always wanted it."

Arthur pushed at both sides of his jaw to try and toughen it up. "You don't think growing up in a wasteland will rob me of my own fertility? It's a frightening time to be alive when the Green Man is so ill, maybe already on the way to his tomb. The King gets his fertility from the land and the land gets its fertility from the King. Maybe this drought will stunt me."

"I've never heard of such a curse, at least not lasting forever. But finding the holy grail will certainly take your worries away. All fertility is restored when the grail is found."

Arthur nodded. "Aye, we *must* find the grail! *Must!*"

Opie the raven flew to the ground, and keeping its cautious distance, it walked around to snoop about the campfire.

"Here Opie! Come over here to me!" The bird completely ignored Parsifal.

Arthur threw a piece of grass at the bird. "Just a few years ago I'd have been a king of all Britannia, protected by many Roman legions. I hear that King Vortigern still calls his soldiers, *centurions*. I like that."

Parsifal huffed out his chest again. "You're safe with me."

"The Romans were very mighty."

"The Romans ran out of oats, so they say, in fact they say they aren't even faring well anymore in their own home country. *Opie come back here!*"

Not finding any meat it could steal, the bird flapped back up into the trees.

Arthur added, "The wicked Saxons have fought them in Rome."

"And thieving Vikings. All the northern tribes. They attack all the lands. I wonder what demons live up in the north to create such evil races of men."

"I'll be the king of a bloodbath." Arthur frowned, hoping he could grow mighty enough to face down such armies. "I'll have to be very strong."

"Maybe you can be clever like the Romans and conquer with the display of might alone. The Romans came in with long parades of elephants." Parsifal got a gleam in his eyes. "That's how they conquered; they impressed."

"Aye, I know the tale," Arthur said. "Merlin described an elephant for me several times but my mind still can't get it in its entirety. I'll never own a parade of elephants. Just one tall horse would please me in nowtimes."

Parsifal smiled. "Aye, tall horses are best."

Arthur said, "Be careful the turnips don't burn."

"Aye, prince, we'll not let you have a burnt turnip." There was an odd sound. "What was that?"

Arthur looked around. "What? What!"

"A person, a woman!" Parsifal pointed to a stirring clump of rushes. "And *unclad!*"

"It's too cold and dangerous in the bog for such a thing." Arthur got up on his tippy toes. "Where? Are you sure it was a woman?"

"I think so. I don't know."

"Merlin?" Arthur called out. "Is that you playing tricks? *Merlin!* Don't run around over there! *Merlin!* You're in the bog!"

Parsifal said, "I don't think that was Merlin. Merlin does not appear like an unclad woman."

"A villain?" Arthur asked.

"Nay, I don't think it was a farmhand." Parsifal gathered up long rushes and bound them to make two torches. He handed a torch to Arthur. "Here. We'll see who it is out there."

"It's not safe in the bog," Arthur warned him.

"Sure it is."

"A bog isn't safe."

Parsifal held out his torch. "I'll not sleep thinking someone is prowling out there to watch me... maybe to steal my breath."

"Or a succubus to steal your..." Arthur dared consider it.

"Don't say that!"

"There!" Arthur alerted him. "I see someone *there!*"

Parsifal grabbed Arthur's arm to pull him along but Arthur stood fast in his place. Parsifal urged, "Come *on!*"

"I think we should wait for Merlin's return."

"It's a woman! An unclad woman! Let's go!"

"That's dangerous!" Arthur warned. "And besides, you forget. We're on our way to a monastery. We're on a quest to learn about what the holy grail is. We shouldn't be up to this sort of thing. I don't think one climbs up onto a milking wench just before he enters a chapel."

"That's tomorrow. This is tonight."

Arthur repeated. "There is often danger in a bog!"

Parsifal laughed. "I'll face such danger as unclad women!"

"Nay, not the woman, the bog!"

"I've hunted in bogs my entire life," Parsifal bragged. "I'm a great hunter. You just have to be surefooted and wary."

Arthur reluctantly followed him. "If it's mischief you're after, you're tempting O' Fortuna. It's a bog!"

"Hurry!"

"My foot is slipping," Arthur complained.

"Don't be so clumsy. Walk like me. Hurry. She'll be enough for two!"

Arthur stated, "Nay! I will not climb up onto an unclad woman. Not like this. Not here! I'm going back to the fire. If you'd like her for your sport, then kindly try not to make too much noise."

Before Arthur turned away, the unclad woman ran up to them, laughing in hysteria. Parsifal stood in utter disbelief.

"Run!" Arthur warned. "Something's not right!"

He smiled. "She's unclad!" He pointed. He grabbed his crotch. He pointed again. He grabbed his crotch again. "Look at that!"

"Give me your kisses," she whispered.

"Don't budge," Arthur warned him. "She'll attack you!"

"With what?" Parsifal asked. "I have the dagger. She has soft flesh!"

"Touch me!" she begged. "Hurry! Touch my body!"

Arthur yelled, "Don't touch her! Something's not right!"

She pleaded, "Touch me right here! Excite me!"

"Don't touch it!" Arthur demanded. When Parsifal reached out to touch her, her skin completely shriveled and shrunk to her bones as she slipped under the moss of the bog. "It's a trick!" Arthur gasped. "A demon!"

"What happened?" Parsifal shuddered, kicking at the moss. "What happened?"

Arthur yelled, "Run!"

With an explosive wet sucking sound, both boys were pulled deep into the mud. They slid down all the way to their necks. The shriveled corpse came back and crawled close to them and gazed oddly into their faces, looking angry one moment and curious the next.

Arthur yelled, "Merlin!"

"Catapults!" Parsifal spat at her crannied blackened face. "Curses on you!"

"Why wouldn't you touch me?" she asked in a soft wispy voice.

"Merlin!" Arthur cried out again. Three brown stags quickly pranced up to her and made snorting noises as they bobbed their heads. The shriveled corpse hissed and then quickly scampered away. With their strong antlers, the stags scooped Parsifal and Arthur up out of the mud.

When the two boys returned to the fire, shivering and dripping with mud, Merlin was eating their turnips. "You look affright!" He smacked his lips.

"Catapult!" was all Parsifal could muster as he tried to shake the mud off himself.

"We were attacked," Arthur cried. "We were almost drowned by a dead demon. Did you send the stags to save us?"

"You're eating our turnips," Parsifal protested.

Merlin merely shrugged, and tossed a skin to Opie the raven who was standing attentively beside him, expertly begging. "I ate them and saved them. They'd have burned on the fire from your neglect if I hadn't. You should thank me. The banshee thanked me kindly."

"The raven's name is *Opie!*" Parsifal corrected Merlin. "It is a raven and not a banshee!"

"The food smells so good," Arthur said with a moan. It still lingered in the air.

"Aye, I agree." Merlin licked his lips.

"Opie! Come to *me*! Come sit upon my hand," Parsifal demanded, and then frowned at the filthy sight of his sleeves. "He won't come to me like this." The raven ignored Parsifal, looked to Merlin for more morsels, and then flew away.

Arthur asked again, "Did you send the stags to save us?"

"Save you from an unclad woman?"

"A *demon corpse!*" Parsifal adamantly corrected him. "Now since you are the great wizard, please cast a spell on my clothes to clean them and make them as good as new."

Merlin looked at him head to toe. "A bit muddy, perhaps."

"Muddy! I'm dripping!"

Merlin looked away. "You look normal for a boy your age."

Parsifal took his muddy clothes off and hung them on a branch by the fire, then shivered near it and pouted. "That woman in the bog looked perfectly fine to me, at first, and I thought I'd go and try to understand her."

"Understand?" Merlin was not amused. "If perchance you should ever come to understand women, you'd never believe it."

"What do you mean?" Arthur questioned. "You don't think a man should have a wife?"

Merlin made a sour face, as he looked out over the bog. "Woman is calamity, but every house must have its one curse."

"You're terrible," Arthur said. "And how did you know to save us?"

Merlin looked confused. Then he burped. "I was walking the other way, squatting where it was far safer. Arthur, you idiot jack, I thought you had more sense than to run off and fall into mud."

Arthur kicked at a dirt clod. "*You've* never been in a bog? There's so many of them underfoot."

Merlin explained, "I've always avoided bogs since I once lost a pair of clogs in one while trying a shortcut."

Arthur said, "I know that bogs are shaky places but… there was an unclad woman enticing *him* into trickery. He cajoled me to…"

"So… if a friend tells you to jump into a bog, you jump into a bog?"

"Merlin! She was unclad!" Arthur reminded him. "We had to go see what she was up to."

Merlin asked, "And when a woman runs astray, man must follow after?"

Parsifal frowned. "She *was* unclad."

"Every square inch of her dead bones?"

Arthur asked, "What do you know of such demons?"

Merlin pulled one side of his moustache. "The bog people can be restless. That's all I know."

Arthur asked, "And what about the stags?"

"What about them?"

"How can hooves stay afloat when our feet sank? How can they care to save us? How can they come to even know we were there? Did you send them?"

Merlin smiled and then made himself comfortable to sleep. "You two carry on. I'm done for the day and will give in to the night. I hope I dream of a beautiful maiden. I feel my body wakening to that urge, too."

Arthur said, "You're too old for maidens. And you shouldn't think such vulgar thoughts as we journey to a monastery. To learn of the holy grail may require men to be pure of heart."

Merlin opened his eyes. "Pure of heart? Don't be tiresome. Don't threaten me. And besides, I can make myself seem any age I want, as angelic as I want, and as randy as I want. I'm only keeping myself old for now, to keep myself as distant in appearance as I can from you."

Parsifal asked, "Tell me of the stags."

Merlin said, "I'm trying to dream of a good wife, right now, why don't you do the same so that you stop thinking of me."

Arthur asked, "What happened in the bog?"

"*Good night!*" The fire flared tall. It brightly warmed the area as Merlin began to breathe with a rattle.

Parsifal tried his best to shake the dried mud off his skin and out of his clothes but when he put them back on, they were now brown instead of yellow. "Curses."

"Look at *me*," Arthur agreed, pulling on his dirty rag.

"But you weren't as richly appointed as I! You had nothing fine to be soiled."

"I will when I'm the King."

Parsifal nodded to agree. "Hopefully you'll be a rich King. Rich enough so it pours off you and onto all the rest of us. And I hope your land is rich with fair women who love the attentions of a great hunter like me." He smirked. "I would like many of them to take their rest just beneath me, where I'll do anything but rest." He lewdly wiggled his hips around.

Arthur blushed and looked away. "We should have pure thoughts. We have to find a holy thing called a grail and pray it can heal the wasteland."

Parsifal sat. "Sure. Pure thoughts. We'll think about my great hunt for the grail. A holy hunt. Do you think this restless bog is a result of the wasteland?"

Arthur looked out at it and wrinkled up his nose. "There are so many bogs. It *must* be a sign of the wasteland."

"The wasteland is a terrible thing when it's only good for sinking into. Maybe next we can invite the Saxons to sink deep."

Arthur questioned, "I wonder what started the wasteland? Does the holy grail cause it by getting lost, or fix it by getting found?"

"My father says the jack-in-the-green had his head cut off. That's what started it all."

Arthur said, "Oh that festival. I didn't know he gets his head cut off. I thought he just gets a bucket on his head. Then he can't see. So he dances until he falls down. And that's the end of the dance. Did you play the May game too rough and it took off his poor head entirely? That poor man!"

Parsifal explained, "Nay, not a May game, but a tale of the jack-in-the-green who's tossed into the river to drown. But he doesn't drown. He floats. And that brings rain for the next season. But one year the dancing was too wild. Then a long sword of sharpness lopped off his head. It rolled straightaway into the river where it sank and couldn't be found after a full day of searching."

"That really happened at your May festival? What a tragic Beltane."

"Nay! It's a tale of a true event of the real jack-in-the-green!"

Arthur argued, "Anybody can play the jack-in-the-green. It's just a part you play for the dancing before the goats are given crowns of leaves and told to give good milk as they drink from the river."

"Nay, my father said it differently."

Arthur added, "It can all occur with sheep. Or pigs for that matter. The animals should be cared for at least enough to be blessed."

Parsifal angrily shook his head. "Nay, nay! I mean I don't remember goats, pigs, and sheep in the story at all."

Arthur insisted, "But you have to bless the animals for the new season. If you don't care enough for your animals to do that, you're cruel. And the one with the power to be cruel has to be most careful that he isn't."

"Nay!"

"Well then," Arthur said, exasperated, "besides blessings for animals and making rain for crops, what's the point of the festival, then?"

Merlin finally interrupted them. "Hush, both of you quibblers! We all know there are many versions of the story."

"Is not!" Parsifal debated. "There's only one version. The *correct* version."

Merlin asked, "And the correct version is the one you know?"

Parsifal broke a stick. "What does it matter? The land about us tonight is a bog of corpses."

Arthur's eyes widened. "And I'd rather not think about hundreds of bog corpses rising up out of the mud while I slumber."

Parsifal crossed himself and began to pray. Merlin began to snore.

Chapter Five

The next morning Merlin awoke to clanking sticks, the two boys practicing their fighting skills. "Just watch the eyes," Merlin warned and rolled over and closed his own again. He hoped Arthur would get a painful whack on the head to teach him something about fighting.

The boys paused and found themselves staring out over the bog wondering how a ghost could rise out of it, since it now looked so literal and placid by the stark light of day. When they looked at each other with blank faces, they had to wonder if any of it had ever happened at all. "The wasteland," Arthur muttered in awe.

"Maybe the holy grail is buried right here in this bog!"

Arthur shook his head. "We could never dig enough to be sure."

Parsifal said, "The abbey had better be able to help us with information, a map with a very clear location. The very spot, marked. We can't dig up the entire kingdom."

Arthur replied, "The monks may not be able to reveal a thing. They may not know very much."

"Catapult!"

"I knew you'd say that. Why do you always say that?"

Parsifal admitted, "It's the only way I can swear and not have my father catapult me across the room. He picked his fighting stick back up. "On guard."

Arthur grabbed his and twirled at him, trying to be fancy. He only got whacked in the head.

Merlin got up. "Curses. You've learned a lesson so soon. Now we must move on and find a new lesson to ready you for when you are the King."

* * * * *

Merlin, Arthur, and Parsifal escaped the western border of the bog without any additional horrors. They passed through a field that had become a mildly diverting maze from a scraggly hedgerow grown wild, to find themselves at the top of a golden colored valley.

Its river had dried to a narrow brown creek that barely supplied a cluster of stone homes, barns, and an uneven row of tarpaulin shop stalls. All pushed up against a tall abbey square. Merlin sniffed. "I smell commerce."

"Ale for Merlin?" Arthur asked.

Merlin pouted. "Nay. Not from that miserable hamlet. Ale is a blessing of the Gods. Ale is proof that there is a God and we might find some small happiness a few nights of our stupid lives with it. There is no happiness here." He sniffed again.

Parsifal asked, "Why isn't this place blessed? It's a charming sight sure enough." He regarded how the roofs were so thatched they almost blended in with the hay fields far yonder.

"You look angry," Arthur said to Merlin.

"Arthur?" Merlin pointed his staff. "Do you see the black tendrils falling out of the clouds and draping over the abbey?"

"Nay."

"Look! Like many smoking chimneys falling backwards and downward? Smoke, dirt, and angry black hornets."

Arthur blinked. "Of course not, but should we go out of our way to avoid it?"

"What is this violence?" Parsifal asked. "Are knights there? Should we avoid this place?"

Merlin assured him. "Nay, not knights. Just the same, I'd very much like to pass through, to spoil their milk at least."

Arthur surmised, "To make it cheese?"

"To make it rank. So the constable can't drink it."

Parsifal asked, "Is it that nasty a place?"

"As nasty as rot," Merlin said. "That church square sits apart as its own pious kingdom, the dreadful blight of Abbey Town. If the constable gets any more gluttonous he'll fall over like a whale. If that isn't a horror in a time of drought, I can't speak of any worse."

Arthur asked, "How do you know of this man? Have you ever been here?"

"Last night in my dreams I was bouncing off a goodly wife, and then I realized I was bouncing off a pot belly. The rest came at me in even greater horror. This town incites the extermination of anybody who doesn't think as they do—sure, that's typical in the dictatorship of a monarchy—but this one takes the turnip!"

Arthur took a step backwards. "Then let's not go in."

Merlin ignored him. They hiked down the slope to the valley floor, flanked a flooded sewer-smelling defensive ditch, and entered an open gate to the abbey square. In the center of the plaza they spotted Mother Hubbard tied fast to a stake. Bundled branches were stacked around it. Men were lighting torches of twisted flax.

"What's this?" Parsifal crossed himself in fear. "A witch? Are we in the presence of evil?"

Merlin stated, "You're in the presence of a righteous mob, and that's evil enough. Horrors! But don't be afraid. Mobs will always be a part of human misbehavior."

Parsifal argued, "Are you to say the mob is evil and the witch is good?"

"I didn't mention her yet. I know nothing of her. She might be very guilty of being a woman. I was only commenting on the nature of mobs."

Parsifal glared at Merlin in irritation. "But is a witch not to burn?"

Merlin ignored him. He asked Arthur, "What do you say?"

"Why is she to burn," Arthur asked. "This isn't just. Is it? What did she do?"

Merlin explained, "Christendom won't abide by witches, we must usually presume."

"Even good ones?" Arthur questioned. "What has she done?"

"Christendom won't even abide by witches who haven't poisoned a king, poisonous assassinations being what originally gave them such a bad name in goodly court. So bad a name that even the kings of the Hebrew Scriptures shuddered at the thought of them."

Arthur looked about at the crowd that was growing louder with such comments as, "Poke her in the eyes so she can't see us! Rip out her tongue so she can't curse us! Cut off her breasts so she can't poison us!"

Arthur finally ordered Merlin. "Stop this. Stop them! Now! Fast!"

"Why? A witch is only one person. Must we go against an entire town that might otherwise be thriving?" He looked about at all the new thatch. "It's doing better than most towns, you must admit, now that you see it so close. Look over there. I see curtains in the window. The house can afford curtains. "

Arthur asked, "But is that witch innocent?"

Merlin pulled on his moustache. "Not of being a witch, I suspect. Toads and warts, she may have a few clever spells up within her. She may be guilty of all that she's charged with."

Parsifal looked to Arthur in distress. "But a witch is not to live. Christendom has no genuine forgiveness for the likes of her."

"Nonsense," Arthur scoffed. "Whoever's teaching you your catechism is daft. It's the God of Christendom's job to forgive. You're thinking of Zeus if you want silly thunderbolts. I can't imagine what else the God of Christendom has to do all day but forgive, now that he's already created the world and already rested from it. Unless he's too busy making it rain across the cold sea in Ireland for him to bother with the rest of us here."

Merlin began to laugh. The wild laughter made Arthur feel uneasy, so he ordered Merlin, "Stop them! Stop them all. I'm the prince and I can order you."

"Do you feel it's that important?"

"Aye. I feel very strongly!"

"And a strong feeling makes it right?"

"Of course!"

"Another lesson might be learned today." Merlin looked down the three narrow dirt streets that led from the plaza. He inspected the piled-up townhouses with their tiers of sagging balconies crowded with chairs, laundry, and potted herbs. He regarded carts already piled high with the day's garbage. He regarded the wattle and daub walls framed by aged timbers. Many tarpaulins and flags made up the shop tents. He decided the bakery oven didn't smell very good. When Merlin spotted a cat, it frightened and bolted off screaming.

He saw laughing boys running towards the plaza since the church school had let out early for the witch burning. "What ugly little warts. This town's a clanking piss pot!"

"What else can be done?" Parsifal defended it. "It seems to be trying to keep itself as clean as can be."

"Brownies couldn't sweep fast enough for what falls out of their bodies and minds. Are you ready, Arthur, ready for a wizard sweep?"

"Aye."

Merlin looked angrily at a plump thatched roof. He pointed his staff at it. Then at his command, Arthur put his tinderbox at his toes and struck the flint and steel from it. "Fire from rock, sky and water, hit the dead fairyless tree—by oak, ash and thorn, so mote it be." Sparks crackled over a rooftop then tongues of fire licked out of the thatch. It quickly grew into a fat orange pillar of fire.

"*Fiiiiiire!*" the townsfolk cried. "To the buckets!"

"There." Merlin nodded with satisfaction, watching the blaze grow even larger. "Toads and warts. If they want a fire, they've got fire."

Parsifal shook. "They didn't want that!"

"They were going to burn a witch. That would have been a fire. They got what they prayed for, but like all prayers, they don't always get answered where expected." The wind began to spread the fire and it flashed and then billowed from rooftop to rooftop, now with no help from Merlin.

"We haven't enough buckets!" the people of the town cried.

Arthur worried. "Merlin? Is it supposed to do that?"

"Do what?"

"Spread so fast."

"Don't you know what fire is?"

Arthur's tinderbox caught fire and he quickly hopped away from it. "My only prize possession!"

Merlin shrugged. "You play with fire, it spreads, you burn things."

"My tinderbox!" Arthur yelled angrily. It consumed.

The potbellied town constable grabbed a burning board from where it had fallen and rushed to Mother Hubbard's kindling. "You'll burn!" he screamed at her in wild fury. "You… you… *witch!*"

Merlin regarded the misplaced anger, "No, *you* will." With that mere regarding of it, and an angry stabbing motion of Merlin's staff, the hotheaded constable burst into blue flames. "A burning whale! Now that's a rare sight!" Merlin chuckled.

Screaming anew, the constable dove into an empty water trough.

"Eee-*ucht!* Rotten eggs! That's what you get!" Mother Hubbard yelled at him, even over the roar around her. She fought stubbornly against her binds. "You give me the evil eye like that, you pay with your own fever!"

Parsifal rushed to the billowing constable to see his condition, acting overly gallant, trying to extinguish the man's cremation that was now also consuming the wood of the trough. "Catapults!"

Merlin smiled. "Now he'll stop eating the food of all the widows."

"Is this just?" Arthur asked, unsure of how to read the great violence unspooling around him. "I don't like the look of such a fire gone wild, now that I see it."

"Why not? It's *big!* The children should be excited." A single red pillar of fire developed and twisted from all the rooftops all the way up to the clouds.

Arthur gasped. "I'm having trouble breathing."

Merlin shrugged. "The fire is burning up all the air. But new air will come in and take its place. Don't worry. It'll pass."

"Put it out or it'll ruin everything for all time."

Merlin shrugged. "It'll be rebuilt."

Arthur yelled, "But that'll make it different! They can't rebuild it the same way!"

"You've always been bothered about the impermanence of things."

"Who wouldn't be?" The ashes of his tinderbox blew across his toes.

Merlin pulled on the side of his moustache. "Did the town not want to unjustly burn a poor old woman? So what's more important? A town's curtains or an old woman's sagging body?"

"A woman?" Arthur answered, not sure anymore, feeling fresh cold air sucking up his legs while hot air blew over his head. Then he thought he saw Merlin's red cap ruffling its feathers as if it were a bird waking up. "Your cap!"

Merlin clobbered his own head, the red feathers became calm again. "The whole town is going up! That's just!" He chortled. "Punish the daft buggers, all of them!"

Arthur filled with doubts. "A woman should be stopped from burning at all costs?" He watched the thatch blow off a roof that hadn't even ignited yet. The voracious pillar of fire pulled it up to the hot clouds, inciting it to sparkle and flash brighter than mad fairies.

Merlin asked, "At all costs? Even if it's the entire shire that's converted to this new Christendom? Even if this new religion would like to have a good crowd-pleasing festival? Woman burning is the festival of this new time. How will you rule then? Will you burn an entire shire to save one woman from indignity, even when there are a few extra women out there to spare?"

"Put it out."

"Sorry, lad, but I can't do that," Merlin confessed, not sorry. "Starting a fire is one thing. Putting it out is another."

"It is?"

Merlin nodded. "Entirely."

Arthur stood muddled, and after Merlin had walked away from him to attend to Mother Hubbard's binds, Arthur finally realized and said out loud, "How can one raise taxes from a burnt shire? Nay. What a fool I was… *am*. Again."

As Merlin unfastened Mother Hubbard's binds, he properly greeted her, "Blessed be."

"Blessed be. Is a storm brewing?" Mother Hubbard asked. "Rain would be lucky for the farmers."

"Nay, it's just the fire blowing off another roof. Have you been tortured?"

"Nay."

"Not whipped and screwed and racked?"

"Nay."

"Not dunked or burned with molten lead?"

"Nay, nay, nay." She rolled her eyes. "They just tried my patience!"

Merlin said, "Then I'll let you live and not kill you for the mercy of it."

Mother Hubbard grinned. "You're so kind, dear wise man. A real gentleman for such concern. I assure you, they wouldn't dare touch a hair on my bonny head."

After a thick waft of black smoke passed them by, Merlin looked about the burning town, bemused. "This is all the wasteland needs, a good fire." He helped her step down off the timbers. "Watch your foot."

She winked at him. "Oh look around. Things are not well these days. Not anywhere."

Merlin felt a bit of glamour magic in her wily expression. He felt his heart leap. "The world isn't getting any worse; it just seems that way now that the carrier pigeons go farther. Are you sure you're not molested by plugs, rakes, and screws?" He looked for bruises. "Hot pokers? Rapid paternosters?"

She wagged her finger. "I said *nay*."

"Then I won't kill you for the mercy of it."

"You sound so disappointed." She looked him over, head to toe. She tapped her fingers on the back of his hand and then slid them up his arm.

Merlin felt his pulse race. It raced around until it thumped between his legs. "Not at all. And aren't you full of spells today, you little pagan. Do have you a husband? And if so, can he be sent away and I'll have my turn with you?"

"I'm all yours. How proper of you to care. You aren't like most men. They've become so religious. Haven't the religious folk become overreaching these days?"

Merlin nodded. "I've nothing against how these religious people would have me think as they think, but it's most appalling as to how they'd have me act as they act."

She tried to smooth her hair. "And they spend so much time in confession. They'd have me confess things I've never even accomplished. The old religion had few sins so we didn't have to hear about it. At least that saved time."

Merlin agreed, "This new religion with its confessors is so popular with the religious, because they like to talk about themselves."

"You're a rare man!" She batted her stubby white eyelashes at him. "Will you marry me and always be so clever as to rescue me whenever humanity draws nigh?"

"Actually, I didn't save you. It was that scrawny lad."

"Where?"

"There."

"The little girl?"

"That one. That's not a lass. Aye *that one*. The one with a face like a slapped puppy."

"Him? He saved me?" Mother Hubbard looked at Arthur, taken aback. "*You?*"

Arthur stepped up to her. "Aye."

"I can't marry *him*. He isn't even old enough to have a billy goat stink."

Arthur stated, "*I* will be getting married only after I've fallen deeply in love."

Merlin looked at Arthur in horror. "Love? You'll be sorry after love has gone." Then Merlin decided, "*I'll* marry this dear woman, for my bed needs some warmer company. That sort of feeling never passes."

"*What?* Why?" Arthur asked.

Merlin looked her up and down. "Marry for the bed, not love. Love is just a delusion that one woman differs from another."

Mother Hubbard elbowed Merlin angrily, "And wisdom, wise wizard, is thinking twice before you say nothing!"

"I'll say—man will not live alone—and while marriage has its solitary pains, celibacy has no shared pleasures."

"So then, you'll marry me?" Mother Hubbard perked, her eyes twinkling. "Really? Really?"

Merlin stood tall. "I said I would. I may be a scoundrel, a cad and double-talker, but by the light of day I usually mean what I say."

"But... but," Arthur protested to Merlin, "You'll be going away... going back to the Realm of the Dragons after my tutorage."

"My *torture?* And what of my bed until then? I should take on a wife since brothels are insufferable and too far one from the other."

Mother Hubbard asked, "Since when has a marriage kept men from brothels? And what did you say about the Realm of Dragons? Do you go there? Do you? Tell me!"

Arthur said, "Adultery is terrible."

Merlin scoffed. "Adultery itself is completely uninteresting. It's what comes just before and just after that makes the legends."

"So you *will* marry me?" Mother Hubbard asked Merlin again. "And I mean a real marriage, not some tricky wizard secret marriage? I want a proper hand fasting now. Then you can take me with you to the Realm of Dragons!"

Arthur pointed out, "Merlin! You aren't alone in life. You have me to tutor! I am your charge now!"

Merlin looked around. "All our lives are a tragedy if we feel, a comedy if we think."

Mother Hubbard busted out into peals of laughter. "You're either wise or a drop of cockle-doodle dung."

"Merlin! Why are you letting her flatter you?"

He shrugged. "Because it feels good? It feels very good!"

Arthur insisted, "I'm not so insufferable that you need a wife to help you along before I become the King! It's only a few years now. And didn't you tell me that flatterers only wish to deceive?"

"You'll be a *king?*" Mother Hubbard asked Arthur, her eyes widening with astonishment. "So you're Arthur? Wait a minute... *that* makes... oh my! So *you* are *Merlin!*"

"Aye."

Mother Hubbard erupted into merriment. "I'll marry the mightiest wizard of all time! I'll marry the man who was the land itself before becoming the first owl who became the first man who became the first wizard! I'm worthy, I assure you. I've many spells of my own! I'm worthy of being married to you proper!"

Merlin looked down at the front of his robe. "Aye, I can see what your love spell has done. What powers." He smoothed his robe to his belly to show how his arousal was pushing out the fabric. She laughed.

Arthur asked Merlin, "You were once an owl?"

Mother Hubbard asked Merlin, "Do you often go to the Realm of Dragons? Let's go there together today! Let's go! Now!"

Merlin nodded. "This flesh that I'm squeezed into has a way of squeezing a man back, and I'll not suffer from it needlessly. Marriage is a lovely deception as mortals need to find some small refuge somewhere. Mortals always have all sorts of mad hungers. Too often the crowd becomes faceless and the night gets dark… the bed too cold and dry. That's why a man takes a wife."

Arthur said, "And love, Merlin. But you need none of this. You're Merlin. Special."

"I'm only mortal now that I'm out of the Realm of Dragons. Now that I'm here I should give in to a few mortal comforts."

"Tell me of that," Mother Hubbard begged. "Not your comforts, but of the Realm of Dragons!"

"*Oooh*," Arthur mocked Merlin. "Comforts. Like when you gave up and gave in and finally decided to start eating food?"

Merlin magically made Arthur trip in his place, and badly pretended he hadn't, and as Mother Hubbard helped the boy up, Merlin said to him, "Don't mock me."

Mother Hubbard asked, "How long did it take you to remember that a person had to eat?"

"After a fortnight I grew weak so I ate a bellyful. And the food went on from there. It was all with repulsive consequences, but flesh is flesh. *Toad* all of stinking earth!"

She grabbed his arm. "And what's your spell to travel to the Realm of Dragons? What is it? Tell me now!"

"It's not as simple as a spell."

"You'll tell me," Mother Hubbard insisted. "As we are a couple now you must teach me everything you know! I'll very much wish to visit the Realm of Dragons. As man and wife, you must teach me these things."

"Why?" Merlin asked.

"Because I'm your lovely wife!"

Arthur regarded Mother Hubbard. "But… she's so old."

Mother Hubbard gave Merlin a dirty look. "Old wizard, your pupil isn't very learned. Have you failed to mention to him how a witch grows old before her time from such hard work, or how that same witch can reverse the effect and have the ability to create a great and timeless glamour? I do have powers and I can do that. But that's fare for kittens, so now I'll learn how to visit the Realm of Dragons!"

Arthur looked back and forth between the two and finally said to Mother Hubbard, "Are you sure you're not simply excited to marry him for the spells you'll gain from him?"

"I already know spells and the glamour spell is easy. A witch is as good at glamour as a wizard, if not better. Besides, I'm in a new youth. They say thirty is the old age of youth and forty is the youth of old age, so youth I'm back at."

Merlin looked surprised. "You look much older. Have you been taxed by spells to get kith and kin through these hard times?" She nodded sadly.

"So, you'll really marry her? Really?" Arthur asked Merlin, doubtful. "As my tutor, should you be doing this right now? What of the grail quest? What of the wasteland? Do you really want a wife at a time like this?"

"Of course."

Arthur felt jealous. "Well then, what'll become of me?"

"Think of it as another lesson. You'll learn that this wizard will have his nook and cranny even if he has to marry for it."

"Oh, I see," Mother Hubbard said to Merlin. "Your little earthly dragon has been sleeping too much, you fear. We'll I'm glad it pokes about now for some adventure, or I'd worry for you."

"Little dragon?" Arthur puzzled.

Merlin told him, "What's awakened during kisses doesn't feel so little."

Arthur turned red. Mother Hubbard smiled at him in impatience, then turned back to Merlin. "Are you sure you're a thorough tutor? Have you told him what a king does with his kingdom of maidens?"

Merlin answered, "He'll fight to keep the many shires Gwynedd, Dyfed, and Powys when that old Vortigern finally gives up the ghost, though I've heard that close-fisted man doesn't give up anything."

"Long live the King!" Mother Hubbard dutifully sang out loudly.

Merlin finally remembered to ask his new fiancé, "So what clumsy witchcraft has brought you to the honor of this town's stake?"

She raised her eyebrows, insulted. "Clumsy?"

"So that they saw it to accuse you. Usually men are blind to cleverness. They always blame the wrong poor milking wench for such hysterical reasons. They leave the real witches to their spinning."

She put her head down in shame. "Nay, I've not been clever. They found me in a very ridiculous posture. I've been taxing myself beyond measure and all for laying goose eggs enough for a town of poor hungry children. They have nothing else to eat. The land is withered since our poor village has lost our grail."

"Holy grail?" Arthur asked. "You had it? You had the holy grail? But what is it?"

"Grail," Mother Hubbard repeated.

"You had the holy grail?"

"Aye."

"What was it?"

Mother Hubbard impatiently explained, "First, dear prince, it's a word. It's a foreign word but common enough in these lands. It means *a meal*, to be small about it. In our case, it's the entire goodly cauldron that feeds the entire hungry town, humble as it is. That is our grail; it is our cauldron of plenty. And it has been stolen by someone with great powers."

Arthur asked Merlin, "Have I heard of that town?"

Mother Hubbard shook her head. "We've been called *the otherworld* before, but that's just because it's *so nothing*, methinks. Most who travel by us fail to notice us at all."

Arthur asked, "How could your cauldron be stolen? Isn't a thing like that mighty heavy?"

"It was stolen by being stolen. And if that isn't enough horror for one dry summer, it seems to have been stolen by a monster capable of turning it affright into a widdershins—a spell turned on its head—an upside-down kettle is good for only one thing."

"A demon bell!" Merlin finished for her, his eyes glowing with realization.

"You know about it?" she asked him.

"Only in principle. I remember something about it now from a past tedious sojourn on this earth. I remember that a goodly article such as a chalice, horn of plenty, or any kettle, any goodly vessel that's used for communal sustenance, but then is stolen by a fiend to be subverted to an unwholesome use, is often done so to become a demon bell. Just as a proper village bell can be stolen so that instead of providing an alarm against danger, it's likewise subverted by being put upside-down. That makes it into a black-magic cauldron to provide danger." Merlin waved his staff dramatically. "It's all very complicated."

Arthur asked, "Why can't it just be simple?"

"Only a clever mind holds two opposing thoughts at the very same time. And only simpletons need things made simple."

Arthur said, "We were on our way to the abbey. What does any of this have to do with the abbey?"

Mother Hubbard jolted. "An Abbey! Eee-*ucht!* That sounds like an evil place to me! I bet it stole our grail for its evil spells!"

Merlin shook his head. "I don't think so. The abbot is a crook but only of forged parchments. We have to go there to ask him if he knows more than he's not written."

Mother Hubbard asked Merlin suspiciously, *"You'd* never steal our cauldron, as a wizard, would you? It's not *you* who took our cauldron of plenty. If you did, I'll have to slay you."

"I may be a scoundrel as a wizard and as a man, but I'm not a monster."

"Nor a thief," Arthur defended him, then doubted, "Are you?"

She asked, "Doesn't your pupil trust you?"

"I hope not. I hope I've at least taught him to not trust anybody, never, not if he's to be the King. Not even his wife or best friend."

Arthur protested. "I'll certainly trust at least two people, at least them. I'd like *some* comfort in my long life."

"Suit yourself."

Arthur sallied, "And you're a cad! It seems you're ready to suit yourself to marry a witch you don't even know."

Merlin stiffened. "I'll be done with you and this earth. I'll be back to the Realm of Dragons soon enough. It isn't like I'm shackled for eternity with mortal arrangements, and until then my earthly dragon needs to roar and rage from time to time."

"You're indeed a scoundrel." Mother Hubbard laughed. "And you must teach me the ways through the gates into the Realm of Dragons! That'll be a fair exchange for such a marriage."

Arthur asked Merlin, "Are you also a scoundrel in the Realm of Dragons?"

"Of course not, men can only do men's things here on earth, but the Realm of Dragons is like living as churning clouds in the sky or as ceaseless water in a brook, it's not living as one with mortal flesh and the puny prison of the ignorant arrogant five senses."

"I can't wait to visit." Mother Hubbard wept. "I can't wait!"

They paused to regard a massive clamor as the timbers of the burning roof of the abbey crashed in. And then the tall grain tower folded inward, and all of its stones crushed the flames that were there. A very grey Parsifal returned, covered in ashes, looking shaken, and regarded Mother Hubbard with great suspicion. "Good day. A bad day we're having. I'm Parsifal." He bowed, not taking his eyes off of her.

"And I'm Mother Hubbard." She eyed his legs "What an odd cut of clothing you're wearing under all that filth."

"My trousers."

She marveled. "Sewn right together into one garment. The right leg with the left. How clever."

"And they were clean once."

Mother Hubbard said, "If you've already made such an ash of yourself, could you go find the granary? We could use this town's grain."

"But is that just?" Parsifal asked Merlin. "We can't just steal their grain!"

Merlin shook some ash out of his beard. "Hmm. Usually when a town is deliberately burned, it's for sacking, nay? But we're here on a holier cause? Saving a fine hard working wench from burning?"

Mother Hubbard insisted, "Feeding dozens of hungry children is as holy as anything."

"What do you say, prince?" Merlin asked Arthur.

"We've made a riot of things here, enough, sure. I think we should leave them some food to carry on, now that I've ruined their permanence of things."

"Charity from the prince, how kind. Will that be your new order as the King? Charity?" Arthur nodded. Merlin continued, "And who'll pull this charity off? Knights?" He laughed.

"Can we stop this fire, now?" Arthur asked Merlin. "There must be some way. Be clever."

"I'd send rain, but there isn't a drop in the parched sky to squeeze out. It's surely a demon bell starving this hide of land." Mother Hubbard nodded to agree.

"The demon bell?" Parsifal asked.

"The holy grail," Arthur said. "One and the same. So they say."

"What?" Parsifal asked. "How can one be the other? Those sound like two very different things! One good. One bad."

Mother Hubbard cackled. "How quickly one becomes another."

Parsifal frowned. "I think the holy grail is something else. Something grander. It has to be."

Mother Hubbard argued, "Nothing is grander to a village than its communal pot. Nothing is grander to a stomach than a meal now and again."

Arthur reiterated, but still questioning, "The holy grail is a pot of gruel? It seems like it should be more."

She teased, "Perchance flanked with the shining doors of Heaven?" Arthur nodded. She grew angry. "Wanting it a certain way doesn't make it so. It is what it is! And you watch your tongue, young prince. You tell any old woman that her pot isn't worth a fart and she'll box your ears!"

Arthur became overwhelmed with discouragement. "So okay, it's a pot. Who knows where to look for something like that? It could be anywhere. Why bother to even try. It would be easier just to leave the wasteland. It would be easier to just walk away and go to some other place. We could live somewhere else than here."

Merlin asked, "What would a king do?"

Arthur answered, "A king would want all of his land prosperous for the next taxation."

Merlin nodded. "We'll go find this demon bell then. We'll turn it back upright and fix this wasteland so you have something to tax. And we'll do this before Mother Hubbard has to lay anymore goose eggs and accrue more wrinkles."

Mother Hubbard smiled, flirting with her eyelashes again. "To do that, you'll be a good husband. And you'll take me to the Realm of Dragons, too."

Merlin said, "Nay, I'm selfish. I don't want you to lay anymore eggs."

"Why would you care about that."

"The work ages you so badly. I'd just rather not mount a woman who has become like a dead tree."

Mother Hubbard slapped his face, then picked up the rope at her feet and handed it to Arthur. "We'll be married now. The prince can do the deed and then we'll holiday in the Realm of Dragons, posthaste."

Arthur reluctantly took the rope. "Are you *sure* you wouldn't want the Church to do your wedding?"

Mother Hubbard said, "Such a prince can marry us and it'll be the highest honor. And this handsome young Parsifal looks like he is of the best breeding. He can be our witness to this handfasting."

Another blazing building loudly collapsed, shaking the ground. Shimmering ashes blew over them, smelling spicy like green tansy and pine, and for a fleeting instant, the ashes chimed like tiny bells.

Mother Hubbard looked up. "Ah, the silver branch is over us. We are blessed; this'll surely be the highest of all high handfasts."

Merlin put his hand over hers. She quickly slipped her hand up to be the one on top. As Arthur tied the rope on their hands, joining them, Merlin slipped his hand back up over hers to be on top. Arthur secured the knot very firmly over Merlin's knuckles, so they'd not be able to switch again, and he prayed, "By the power of two, one you will be, and the one who becomes will want out and to flee, so this knot lasts till then, then till then you agree, that a marriage is best, so mote it be. Transform, fath-fith. Transform, forthwith. And now I apologize," Arthur quickly added, "for not having caraway seeds to toss over you both to make you lustful."

"What kind of unholy clap-trap is that?" Mother Hubbard gave Arthur a frown. "Who taught you that handfasting spell?"

Arthur regarded Merlin, puzzling at how she'd somehow managed to get her hand back up on top of his again. "It's how the wizard taught it to me, since as the King I'll be joining many daunting couples, tying their knots."

"And *you* think a marriage is untied as easily as a knot?"

"Aye. Well, *nay*," Arthur rethought. "*I* would never think such, for myself. True love isn't a rope with a knot."

Merlin asked her, "What kind of a marriage is this going to be? There's so many kinds we can choose from these days. Is this a Roman marriage or a Celtic marriage? In a Celtic marriage the arrangement is only for a year and a day, and even then an easy divorce could be requested from the Druid in charge once the clan got tired of hearing all the quarreling."

Arthur frowned. "When I marry my queen it will only be for a year?"

"A king's marriage is for a lifetime. That's because kings don't live long. We commoners have a different set of rules."

Mother Hubbard said, "So be it. I've got you for a livelong year, at least, starting tomorrow. I'll just stay in the Realm of Dragons after that, probably, anyway. I'm tired of dirt. But, wait a minute. Isn't *fath-fith* used for an invisible spell?"

"Where are you?" Merlin called out, pretending to see past her. "My wife is already out of my beard, how prosperous for me."

Mother Hubbard tore the knot away from their hands. "Scoundrel!" She turned to Parsifal and ordered him, "*You* have a strong back; we'll cart away our bags of grain now."

Parsifal looked to Arthur for confirmation of that order. Arthur nodded and added, "Leave a few bags behind so this town can carry on."

The abbey collapsed completely and a new cloud of ash rolled over the square and covered the rest of them in a film of grey.

"*Eee*-ucht! What a corker of a day!"

Chapter Six

That same evening, as the purple and gold of a languishing sunset cloaked most of the stars, Nimm wandered about the village square with a blank look in her eyes. "The dragons! Do you hear the dragons? I must find them! I must go to them. I must be where they are!"

"Mum." Rafe took his mom's arm. "Why do you look so lost? You're home, now. You're back. Just relax. Just sit somewhere. Stop it. You're making me nervous!"

Nimm looked at her son oddly, and then quickly pulled the scarf off her head as if it was burning her. "Dragon roars. I hear them." She put her hands to her ears.

"What?" Rafe asked.

Nimm nodded. "A great battle—*a war!*—a violent fight in the Realm of Dragons."

"What do you mean?" Rafe asked.

"The veil between the worlds is parting and then closing. I don't know what I'm seeing but I must go to it. I must find that place again."

"Nay! You won't go anywhere! You're my mum! You'll not be led off by a bell one night and then by a big roar, the next. You're to stay with me! You have to!"

Nimm whispered, "I heard it but now it's gone."

Rafe took her hand. "What?"

She squeezed it. "Now I wonder if it was just a dream. But the blood was so delicious. Dragon blood. I don't know how I'll ever forget the glimpse of it—the taste of it—the sight of such a bounty of red."

"Nay, it wasn't real," Rafe insisted. "You're my mum and nothing more."

"The dragons want me. I'm special. I'm destined for a life more than an earthly one! Earth floats on the dragon blood of old and I fear, I feel, I'm sinking deep into it."

"What? Nay! Stop it Mum. Please!"

Nimm put her finger to her lips. "The very edges of this land are melting away. The edges fall in great thunderous avalanches. Middle earth is crumbling down into dragon's blood. It's melting from below. The mantle is thinning. Soon we'll all swim in blood!"

"Stop it!"

"I've been kissed by the Goddess; I've been kissed by the dragons. I've been *kissed!*"

"Nay!"

"*Kissed!*"

Rafe stamped his foot. "You're my mum and nothing more! And you must act normal or the men of the inquisition will see you and want to burn you!"

"Burn who?" Mother Hubbard called out.

Merlin, Arthur, Mother Hubbard, and Parsifal walked up to them tugging a cart of five sacks of grain. Rafe grabbed his mother and pulled her impatiently to them, along with the other children who poured from the barn. "Blessed be! You all smell like you've been at a nice bonfire. Where did you find such splendid wood?"

"Put your hair back up," Mother Hubbard chastised Nimm. "You look like a bewildered slave." She helped her twist and wrap her long auburn hair around her head and retie her scarf. "You know how you hate to get anything in your hair, anyway, even a piece of straw. You go mad."

Priest Owen came out of his round house. "What a blessing! Our woman who feeds the land! Of course we couldn't find a single goose egg all while you were gone. Blessings on you as on me!"

"The food we bring is for the children," Mother Hubbard told him. "Don't think for a second that this is for you."

Priest Owen eyed the sacks of grain in the cart. "But you must tithe to the church."

"Why?"

"It's the law."

Mother Hubbard asked Arthur, "Do we have a bag of thistles back there?" Arthur shook his head. "Alas, the lucky Christian gets half a bag of grain."

"A *whole* bag of grain," Priest Owen bargained.

"I know what a tithe is, you old cheat. *Half* a bag. Now let's make some porridge. And children, chew the grain to dust so it digests well or I'll make you eat the same bowl over again and again until you get it right. My new husband Merlin will spank you, too."

Priest Owen looked oddly at Parsifal. "What strange pants."

"They've been sewn into one piece," he demonstrated, tugging at where they joined.

"It looks sinful, I fear."

"Rotten eggs! Sin in pants? You're all daft!" Mother Hubbard left them and scampered off to the barn. She climbed up the ladder to the barn loft and dug through the straw in the corner to unbury her staff that had an inlaid crystal shard at its top. She smiled in relief that nobody had discovered it, and then nervously hid it again.

Still in the greensward, standing in shock at the sight of so many children and in alarm of the sound of their loud little voices, Merlin frowned. "A sea of warts."

A little girl skipped up to him and said, "You're a nice old man. May I sit on your lap?"

"Come closer," he enticed her, bending down to her. A few spiders rushed out of his beard.

The little girl screamed and ran back to the barn.

"You're a cad!" Arthur said, but Merlin couldn't hear him through his own laughter.

As Mother Hubbard returned from the barn loft, Nimm exclaimed to her, "If you have a husband now, then we'll have a festival for it! A wedding festival! Something worthy of dragons!"

Rafe smiled big with relief that his mum's mood had finally brightened. "Aye! A festival!"

Priest Owen protested, "*I* didn't bind your marriage for you."

"A prince did!" Mother Hubbard bragged. "And it was witnessed by a wealthy young inheritor, which is better than anything a priest in this village could have offered." Then she nodded eagerly at Merlin to add, "And it would be nice to have another wedding in the Realm of Dragons! Let's do as Nimm suggests and go there now. Let's go to the dragons!"

Priest Owen made the sign of the cross on her. "Blessings on you as on me. I hope."

"You're so blessed!" Nimm grabbed Mother Hubbard's hands in excitement. "I don't care about dragons anymore today. My head was full of them just a moment ago but now we have this. You're a bride! That is such good news! I don't care if you've already tied the knot; you'll reenact your wedding in the tradition of our own town. We'll have a grand festival full of proper tradition!"

Merlin grew irritated. "One wedding per marriage is more than enough."

Nimm adjusted her head scarf. "We must do it properly for all the children to see! They need inspiration so very badly!"

Merlin gave them all a nasty look and they backed away. "The tiny little children will do well enough without a festival at my expense. Children hate dancing, games, and treats."

"Nonsense!" Nimm protested, stepping closer to him in defiance. "We *will* have a wedding festival and only your funeral festival can prevent it!"

Merlin said, "We were on our way to the abbey and would like to get there before reincarnation sets in. Young Parsifal has to punch someone in the nose on behalf of his father. The violence involves coins and pride; so it is just."

Nimm put her hands on her hips. "You can all go on some fool men's adventure tomorrow."

Parsifal sadly said, "It's only a holy grail we're looking for, anyway, and I don't know anymore if it's anything as grand as I first thought it might be."

Merlin shook his finger at him. "You might be surprised, lad. If restoring one lost cauldron cures this shire of drought, it'll be just what you were looking for. And the abbey may still give us a clue as to how to begin."

Mother Hubbard shooed them off. "You can all prepare for my party while I ready some of this grain for a marriage feast!"

Parsifal pouted. "That's all we'll eat? Just that? In my father's house a feast is ale and meats and cheeses and white bread."

"Yeah! Ale!" Merlin smiled. "Pour me a yard of it!"

Nimm frowned. "We have none of that here."

"Soon," Arthur assured Merlin. "In my reign, there'll be no wasteland and even the peasants will eat plenty and will have ale."

Merlin scoffed. "By then, I'll be out of here. I want a yard of it now!"

Mother Hubbard winked. "And I'll be with him… in the Realm of Dragons!"

Merlin pouted. "There is nothing sadder than a wedding without ale."

* * * * *

As wedding preparations began, Rafe showed Arthur the barn. "That's Palag." Rafe pointed up into the rafters at the big yellow cat. The cat regally turned his head away.

"He's so fat!" Arthur marveled. "Where does he find all his mice?"

"Cat magic, I'm sure. They say he swam all the way from Ireland as a kitten; he's that ferocious."

"Is that possible? *Naaay.*"

Rafe added, "He'll soon be so big we'll have to slay him."

Arthur climbed up onto the mount of a log horse that the children had fashioned. He looked down on Rafe. Arthur carefully eyed him head to toe. "How old are you?"

"I don't know. Twelve Samhains. Thirteen the next one, methinks. Ask Mum. She would know for sure."

Arthur asked, "Do you worry about not growing up all the way?"

Rafe said, "Don't be daft. Everybody grows up all the way."

"But, I mean… how it'll be? Do you know?"

"I don't know if I'll live that long. *You* can worry about it because you'll probably get all hacked-up and skewered or chopped into kibbles. All in a great glorious heroic battle. But people like me often just get lice and starve to death and that's that, no glory, and no one notices."

Arthur winced. "Hacked doesn't sound like glory."

"It's something to do. It's about the only thing to do around here that people will talk about. Consider yourself lucky."

Arthur straightened his back. "Do you think I'll be tall when I'm full grown?"

Rafe shrugged. "Tall and other things. You know what a man grown all the way up looks like. Taller than you, for sure."

Arthur asked, "If you do grow old enough to be a man, fully grown. What do you think it'll be like?"

Rafe chewed on a piece of straw. "Be like? It'll be like being big and strong I guess, and make a wife have my babies. Lots of them so I'm not alone if I do live long. Your children have to like you, you know. When you have children they're stuck with you. That's what Mum said once."

"What do you think that'll feel like?"

"*What* will it feel like?" Rafe said. "Making a wife have babies? Good, I suppose. They say it's the only good thing you get in life—that, and cheese—that's what the priest says."

Arthur shook his head. "I mean, having a wife. Will you be afraid?"

"She's the one who needs to fear. They usually die trying to give birth. But anyway, I'm afraid of everything and I don't know if I'll live to be old enough to have a wife. I don't like thinking about it."

Arthur felt frustrated that he couldn't say what he was feeling. "What I mean is… I don't know."

"And your questions are not nice. I think I'll go now and help Mum with the wedding." Rafe spat the sliver of straw out and hurried away.

Arthur sat alone on the log horse. He didn't feel like he belonged up in such a lofty position. He tried to imagine that he had mounted his horse and was high over a valley. It was flooding with ferocious Saxons and he alone would lop all their stubbly heads off. Then he'd pause and acknowledge that his enemies were men that fought with bravery and he'd give a humble prayer of thanks to the Goddess Victory so she wouldn't drive him mad for being a monster, at least not in matters of slaughter.

"Ride me to Summerland," he told the horse. "I am a fierce King! I am mighty!" Since it didn't move, he slipped off, scratching the tender inside of his leg on the rough bark.

* * * * *

Mother Hubbard deftly took the grain, cracked a large portion between two stones then soaked the flour and carefully placed cakes of it on the coals. "Rotten eggs. If I'd a proper grail I could make this into the most runny and sloppy gruel."

"You're doing marvelous." Nimm helped keep the cakes from burning. "Considering that we don't even usually have a pot, this is clever of you."

Mother Hubbard grumbled, "I should've had Arthur take a pot from that last town that tried to burn me down. Why didn't I think to do that! They had soup pots, and even piss pots I bet. Rotten eggs. I just burned my finger."

Nimm blew on her fingers. "You've done enough today and you've yet to get married for us. So rest. Let me turn all the cakes. You just relax and watch. *Ouch*!"

"Eee-*ucht*!"

The women finished their cooking and then passed out the cakes. The communal meal was eaten with reverence. While the twilight of the purple cloudless sky slipped into a raven black eventide of bright crystal stars, Nimm and the children snuck away and finished preparing the greensward for a wedding of proper old-fashioned rituals.

"We're done! It's time!" Nimm clapped her hands for attention.

Merlin griped, "I suddenly want to be a Roman. They were such a practical people."

Nimm led Mother Hubbard and Merlin to the barn. "Come into the sacred grove!"

"Sacred grove?" Merlin asked. "I'd love to see one of those around here. The Romans turned our last one into lumber for their fort."

Nimm said, "It'll be a sacred grove of the children's imagination."

"How charming." Merlin was not charmed.

Rafe got on his knees to slip crude wooden clogs onto their feet. "Put these wedding shoes on first. So you don't touch earth."

Merlin winced. His were too tight and pinched his toes. He fixed his face and tried his best to look like he was walking on air, only to help hurry things along to their climax.

At the barn door, Mother Hubbard screamed, "Bones!"

"Aye," Nimm nodded proudly. Hundreds of sheep bones dangled from strings all about their heads, with a few lit tallow candles and small whale oil lamps also on strings, amongst them.

Merlin chuckled. "I forgot how some children have true imagination. I *am* impressed."

Rafe nodded proudly. "Aye, these aren't bones today, but the golden boughs of the sacred mistletoe. Come and walk to its magic center."

"*Blessed be. Blessed be,*" the children sang and danced in circles around them as Merlin took Mother Hubbard's hand, so she could help him walk in the horrible clogs. "*Blessed be, the old oak, ash and thorn tree.*"

Priest Owen rushed in like a crazed zealot, splashed them all with water from a small clay bowl, and hastily pronounced, "The pagan devils be gone!" He quickly raced back out.

"Oh break wind!" Nimm yelled after him. "If you can't be nice then at least shut your porridge hole!"

After the children stopped laughing, Rafe led them in song,

"*In life after life, the cycle of seasons
there's the seasons for marriage and frolic
to the sacred grove we walk in honor
to the sacred well we drink and are full
to the sacred fire we're warm and safe*

*In birth and rebirth, born again to another
there's the festival of marriage and new babies
and when the marriage grows old and the wheel turns
and new lovers have babies for our souls
and soldiers to fight, to die, and be reborn.
Fee-fidel fee-fidel fee-fee-fee fidel-fum."*

Mother Hubbard stepped out of her clogs and joined the dancing, hiking up her apron and kicking her legs up high to show the folks how youthful she could be. Merlin watched, growing happy at the sight of her strong legs.

They sang the song over and over.

"*In birth and rebirth, born again to another,
there is the festival of marriage and new babies."*

Mother Hubbard began to laugh loudly as Merlin began to protest the song, "Nay anymore babies! This town and this woman have enough children!"

"I still have my eggs!" Mother Hubbard howled.

Merlin turned away and a dangling sheep's rib poked him in the eye. "Is this the end of the festival so I can get on with my wife?" he asked them, blowing a magic-enough breath to disturb all the hanging bones in the barn.

"Nay," Rafe said. "We have to burn you to death."

"Again?" Mother Hubbard chuckled. "All the naughty Spirits of the wood, water, and air are already confused at my being at a stake already once today."

"They saw you saved," Nimm warned her, "but this time we'll trick them good and you'll spend the night in peace and not have your new husband cursed with impotence."

Merlin protested, "I'll not beg your pardon. You'll simply know that a man fresh from the Realm of the Dragons has no trouble with his own roar, no matter what imp may be near to curse me."

Ignoring his manly crowing, two empty gunnysacks were pulled down over both the bride and groom's heads to disguise them.

"Careful!" Mother Hubbard gasped. "Leave a lot of room for air. I'm breathless!"

They were led outside of the barn to the greensward where a carefully prepared bonfire was lit. Larger than life-sized effigy scarecrows of Merlin and Mother Hubbard were tied together up on it.

"Burn the bride, burn the groom!" they all chanted loudly, so the spirits of the air were sure to hear. "Burn them so the rest of us can live another day! They're dead, they're gone, the tricking spirits watching are left with nothing and can go home!"

Priest Owen ran out to them again with his small bowl of water and baptized some more of them in messy haste, again, hollering prayers that couldn't be heard over their howls, "Blessings on you as on me!" and then as quickly as he came, he ran off into the dark again as the scarecrows of Merlin and Mother Hubbard were set alight. The crowd whooped and hollered louder as the scarecrow arms came alive and waved as they burned and it seemed to everyone's ripe imaginations as if two giants had been killed.

Nimm shouted, "To the magic land of man and wife!"

The children hoisted the real Merlin and Mother Hubbard high into the air, with the sacks still over their heads, taking them over a pile of broomstraw, chanting, "These are only sacks of cobs, all you tricking spirits leave these sacks alone. The tricking spirits watching us are tired and are left with nothing and can go home."

Merlin and Mother Hubbard were carried into the barn where they were dumped into a manger of fresh straw, love spell herbs, and threadbare blankets. Then they were left alone to play as the crowd stood outside the barn and sang, *By the power of two, one you will be, and the one who becomes will want out and to flee, so this knot lasts till then, then till then you agree, that a marriage is best, poof-poof ho ho, so mote it be.*"

Then songs that were very bawdy and lewd to encourage baby-making continued to be sung outside in a manner that would confuse even the Devil of Christendom, along with Priest Owen who ran around the crowd and vainly tried to stop them.

"I wish I had mint," Mother Hubbard said, adoring the traditional music wafting in from all around her.

"For your breath?"

"*Nay*! To make the spells more exciting."

"Oh. Aye, mint is exciting to spells. So we'll have a bland peace, instead." He reached over to Mother Hubbard, found her and petted for a few minutes like a fragile kitten. "A bland peace until my dragon makes up for a lack of mint. Let's take these hoods off."

"Not yet, it's bad luck."

"Aye."

Mother Hubbard asked, "When will you teach me the magic to enter the gates to the Realm of the Dragons?"

"Did I say I would?"

She chuckled. "You are a tease, a rotten egg."

"Before you take off your sack, make yourself an enchanting spell and when you have the glamour of a lass, I'll gaze upon you. Make yourself as young as you wish and I'll match it, and we'll be young lovers sprawled in lofty heather." He waited a moment and then asked, "Are you ready?" He began to smell the heather already.

Mother Hubbard said, "I'm only forty four. And that's not old when you know spells and herbs. But I look old, I know. It's just from all my hard work of laying all those eggs that has made me seem older. But aye, I can make myself be sixteen for you, if you make yourself twenty-five for me."

Merlin finally pulled the sack up off of his head. "Hello? Wife?" He pulled the sack from Mother Hubbard's head to find her looking her age of forty, and fast asleep. "You worn out old slag."

He shook her, but she woke up only enough to point her finger in the air and babble angrily about the rotten cakes burning when it should be boiling gruel, and the rotten cauldron had been stolen so she was at a sorry loss, and then she slipped away again into a deep exhausted sleep, snoring as if it hurt.

Since he decided that she was now as if dead, Merlin thought he'd put a common *dancing dead* spell on her and still have his randy fun, but as he tried to remember how it went, his thoughts slipped away to a time he entertained an entire seaport brothel as a ferocious lad, and he began to snore himself.

Chapter Seven

Morning came to find Nimm in the greensward hollering at the top of her voice down into the well. "A well of dragon's blood!"

"Put your hair up!" Mother Hubbard shamed her, hurrying out of the barn with a scarf for her. "Have you lost all sense of decorum? Only the slaves were once seen like this so uncovered under the sun!" Nimm ignored Mother Hubbard as her hair was quickly twisted into a wreath on her head. "Hold still! What do you see down there in that water besides your own slovenly reflection?"

"The trees! The bell! The sounds of dragons! The water! Blood! A well of dragon's blood! And the ether is so very charged! It smells like Merlin! It is powerful wizard ether."

Mother Hubbard shook her head. "The true Realm of Dragons? Impossible. It's just your imagination from too much fun last night." After tying the scarf on Nimm's head she walked away, grumbling, "You'd think the Romans had never been here the way she lets her hair go wild like some rumpled brownie pagan."

Rafe asked her, "Aren't you going to help my Mum?"

"Eee-*ucht*. She needs to scream awhile. She's been a bit touched ever since the sound of the demon bell dragged her away. And now she thinks she can hear the Realm of the Dragons. How absurd. Only Merlin's power can reach that deep, and it'll soon be shared with me. Soon. But your Mum knows nothing of it, for sure. She's just touched."

Rafe asked, "How's Mum touched? Touched by what?"

"Touched by things that have no fingers, I presume. Now just let her scream. It sounds affright to you and me but it'll be good for her. Let her scream."

Then Nimm screamed so much she flipped over the lip of the well and fell headlong down into its black depths. Rafe screamed for Mother Hubbard. "Help! Mum's gone down the well!" Opie, the raven, flapped down and stood on the edge of the well to peer into it, and then looked about at all the people, turning its head sideways at them like they were all mad, and then he flew off.

"Eee-*ucht*!" Mother Hubbard peered over the well's edge and could only make out Nimm's pink toes just below the surface. They wiggled for a short while and then were still. Mother Hubbard rushed to the barn for the rope, made a noose, and then all the village's children pulled together and fished her back up. "Heave-ho!"

"Mum!" Rafe screamed. "Breathe!"

Back up on the greensward, Nimm vomited up great amounts of water until the water began to contain a few dragon's scales that popped into fire and vanished with the touch of the sun. Then Nimm smiled and said in the simplest and most innocent tone, "I think I feel much better, thank you." She reached up and felt that her scarf was still in place. "Blessed be."

* * * * *

In the barn manger, Merlin awoke in horror to see Palag the cat sitting heavily on his chest. "I can't breathe!" Merlin tried to grab the cat to brusquely toss it off, but the big yellow cat leapt onto his face and bounced away.

He noticed his bride was up and gone, so he couldn't roll over on top of her and wake her with his desires. So he stumbled out to the greensward. When he saw Arthur, he moaned, "I feel sick."

"You're still sleepy. That's all. But you still have your beard. Did you not make yourself a young man last night for the glamour of a marriage bed? All I see of activity are cat scratches on your face."

"Don't ask me about cats, brides, or last night!" Merlin spotted a dripping wet Nimm. "What were you doing down there in the well? Shame on you for drawing such attention to yourself!"

"Didn't you hear it?" Nimm asked him.

"What?" Mother Hubbard looked about in alarm. "Hear what? The demon bell?"

"The roaring. The horrible wonderful roaring."

"Of dragons?" Merlin continued for her.

"Aye, roaring and…"

"Fighting?" Merlin finished.

She went to him and took his hands, squeezing knowingly. "Aye! With …"

"Much blood!"

"Dragon blood," Nimm said.

"Blood everywhere!"

"Dragon blood!" Nimm laughed. "Delicious blood!"

Merlin warned her, "Blood to confuse an earthly mortal."

"What's this?" Mother Hubbard now felt jealous. "What do you know that I don't know? What's going on down under that well with my husband?"

Merlin pulled on his beard. He pulled out a spider and squashed it. "It seems that your well is poking through a thin piece of this earthly dirt and it obviously reaches just to the edge of the nether world of the Realm of Dragons. Are there springs nearby?"

"Aye." Mother Hubbard pointed. "There used to be one locked deep within the forest. The forest is gone now, all gone to firewood, and it's all muddy and only good for frogs. But under the water at the far end is a drowning pool. It is as far deep as you can swim and you can't swim deep enough. There's caves under that water that go down to the heart of the earth. Why? What does this have to do with me? Will that make it easy for *me* to go to the Realm of Dragons?"

Arthur asked, Merlin, "This well could be a portal?"

Merlin quickly corrected them, "As a well, not in particular, and in particular, not in any ordinary way. You'll find that if you or most others fall headlong into this well, you'll quickly drown, and then you're dead, and that's all."

"But she didn't." Mother Hubbard became jealous again and glared at Nimm. "How do you see so far into the Realm of Dragons? What's your spell? Share your spell with me and don't be stingy! We womenfolk need to stick together and share our spells for the commonwealth of the land!"

Merlin took Mother Hubbard in his arms. "Are you sure you wouldn't like to go back to the manger to make up for last night?"

"Are you in such a mood?"

"Why else would I get married? Why does anybody bother to get married?"

She smiled and batted her eyelashes. "And what will you do in the manger?"

"*Mum!*" Rafe screamed in dire warning.

Mother Hubbard kissed Merlin's nose. "I'll make myself sixteen and you'll have such joy in me." They joined hands and started to the barn.

Nimm leaned too far over the edge of the well and flipped down into it, headfirst, and was gone again. Mother Hubbard turned her head in time to see Nimm's feet go down. "Eee-*ucht!*" Merlin climbed up onto the well to jump in after her.

"Merlin!" Arthur called out. "Halt! Where do you think you're going?"

"After her."

"You can't leave me yet! I'm not well tutored."

The wizard caught himself at the rim to say, "I only have to add that a square table is for lovers and a round one is best for friends."

"*What?*"

At that, Merlin jumped down the well and was gone deep beneath the dark water. "Rotten eggs!" Mother Hubbard added, gazing down after them and not seeing anybody. "Oh my. What did they do that for? Are they gone for good?" She began to cry.

* * * * *

That night, as Arthur curled up in the barn straw with the other children, he prayed to the stars that he wouldn't dream so that he might wake up for once not feeling so sad. "You don't get a horse," Uther told him, but he couldn't see his father's face, there wasn't one, just a shadow.

"Oh, I'm dreaming," he told his father. "Go away now. I've never known you and to remember you ruins my feelings. Every King needs a father but I had you." He was upon the log horse and it became a real horse and then he was upon a sack of oats that began to dance under him and the children danced around him and sang lewd wedding songs until he hugged it so tightly it became a forceful stream of boiling milk.

Merlin shook him. "Blessed be."

"And same to you." Arthur asked, "Am I dreaming? You're *back*! Have you come to take me away from my father?"

"Wake up."

"You?"

"Aye, it's Merlin. I'm back, aye. You're all wet. Do you have a fever?"

"Do I?" Arthur asked.

"Nay, I see you've just been attacked by a succubus."

"Horrors. What is happening to my body. I'm leaking! I must have an infection."

"It's just your seed and nobody wants to hear about that."

"My what? I'm okay?"

"You'll live. Wipe yourself off with a bit of straw and come with me. It's time to leave this village. We'll go to Abbot Babble Blaise straightaway where we haven't worn out our welcome."

"Am I dying?" Arthur asked.

"Wake up." Merlin angrily pulled on him.

Arthur woke up fully. "The abbey? Why there of all odd places? Now?"

"I'd like to hide from my wife, and we have yet to take Parsifal to find the meaning of his father's shoddy scrolls."

"How'd you get here? You went down the well with Nimm."

"And it was great fun. She's a marvelous goodly wench."

"Did she drown?"

"Nay. She's very alive."

Arthur asked, "Where's she now?"

"Still in the Realm of Dragons, guarded well, but she'll be back in due time."

"How are you so sure?"

"I'm not," Merlin admitted, "but she doesn't belong there."

"What's wrong with your ears, why do you keep rubbing them?"

"I almost had them pulled off by the three crones of Camelot."

Arthur asked, "What's Camelot?"

"You'll know soon enough. Now let's sneak out before Mother Hubbard finds out what a rascal I've been."

"Been a what?"

"I'm supposed to be her husband today, but I married a fairer wench in the meantime."

"Down the well? With Nimm? Am I still dreaming or do you make no sense."

"Nimm will explain our secret when she returns. I'm sure she can't wait to wag her tongue against me. And I will be charged with bigamy. I am guilty. My punishment is that I must be shunned. Good. Hurry. I must be gone."

"Are you sure Nimm will return? Poor Rafe is so upset! We all are! It's so horrible to see a goodly woman fall headfirst into a deep well! Twice!"

"She will be back, unless she dies in the meantime. That happens to people sometimes too, and then my Mother Hubbard will never find out what a cad I've been."

Arthur asked, "Will Nimm come back and think she's married to you?"

"I won't know what memory she'll have of the Realm of the Dragons until she stands on this mundane earth and opens her mundane mouth."

Arthur said, "And you hope she's dead so that it never opens."

"Nay!" Merlin slapped the top of his head. "I'm a mischievous wizard but I'm not one who'd profit from another's death. I only hope Mother Hubbard doesn't find out what I've been up to in my absence, for the sake of her hurt feelings. Who cares about mine."

"What have you been up to? You've only been gone a few hours."

"In the Realm of Dragons it was a year or two or six or twelve. But, nay, it hasn't been too long up here on middle earth. You're still scrawny and losing your seed in your sleep."

Arthur rubbed straw on his belly to scrape away the last of his nocturnal emission. "Grown men don't have this happen?"

"Only on purpose, deliberately, while awake."

"Why?"

"Things are usually more fun for you when you're awake."

Arthur frowned. "They say I'll grow into a man someday no matter what, though I worry."

"For now, we'll only worry about the abbey."

They quickly gathered up their few valued things, including Parsifal, and scampered off like outlaws into the night.

Chapter Eight

A thick salty fog hid the morning sun making the world look like the inside of a grey crock. Parsifal, Merlin, and Arthur walked a tight curve in the narrow rocky path above a stream. "This is the kink of Kinker Creek," Parsifal pointed out.

"So. Is it important?" Arthur asked, tasting the fog on his teeth. "I sure am hungry."

Parsifal shrugged. "It's well known. Because there's a town near here. It's a town that is known for their hospitality."

Merlin turned to Arthur to speak but fell to his face. His staff flew out from his grip. "My foot! My foot has fallen off!"

"Nay, it's right there," Parsifal assured him, picking up his staff and returning it to him.

Merlin tried to get up and walk but couldn't put any weight on his swelling ankle. He lay back down on his face, moaning, "I want to die."

"Nay," Arthur said. "You don't die from just twisting your ankle."

Merlin punched the ground with his fist. "What do I do then if I'm not to die? I feel such an overwhelming sadness in my heart. I'm sad. *I'm sad!* I fear that my sadness is what really tripped me onto my face."

"Sad or not," Parsifal said, "you're not going anywhere for a few days. Let's care for you here. Your foot will mend only if you stay completely off of it."

"I want to die. I want to go back to the Realm of Dragons where I'm like a cloud, not an old pile of crunching bones."

"There's a town near," Parsifal reminded him. "It's filled with healing women, all of them, and soldiers would go to it to be healed of their wounds. I'll have one of them come and nurse you."

Arthur sat down. "I'll stay behind to keep Merlin company."

Merlin moaned. "Anybody but you." Arthur sat anyway.

Parsifal set off alone and when he came to the town, all was quiet. Not even a dog snooped about the street. "Hello! Hello?"

When he came to the square, he saw the town's women hanging from the branches of an immense oak tree, all ages, young and old. A notice on the trunk, a parchment proclamation, said they'd all been hanged for witchcraft. "Catapults!" He crossed himself. He looked up to a house roof and spotted Opie the raven watching them, but keeping far away. "Opie! Come to me." The bird was silent. Parsifal was ignored.

He went from shop to shop to find them all closed up and soulless, but when he returned to the hanging women he saw many fresh footprints circling around and around the tree underneath the dead bodies. He swept the footprints away and then went back to Merlin to tell him what he'd seen.

"Why did you sweep the footprints away?" Merlin asked. "That was an odd thing to do."

Parsifal said, "They were the footprints of women. Could it be the footprints of the women who were hanging?"

Arthur suggested, "Maybe they were paraded around before they were hanged."

"But it seemed as if the footprints were fresher than the corpses, which were all shriveled and leathered."

Merlin asked, "The ravens hadn't picked their bones?"

"That's odd, but nay," Parsifal realized. "Not a scrap of rotting meat had been stolen from any of them. They just hung withering. Opie was even there but stayed far removed from the tree."

Merlin pulled his hat over his eyes. "So the hungry hawks and ravens won't dine. Well, that's their empty belly, not ours."

That night they ate nuts and roots and then as they slept by a small fire, Arthur dreamt of the town square and the hanging tree. At the hour of midnight, all the hanged women reached up and pulled their heads out of their rope nooses. They fell to the ground, and then danced in a circle about the giant tree. It was such an alarming sight that he woke up screaming.

Merlin dismissed it. "It was just your imagination run unruly. If Parsifal had said nothing of what he'd encountered, you'd have dreamt of something else."

"But it seemed so real; it was most frightful."

Merlin said, "That's how vivid imaginations are. Dancing dead witches? That *is* rather frightful."

* * * * *

The next day, both Arthur and Parsifal left Merlin alone with his swollen ankle as they went to the empty town. All the hanged bodies were still up on their nooses as they'd been the day before. "All is the same, and quiet," Parsifal said, taking in the sight of how young some of the lasses were who'd been hanged.

"Ghastly!" Arthur felt faint at the sad sight. "Hold my hand." But then he was distracted by an observation. "Look! Footprints!"

"But I'd swept them away, as I said."

Feeling lightheaded again, Arthur grabbed Parsifal's arm. "We'll be returning to Merlin now."

When they returned to Merlin, his ankle was floating an inch from the ground. "You're both pale."

Arthur blurted, "The footprints are back! It's as if my dream really happened. It's as if they really did dance, though dead!"

"I could so use a mending spell on my ankle but I'm not sure I'd like that."

"What?" Parsifal asked. "If you can heal yourself then why don't you?"

"You lads are too young to know the pain I feel and this twisted ankle is tortuous to me, which is a blessing, since it distracts me from the worse pain of memory."

"What?" Arthur and Parsifal just looked at Merlin, worrying that the old man wasn't in his right mind.

"Nay, I'm *not* in my right mind," Merlin pouted. "*I feel so sad!*"

"Why?" Arthur asked.

Merlin merely groaned and rolled onto this face.

"Why?"

"I'd like to be a young man. Not as young as you miserable lads, but five years older than you and locked inside a giant brothel."

Arthur asked, "You're not sad for your wife? Wives?"

"I'm sad for women. They make a man's heart ache so that even an injured foot can hardly distract me enough."

Arthur said, "We can't stay here. We have to get to the abbey."

"Aye," Parsifal agreed. "I need to carry out this mission, for my father at least. My father's pride is so important to me."

Merlin asked, "Is that an order from a prince and a lord?" They nodded. "All right. But one more day for healing and to enjoy my pain. The pain in my ankle. And there's the mystery of the hanging tree and whose footprints are circling it. You two will set up chairs in the town square and wait and see with your own eyes."

"*Nay!*" Arthur protested. "If anything frightful is unfolding, I'll be sleeping very far from that town square. Why ask us to do something so utterly frightful?"

Parsifal nodded along. "Yeah!"

"As the King you'll be required to do many frightful things, a dead dancing witch will be hasty pudding to you in comparison to what your future holds for you."

"I'm not a man yet," Arthur reminded.

Merlin squinted at him. "Aye. You're not. But one doesn't grow up in a day."

"I know how we'll find out if it's the hanged corpses leaving the footprints," Arthur said.

"How?" Merlin questioned.

Arthur explained his scheme. "We'll be clever and set a trap. We'll take sand from the stream here, and tie it in all the hanged women's aprons with a hole put at the bottom."

"Go then and see what this trick proves." Arthur and Parsifal went back to the empty town and made leaky pockets of sand in every apron, swept away all the past night's footprints, then returned to Merlin.

* * * * *

That night, while sleeping, the gurgling of the creek's water seemed to sing to Arthur, over and over again, "*Diamonds and Toads, I will do harm to you or leave a gift, that is the way of night magic.*"

"Can I choose?" Arthur asked the water. "Can I choose if I get harm or a gift?"

"You're only dreaming, fool. Your father was a fool and you'll fall into his grave, the same fool."

"Who's speaking to me in my dream?"

"O' Fortuna. The wheel spins. The wheel of fortune doesn't know when it'll stop. Your story will be one of impossible love and thwarted fertility and familial doom on one half of the wheel. And true love, friendship, and a long life on the other half of the wheel. But the wheel doesn't know where it stops."

Arthur wept. "My father didn't tell me anything. He didn't even watch me as I sat on the floor, or do whatever it is a real father does. Will I grow to be a man? Can you tell me that much? Can I grow to be a man even though my father didn't watch me? I don't even know what he looked like. Will I still grow more?"

"That'll be your first curse."

"How can that be a curse?"

"Petty passions, and what's within the reach of your hand, and jealousies. They always take a man's mind away from loftier matters."

Then he was walking through an orchard. He had the oddest feeling his mother and father were ghosts walking by, and they didn't recognize him. He saw an old woman picking plums. She said, "They'll never know what you looked like. Their ghosts are looking for you but they don't know how. Parents usually spend so much time looking at their own children. But yours didn't ever look at you. So they walk by you now, but don't see you."

When morning came, Arthur was exhausted from not sleeping soundly, and Parsifal had to shake him. "Wake up! Wake up! Stop crying! Let's go see if the dead were dancing!"

"Parsi, what? Did you come to take me away from Uther?"

"Wake up!"

Arthur sat up. "Have you come to teach me how to hunt?"

"Why are you so odd when you wake up?"

"My father didn't teach me how to wake up."

Parsifal questioned him, "Why would you need to learn to wake up?"

Arthur didn't know what to say. "Don't we learn all we know from our fathers?"

Merlin said, "He's a mad prince. Maybe that'll help him be a mad king. They're all mad."

"May I rest another hour?"

"I'd like us to get on to the abbey," Parsifal said. "We'll learn nothing about the grail at this creek."

Arthur and Parsifal went back to the town square and saw that all the sand was in a ring around the tree, with fresh footprints in it, having all leaked out of their aprons. "They *are* dancing at night; it *is* the corpses who make the footprints!"

Arthur asked, "How can the dead quicken?"

"Night wraiths! We should bury or burn them all to stop this restlessness!"

Arthur pulled Parsifal away. "Let's forever leave this sorry spot, and let them dance if that's what they must do. We'll soon be far from here and it won't matter to us."

"You'd leave the dead to dance?" Parsifal wrinkled up his nose in snobbishness.

Arthur shrugged. "Why not?"

"You must stop this. You can't have a town in your kingdom like this. What if they are still doing this when you are king?"

"You're correct. I can't have a kingdom taken over by knights on one side and dead women on the other. But I'm scared. I don't know what to do about it all now. We can decide later in the safety of the abbey. Let's go."

* * * * *

Returning to Merlin, they told him of the sand and insisted he heal himself quickly so they could continue their journey.

"But I feel so sad!"

Arthur pulled on him. "So what. Feel sad somewhere else."

"I want to be back in the Realm of Dragons!"

"*Now!* As the prince, I order you. We go! Posthaste!"

Merlin grumbled to Arthur, "Someday when your heart has a heavy ripping pang, you'll want a sprained ankle to distract you, and you'll know what I'd felt."

"I'd never marry twice," Arthur said. "That's begging for trouble."

Merlin stated, "Second marriages have always been thought of as hope over experience. I should receive praise for my efforts to live in hope when I should know better. Go ahead and marry only once. If you get a good wife it'll make you a good man. If you get a bad wife it'll make you a good King."

"You sure?" Arthur frowned.

"The only thing that's sure is that earth is a nightmare of mundane dirt."

Parsifal said, "The world isn't so terrible to me!"

Merlin made a face at him. "Aye. To be so young, handsome, healthful and rich, the world is your baked turnip. How happy we all are for you. I'd sing and dance for you but I might hurt my other ankle." He pointed his stick. "Let's go."

After walking an hour in silence, Arthur asked, "Is it fitting for a wizard of the wild to take the hospitality of an abbey of Christendom?"

"They have ale."

"That's your reason?" Arthur asked. "But what if they want to burn your thumbs or screw you to the stake, whatever it is they do to wizards?"

"I know Abbot Babble Blaise well, and he already knows that I'm Merlin and I don't have to hide anything from him. Remember I had him scribe for me. My only true complaint about the monks is that when they're not drunk, they're sober."

Parsifal was dismayed. "What kind of a monastery doesn't care about Christian ways?"

"The true mission of that abbey is to provide sanctuary for all the poor orphans of the demon bell and wasteland blight."

Arthur was impressed. "Really?"

Merlin said, 'Nay, it's really just to make a very happy ale."

"Nay," Parsifal disagreed. "It's to pray for our souls and make ale."

After skirting the lands of the gluttonous wicked knight Melwas so they wouldn't be chopped and boiled in a pot, they arrived at the abbey compound.

Merlin marveled. "It's been all redone. Expanded. Surely to make room for more and more orphans."

The oldest buildings were crude but very sturdy in the drystone technique, rocks piled carefully without mortar. With nothing between them to crumble they could last forever. The old drystone oratory was the shape of an upturned boat that would have only held a dozen monks at one time. Surrounding the oratory were individual cells of drystone beehives. Nobody wanted to live there now. All the young monks poured out of the nearby large long modern barn and new houses, built in a ring, securely surrounding a three floor keep tower.

"What's this?" Arthur asked. "Oh toad! Do they do that to themselves to show they're monks?"

"They're bald as fish!" Parsifal said.

The sight of the monks was shocking since the young monks didn't even sport eyelashes or eyebrows. Arthur asked, "Where's your hair?"

The monks shrugged. "One day we all went bald." One monk pulled the front of his robe all the way up to his chin. "Bald from head to toe."

"Catapults!"

"That's indeed bald," Merlin agreed.

Parsifal repeated, "Bald as a fish."

Another monk asked, "Have you ever seen such a bald crowd?"

Arthur shook his head. "Nay. Has Abbot Babble Blaise also grown so bald?"

"Nay, he has all his hair from head to toe, and aye we saw bristles of hair even on the tops of his toes, swear to the Virgin! And so it seems he escaped this curse."

"Good," Merlin said. "Then we can presume you've been cursed, proper, and it isn't just a case of poisoning from bad food or water. Now hop, and hop fast, and bring me a tall happy cup of your best ale. A yard of it to start with."

A monk said, "We have none. The drought has ruined our supply."

"*What?*" Merlin felt panic.

"Aye." a monk added, "It rotted and went thick like glue."

All the black squirrel tails jittered on Merlin's robe as he fell to the ground. Arthur kicked his arm gingerly and ordered, "Ale or no ale, you'll help us solve the mystery of the parchments and the holy grail."

A monk said, "Nay, solve the mystery of our baldness!"

Merlin said, "My heart is broken."

"Stop it." Arthur pulled on him.

Merlin got up and told the gathered monks, "Take me to your abbot."

Abbot Babble Blaise hurried out of the main long house with a big smile. He put his arms out to Merlin. Then he saw Parsifal and turned red and cringed with guilt. "Aye?"

"Look at him squirm," Parsifal said, "at the very sight of me, and having come with a prince and a wizard who can read. He knows he hasn't sold my father the secrets of the holy grail!" He raised his fist to punch the abbot in the nose as he'd been waiting so long to do, but then wondered if a lord can punch an abbot in the nose without burning in Hell for it, so he paused.

Merlin yelled at the abbot, "What happened to your ale!"

"It went to Hell in a crock. And *oh* my poor head has been too clear ever since."

"Aye, and it seems you've found a lucrative business selling parchments for gentlemen's libraries."

Abbot Babble Blaise said, "O' Virgin. Don't be such a cynic."

"A cynic is a man who when he smells sage looks about for the funeral. The gentle Parsifal only asks about a false parchment about the holy grail, since he has the morality not to lie, cheat, and steal, not being old enough to have yet figured out how."

"Morality!" Abbot Babble Blaise said. "*That* is only the attitude we take against those we dislike."

Merlin asked, "Do you have any proper parchments you can repay this lord's son with?"

"Repay? I've nothing written down presently. But I *do* have a Goliardic poet, Fisher Minstrel is his name, who stays in the keep tower. He's penning a masterwork, or so he excitedly claims. And by his excitement alone, I've no reason to doubt him."

Arthur asked, "Why is a commoner bard in your keep? Is he locked away there for a crime?"

"Nay, but he won't step out. He's too afraid. He's been there in the stronghold since he came to us, said he was walking through a fine summer's field where he found a plum tree. He ate and ate. Then he was suddenly in the ill fortune to find himself caught between two armies. We tended to his many wounds and he's healed, but he won't step outside ever again. He thinks he's being punished by God for finding such bliss in ripe plums."

Merlin stated, "We won't wait for Fisher Minstrel to finish a masterwork. Why aren't you working on *your* parchments?"

"O' Virgin, my hands hurt far too much to write but for a minute." He held them up and it was clear that the joints of his fingers were all swollen. "That's why my penmanship has been a bit of a fraud."

"A hanging fraud!" Parsifal said.

"But can I tell you with my tongue instead. It'll be three gold coins to hear it."

At that offer, Parsifal punched the abbot in the nose.

"I'll tell it for free."

"And a warm supper," Parsifal demanded.

"Aye, of course, our hospitality is never lacking. You never know when it might be the Christ, himself, at your door, disguised as a beggar. Or a lad such as yourself."

Chapter Nine

They were shown to their private beds in their small apartments within the monastery compound. The rooms were well appointed with pillowed beds, piss pots, washbasins, and narrow stone hearths for coals when winter became cold.

At the touch of his bed, Merlin passed out and would have stayed that way until breakfast, but a monk slipped into his room and blurted, "Teach me how to be a wizard!"

"*Wa- wa?*" Merlin bolted upright and swung his staff. "Wolves at bay!"

"Nay, I'm not a wolf," the monk called out, ducking. "You're dreaming. It's a monk, *me*, and I want to be a wizard!"

"Put your robe back on and go to sleep."

"I want to dance naked in the greenwood to a sacred grove and fly to the full moon with mistletoe and ivy in my hair—when I have hair. I used to have such thick hair before it was cursed off."

"Fly to bed!"

He danced in a gangly manner at the end of the narrow room. "You have to show me magic. I want to know a few secrets of the wild."

"If you don't go to bed, I'll poke out at least one of your eyes. How will you explain that to your master? Now *go*! This is a monastery for your Christ's sake."

"So?"

Merlin said, "Abbot Babble Blaise will birch you for even asking me for such knowledge."

"Abbot Babble Blaise doesn't even know what we monks do, and I don't think being a monk should condemn us to ignorance."

Merlin gave him one of his searing dragon looks and the man scampered out, slamming the door.

In the hall, Merlin heard the monk yell through the door, "Take me with you! I'd just die for an adventure. This abbey is so boring."

Merlin yelled in return, "It's your job to be bored. Now go and let me rest so I may at least chance to dream of pleasure."

"I'd make a brave warrior at your side and protect you from knaves."

Merlin answered, "I only want to be protected from bored monks. Go pray to the Blessed Virgin."

"Why?"

"That's your job."

A different monk dressed in tree branches pushed through the door. "We want to be Druid monks! Teach us how. Give me advice!"

"When men want advice, they really only want praise."

"Give me a wizard's grand advice!"

With a fierce bark and a stamp of his staff on the floor, Merlin made the man's tree branches splinter and fall apart. The monk yiped and ran out of the room. Merlin yelled after the monk, "A good scare is worth more to a man than good advice."

The man came right back, rubbing scratches that the breaking branches had left on him. "You would have killed me! Stabbed me alive!"

"Still, alive you look like a fool. Go now or I'll tell Abbot Babble Blaise of your rude insult to me."

"You wouldn't tell!"

"Run away now and I may mistake this for a stupid dream." Merlin looked down the hall. From the far end several other naked monks were looking curiously at him. Being so bald, they seemed to him in the dim light like odd leggy fish. He gave out a mean bark and they ran off like deer.

"Mice!" Merlin yelled after them and slammed his door as loud as he could to make a big bang, then pushed two chests in front of it. When he curled up in his blankets, he thought about how tired he was.

The door pounded urgently. Merlin bolted up. "What is it?"

"It is I!" Abbot Babble Blaise yelled through the door. "And a dragon is upon our walls! Or a questing beast!"

"What?" Merlin pulled the trunks from the door and opened it, then glared at Abbot Babble Blaise's tired red eyes. "What!"

"A monster!" Abbot Babble Blaise repeated.

"If it's one of your lads playing a trick, I'll staff him through like a stuck pig!"

"A monstrous beast of some sort is bellowing down our chimneys. It blasted down my chimney! It's terrible!"

"And you ask me to slay it?" Merlin heard a bright trumpeting blast down his own room's chimney. "*Toads*! That's *horrible*!"

"A questing beast?" Abbot Babble Blaise asked, pulling Merlin towards the door. "O' Virgin! We must get to the keep tower where we'll all be safe. What if the monster crawls down the chimney?"

The horrible sound roared again, but then it chirped, stopped and they heard a clang. Merlin looked back to the hearth to watch a long brass musical horn fall to the bottom.

"What? A trick?"

Merlin gritted his teeth. "I'll like to sleep for at least one minute this night. Your retched little monks are—retched. May I birch all their naughty little hinders in the morning for you? I promise I'll not remove a fleck of skin but will have them thinking I've done so much worse. I'll have them thinking I've birched them to bare bone!"

Also angry, Abbot Babble Blaise nodded, pulling the horn out of the hearth and blowing a bit of soot off it. "I'll birch them all."

"Nay, let me do it."

"You may birch them. Birch them good until the goodly Virgin comes into their hearts."

* * * * *

As they sipped their breakfast broth of lard and gruel, a monk ran into the room screaming, "We've found a dragon's head!"

"O' Virgin." Abbot Babble Blaise wearily rolled his eyes.

"It's true! It's true! It's true!"

Abbot Babble Blaise jumped up, red faced, and screamed right back, "What kind of fools do you take us for? Go away and let us eat in peace since we didn't sleep in peace, or is my monastery a prison of torture and Hell and endless agony for anyone over the age of ten?"

"Nay! It's true!"

"You're all getting birched for last night's pranks! What more punishment do you want from us?"

The monk insisted, "Nay it's a dragon's head! All bones now! It was found in the field that's washed away to stones. We found it last night after the horn dropped and we ran away. But now it's true!"

Arthur began to cough, swallowing wrong.

Parsifal asked him, "Are you going to live?"

"You lie," Abbot Babble Blaise accused his monk.

The young monk desperately shook his head. "I swear to everything holy, unholy, and indifferent that there's a dragon skull out in the rock!"

Merlin asked him, "Have you ever heard the story of the boy who cried wolf? That's why we don't believe you until you actually get eaten."

"It's true though! A ferocious looking skull with sharp teeth is resting in the stone!"

Merlin shrugged. "Maybe it's an old horse head. Old bones can fool some people into a good fright. Especially idiots, hysterics, and monks under the mental age of ten."

"Nay! It's not a horse head."

"Let's go see," Abbot Babble Blaise said. "And if it's another hoax, you will all go four days without eating and thanking the goodly Virgin for it."

Merlin said, "You better hope it's a hoax then, Abbot. Just think of the food you'll save."

* * * * *

They all trudged together to join those monks already gathered at the field that had long washed to stones. They pointed and at first it was difficult to see, but close thoughtful inspection showed an odd large long skull on its side, with sharp teeth, but it was half buried in solid bedrock. Arthur gasped, "A ferocious dragon! And it's lived and died with bones on earth."

"How can that be?" Parsifal asked.

"It's not a dragon," Merlin stated. "Not one from the Realm of Dragons, anyhow. But whatever this was, it was a terrible monster. And indeed just like a big oversized lizard."

Arthur said, "But half its head is *within* stone. Like Excalibur was before I took it! Is this another test? Am I to pull the dragon skull from the rock to further prove my worth as the next king?" He tried to pull at the skull but it didn't slip out.

"Stop it," Merlin ordered him. "I've never heard of such a task from the Gods as to pull a dragon's head out of anything for the peasant's amusement."

"Is it a dead questing beast?" Abbot Babble Blaise asked. "Or is this how the stones speak? Even the Christ said the stones would sing out to praise him. The stones do speak to us, and is this how?"

Merlin asked the abbot, "If you were to have to add a body to the skull, how large a monster would you surmise we would have?"

"As big as a tree!" Abbot Babble Blaise guessed.

"If it had a tail, bigger!" Parsifal said. "Big!"

Merlin scratched at it. "Hmmm."

Abbot Babble Blaise asked, What's wrong?"

Merlin detected, "But this isn't bone at all. Surely a hoax."

"What?" a monk asked. "What is it?"

Merlin scratched some more. "The skull seems to be made of rock, not bone." The wizard boldly laid his hands on it, feeling no trace of spirit, nothing, no life, no memory, no vision of the recent past.

"Another hoax?" Abbot Babble Blaise asked in fury.

"Nay, nay," the monks cried. "We did *not* make this! We found it like this!"

Arthur said, "This isn't a carving these jacks could have accomplished. It's too uncanny."

The monks cried, "We didn't do it!"

Arthur said, "It *is* too skilled a creation of a skull. Merlin, you can see that."

Abbot Babble Blaise asked, "Then who carved this skull into the stone? And why?"

Arthur suggested, "Maybe it was turned into stone by a brave magic warrior with snakes for hair!"

Abbot Babble Blaise admitted, "It *is* a convincing vision of a skull."

Arthur agreed. "It's truly a mystery."

"Last night was a trick though," Merlin reminded them. "Who was on the roof blowing a horn down our chimneys? Not this creature, stone or bone."

They didn't answer.

Abbot Babble Blaise looked them all in the eye. "Nay anyone? Then you all get a birching from Merlin!" They followed him back at the abbey.

* * * * *

In the abbey hall Merlin asked, "Where's a bit of thin cord to tie these birch branches? I'd like my whipping done properly and they should be bound with magic so the pain is unique."

A thin rope was brought to him that had been evenly knotted from end to end. The feeling of it shocked Merlin with its dissipating energy. "*Knots*! *Toads*! *Warts*! Where did you get this cord? It is charged!"

One monk pointed to a barrel of fabric and rope scraps. "There."

Abbot Babble Blaise asked, "What's wrong?"

"It seems part of a spell," Merlin said, shocked. "A skipping stone spell, or a mirror spell. Odd."

Abbot Babble Blaise looked angrily at the monks. "Who cast a spell? Who wants to be flogged more than all the others so that you'll only find your hinder in the afterlife?"

They all looked to each other in confusion. "We don't know how."

Merlin raised his hand for quiet. "This feels too clever for any young monk, for any young anybody. An old experienced wise spinner of strong magic has done this trick. And somehow left it here."

One monk asked, "Can a warlock feel such things?"

Merlin impatiently shook his head, his cheeks flushing. "*Nay*! I'm not a *warlock*! A warlock is a liar and nothing more. The word *warlock* means *one who breaks oaths*. I'm far more than that, as you are all far more than a den of naughty whack and wankers. Who here knows anyone who knows knotting spells?"

The monks slumped, confused. "No idea."

Abbot Babble Blaise bellowed, "Tell me or I'll make you all go a year without food!"

Merlin put up his hand. "They all look too vapid. Have you had any visitors to this place besides me? Has there been anyone who could have cast the spell to meddle with you before they then went on their way?"

Abbot Babble Blaise remembered, "There was an old bald woman who stopped by on a terrible windy night. Her accent was most odd and her skin was so blue; she was so cold and in ill circulation, the poor crone. And she was covered in head to toe tattoos of roses. She was surely a Pict."

Arthur said, "She could have painted herself blue with the woad leaf."

Merlin added, "Aye it makes great wool dye also. It's quite blue."

Abbot Babble Blaise asked, "Why do the pagans paint themselves blue? I've always wondered that."

Merlin explained, "There's a medicine in the blue that keeps the nooks and crannies of the skin from turning into a toadstool garden and like-minded skin ailments: crumbly itch, toe sponge, scab-scales and ringworm, which has absolutely nothing to do with worms. The more the pagan folk are pushed back into the swamps, the more blue medicine they'll be needing to wear."

"This wasn't paint," a monk insisted. "I could see that the Pict witch was blue to the veins."

Another monk said, "And her tattoos weren't of roses but of dragonflies. I saw them clearly."

"Nay, they were dandelions," another monk remembered.

"Nay," another monk protested. "They were squares, like chests of gold."

"Nay," yet another argued. "I saw her tattoos clearly and they were woven vines."

"Nay, they were chains with spikes. Cruel spikes."

Merlin put up his hand for silence. "Her tattoos were ever changing, how odd. She wasn't a mere Pict but a sly mystical one, to be sure."

"What's a Pict?" a monk asked.

Arthur explained, "An ancient tribe from the northern highlands. The Romans called them Picts because they were covered in pictures, their tattoos. But the Romans couldn't conquer them so they put up a wall at the edge of the highlands. They announced it the end of the empire, which was the end of the world."

Abbot Babble Blaise added, "And our present King Vortigern brought the Saxons into our land to help fight the nasty Picts, since with the Romans gone, they're growing mighty again."

"Aye, aye, aye," Arthur frowned, irritated. "I keep hearing about it! And now because of what my dad did, I'm going to someday have to rule a land crawling with Saxons, too."

Merlin asked Abbot Babble Blaise, "What did this old Pict woman want with your abbey?"

"It was odd. Odd, indeed. O' Virgin, I'm not quite sure what we've been through."

"Just tell me as it occurred!" Merlin asked impatiently. "What happened?"

"She came and I had to let her in. Sometimes I hate hospitality—sometimes it's such a bother—but I do know how very sacred it is, and I'll not blaspheme, since we don't know if it isn't God in disguise who comes to our door. This time I got a nasty rotten witch of a Pict—lucky me—O' Fortuna doesn't smile on me."

"What happened?"

Abbot Babble Blaise took a deep weary breath. "The old tattooed wench got her warm bed for the night, and a bowl of onion soup, but she kept asking us about our kettle, and asked us when we'd get our bell. And she had gold and bought up all of my parchments about the holy grail, frauds all of them. But she said she couldn't read Latin."

"Aye, you already mentioned selling those off to a crone." Then Merlin jolted again.

"What?"

Merlin stated, "It wasn't a wholesome witch you entertained, but a meddlesome thief."

"What'd she steal?" Abbot Babble Blaise asked. "I told her the parchments were all frauds and I got gold for them."

"She wanted to steal your monastery bell to turn it affright and then use it as her cauldron, as she has certainly perverted the goodly cauldron for her demon bell! But you don't have a bell yet, lucky for you."

"And she cursed us with baldness?" the monks cried.

Merlin said, "Why she'd bother cursing you with baldness, that's another story, and very odd. Did any of you play a trick on her? Be honest."

One monk admitted, "She was bald, as we said, but she had a wig made of a pony's tail. We stole it and hid it in plain sight on one of the pony's tails. She couldn't find it and cursed us, but we thought it was just in jest and she'd find a new pony's tail, they're not hard to find."

"A witch is terrified of ponies, that's why she didn't find her wig on your pet's hinder. And anyway, I can assure you that it wasn't a wig made of such an animal. It was certainly the hair of a human that she'd killed merely for her own vanity."

Parsifal gasped. "Catapults!"

"Nay!" the monks agreed.

"Aye," Merlin said. "You all crossed a nasty mean witch from the highlands."

Abbot Babble Blaise guessed, "And she knotted this spell before she left us to curse us?"

"Aye." Merlin nodded. "So the final trick has been on all of you! Bald monks."

A monk rubbed his head. "Horrible!"

Abbot Babble Blaise asked, "How do we break this spell?"

Merlin handed the monks the rope. He waved his staff about in wide circles over his head and chanted, "Uncrossing, uncrossing, undo curses, hair catastrophe. Let my words have power over spells cast in ill temper, baldness was the fee. By oak, ash, and thorn, so mote it be. Stupid monks, stupid monks, you've now paid for your foolish filching spree."

"Is that it?" a monk asked. "You mock us."

Merlin hushed him. "I mock everybody and you know you deserve it. Now, all of you take turns quietly untying this rope, there's a knot for each and every one of you here, so don't fear you'll be left out. While you do it, think hard about how disobedient you've been to your goodly abbot, and you'll then find that you'll grow your hair back in a month's time. The spell will be uncrossed."

"But," Abbot Babble Blaise asked, "will these terrible monks be cured of their terribleness?"

Merlin frowned at them all. "Nature is nature. But this spell had pushed them over the edge of all sanity and made their behavior worse than average for their age."

Abbot Babble Blaise said, "Still, there's no excuse for blowing horns down the chimney at night to scare us all,"

"I did it," Arthur finally confessed.

"What?" Parsifal gasped.

"I admit it. I was playing with the monks and helped with their tricks."

"I've always warned you to carefully choose the company you keep." Merlin wearily wagged a finger at him. "When a good boy and a naughty boy play together, the naughty boy never becomes good. I'd birch you but you're the prince, so I'll just birch the others extra for you, and then they'll see what they think about what kind of a King you'll be for them."

A monk insisted, "The skull in the rock isn't our trick."

Merlin agreed. "That was a genuine find. There *really are* enough real monsters in the world. Remember how your parents were all taken."

"The demon bell?" a monk asked.

Parsifal asked Abbot Babble Blaise, "Did the horrible Pict witch ask about any other parchments?"

"Aye. I told him your father had most of them."

"You *didn't*!"

"I did."

"You told her? Because of you she now knows of my father?"

Arthur warned them, "She's gone to kill him!"

Parsifal put his hands on his hips. "My father would cut her into bits."

Merlin agreed, "We'll go back to the manor of Baron Bearloin right now to see who's in bits, and the sooner we go, the warmer her trail will be."

"To slice off her head?" Arthur asked.

Merlin corrected, "I think it'd be best to find her alive and for her not to find us at all, so we can follow her to her demon bell."

Parsifal said, "We'll slay her and throw her so she's found in four different shires!" He laughed.

"Don't be irritating," Merlin warned him. "She's our enemy. Desecration of the vanquished is always unsavory. We'll be restrained and kill her at a proper time and be honorable about it." Merlin turned to Arthur. "To desecrate your enemy always brings on madness. A man who will be King must be warned of that, so I warn you now."

Arthur nodded. Merlin had warned him about the evils of desecration before.

Parsifal looked down at his boots in shame. "Aye, I'd like to be an honorable warrior like the Spartans."

"I must come with you," Abbot Babble Blaise implored Merlin. "I want to be a part of the grail quest."

Arthur asked him, "What about all the monks that need your care."

"And need firm birching," Merlin quickly added.

Abbot Babble Blaise pointed to the keep tower. "Fisher Minstrel can be temporarily in charge."

Arthur asked, "How can anyone be in charge from the top of a keep?"

Abbot Babble Blaise smiled. "He'll have to wander out to see what's going on. And I assure you, these monks are so mischievous that he'll have to wander out to see what's going on many times."

"Grand idea," Merlin said. "It'll be what he needs to get over his fears and get him back out into the world."

"And to get on with *my* life," Abbot Babble Blaise said. "To the grail quest! You need an abbot along to bless the path, bless the find, and bless the slaughter!"

Arthur assured him, "We have Merlin for all that."

"Let me come! O' Virgin, it's evil out there, I can just feel it! You need an abbot at your side!"

"He can come," Merlin agreed. "If nothing else, he's got guts. Lots of guts."

Merlin, Arthur, Parsifal and Abbot Babble Blaise hurried off towards the manor of Baron Bearloin.

* * * * *

Carefully skirting the lands of the wicked ravenous knight Melwas, Arthur grumbled to Merlin, "What'll a king do with such a perverse knight as this one?"

"A knight so rabid as Melwas can't ever be reasoned with. Boiling grown men in pots for dinner isn't the way of Druids, Romans or Christendom. Someday, somebody will have to come by and string him up."

"Here's father's lands." Parsifal pointed ahead. "I hope everything's all right."

Merlin grumbled, "I'm tired from such a roundabout journey. I'll have to burn down that knight's house and barn when I find the time. No wizard should have to suffer such indignity."

They walked through a gate in the hedge row and Parsifal gasped, "My father! Is he dead?"

"He looks dead," Arthur said.

Merlin nodded. "He looks peaceful. I wish I could look so peaceful. Toads on him!"

"Father! Now I really am an inheritor and I feel so ashamed; I didn't appreciate my name! I was such a poor son!" When they came close to where Baron Bearloin was sprawling under a large tree, Parsifal repeated, "I'm so unworthy a son! I'm so ashamed to be so unskilled compared to him. He was the greatest husband to my mother and most professional warrior to my enemies and kindest father to me!"

They found he was merely napping contently. "I love you too, son."

"O' Virgin!" Abbot Babble Blaise gasped. "Blessed! You're alright!"

"Why?" Baron Bearloin was perplexed that he was being gazed down upon so ardently.

"You're alive!" Parsifal said. "You weren't destroyed."

"What?"

"Assassinated!"

"I wasn't *what?*"

"Was a horrid Pict witch here?" his son asked him. "Did she try to steal your library?"

"Her? Is that what she was? Is that why you've come like this? Her accent was so odd... so very odd. And she was so blue I wondered if I'd soon be burying her if she didn't start breathing."

"O' Virgin! That's her!" Abbot Babble Blaise crossed himself. "O' Virgin! It's just evil! I can feel it!"

Arthur said, "Where's your library? Did she steal it?"

"Nay." Baron Bearloin chuckled. "She came with a mighty fine, *fine* wagon and asked if I had parchments that I'd bought from the abbey, writings that gave a prayer against the demon bell. I told her I bought many from the abbey but couldn't read to tell her what was what, but she could purchase the entire library from me and haul it away for ten gold coins. Before I could blink she had ten gold coins in her hand, and in my face, and I sent her off with every last piece of nonsense parchment I'd been cheated on by you, you cursed bastard lazy thief of a buggery monk abbot. But… but…" he burst into joyous laughter, "I cheated her, and now I've more gold for it than I started with."

Abbot Babble Blaise pointed out, "If she finds out she gave you ten of her gold coins for a chest of frauds, she may curse you mightily."

He stopped chuckling. "I never thought of that."

Merlin asked, "In what direction did she head off in?"

"North."

Parsifal said, "Let's go catch up with her and strangle her, forthright."

"Find her, to be sure," Merlin agreed. "Then follow her cautiously to her lair."

* * * * *

Leaving Baron Bearloin behind, the four followed the tracks of her wagon northward until they came to a burnt trunk filled with large flakes of ashes of burnt parchment. "Father's library!" Parsifal cried.

Arthur sympathized with him. "And such a fine chest ruined with it."

Parsifal agreed, "I'd have liked such a chest to put all my weapons in that I'll someday possess!"

Merlin poked at it with his stick. "Forget the trunk."

Arthur said, "Let's hope she didn't see what frauds the writings were, before she burnt them. If she didn't then we'll have no worry of her cursing your father."

"Nay, fear not," Abbot Babble Blaise assured Parsifal. "I remember her saying she couldn't read Latin. She was as ignorant in such a thing as Baron Bearloin."

Parsifal raised his fist to punch the abbot but stopped himself, and said instead, "My father isn't ignorant!"

"Merlin?" Arthur pointed out. "Look! Nothing! Where's the wagon tracks? They've disappeared."

Parsifal asked, "Can a wagon be made to fly?"

"O' Virgin!" Abbot Babble Blaise looked up at the sky and quickly crossed himself. "I feel evil! I feel a great evil all about us! A terrible Pict evil!"

Parsifal said to him, "It isn't like it's going to drop on your head."

"Nay," Merlin agreed. "Whatever evil there may have been here is long gone." He walked around in the dry dead grass and kicked at it here and there. "She must have noticed what an obvious path she was making so she paused long enough to burn the library. With nothing but her in her own magic cart, aye, she can fly in it so the wheels won't leave tracks. She's now hidden her travels." He put his staff into the breeze and tested it. "But I feel she's gone this way, to the west."

"Why west?" Arthur asked Merlin. "Couldn't it be a trick and she really means to head all the way north into the highlands and back to her nasty unbathed people?"

"Aye, it could. But in stories from before the Romans came, the west has always been connected with the dream of the cauldron of unending supply."

Arthur asked, "What does that have to do with today?"

Merlin said, "In our grail quest that seems of nowtimes, we may only be re-stepping in the old deep footsteps of ancient myth."

Greatly bewildered by that, they followed Merlin west.

Chapter Ten

At another wide stretch of bog, Parsifal spotted a squirrel darting about between the rushes. "Look!" He raced after it.

"Don't run out there!" Arthur warned him. "Have you learned nothing from the last bog we were in?"

"Nay! It's daytime now and I know my footing. I've hunted in bogs my whole life, and all bogs can't be as horrible as that last one."

Arthur insisted, "I've heard you say that once before."

"This is a squirrel, not an unclad woman!"

"The creature might be a trick!" Abbot Babble Blaise warned him. "These bogs are haunted on a regular basis!"

"Hunted?"

"Nay! *Haunted*!"

"What?" Arthur asked the abbot.

"Aye. Time and again. Haunted."

Arthur questioned, "But not by the light of day." He called out, "Come back! You'll get all muddy again!"

Parsifal ignored them and raced away, laughing. He was so spry he ran farther and farther from them, keeping up with the squirrel.

"Come back *now*!" Arthur yelled at him. "It's a trick, I can feel it and you'll ruin your boots!"

"Help!" Parsifal cried out as he was yanked below the surface of the bog.

"Time and again," Merlin moaned as Abbot Babble Blaise and Arthur raced out to save him. "Toads! I can't abide slipshod children!"

"Where is he?" Abbot Babble Blaise yelled. "He's gone entirely!"

"Merlin!" Arthur hollered, feeling the ground wobble. "We may be next."

At a different spot from where Parsifal went under, he came back, seeming to be pushed up forcefully. He spat and lay gasping, covered solidly again in mud.

"What just happened?" Arthur asked. "You were torn from us and thrown back as if by a dragon!"

"It was the unclad woman! The same dead bog woman as before! Restless! Angry! My sleeves are gone! They've been ripped right off of my arms! How can I be alive?"

Arthur turned to Merlin in confusion and asked, "But we're so far from that spot we were last attacked!"

Merlin smiled. "Maybe a dead woman can swim farther when she's unclad."

Arthur stomped. "Don't mock us!"

"This is a curse!" Abbot Babble Blaise gasped. "O' Virgin! There's life under this bog! I warned you it was haunted! I can feel the evil!"

"My sleeves are gone! My hair! All mucked!" Parsifal fought back tears as he tried to scrape the slimy mud off his trousers.

"Toads and warts." Merlin turned to Abbot Babble Blaise. "I know this isn't a habit of Christendom, but I'll need to do a ritual, posthaste."

"What? Why? A what? O' Virgin! That sounds evil!"

"Do it!" Parsifal urged him. "Kill the rotten wench! Rip her to shreds!"

"Her?" Merlin asked. "Was it really a her? How do you know for sure what it was?"

"What did you see under the earth?" Arthur questioned, helping him wipe mud out of his hair.

"It's too terrible to say. And now that I'm here above ground, I don't know if I was only dreaming, other than my clothes are ruined with mud again to tell me it was real, and I've no sleeves."

"What did you see?" Arthur pressed.

"Well, I'm not sure, but an angry she-wolf was racing back and forth, upside-down, across the field, and her mouth was foaming so badly I couldn't see any teeth. And the foam fell over all the crystal pieces of stars and dirtied them. I couldn't breathe. The mad she-wolf came at me, but I kicked hard against her head and jumped away. I jumped away!"

Abbot Babble Blaise shook his head. "How could you see *that* under the cold dark earth? You were touched by a devil into confusion. Pray to the Virgin so that you don't lose your soul."

"I could lose my soul?"

Merlin chuckled. "You *almost* just did. But it looks fast inside of you now. A ritual can answer all this nonsense if we take the time."

"What'll a ritual solve now," Parsifal asked, growing afraid for his soul. "Let's just run from this spot and never come back."

Arthur asked him, "Don't you care who did this to you? And what if this dead ghost woman swims, and swims after us under the earth all the way to the sea?"

Merlin poked at the ground. "Dead things aren't supposed to act with such vigor. I'll stop this now so that someday Arthur can build a proper road across here to join London with the western sea. A safe road here would be proper. A road so the poor peasants aren't always being yanked under to the netherworld."

"Aye!" Arthur nodded. "My realm will have enough trouble with outlaws and brigands. Until then, let Merlin clean up a few dead things."

Merlin said, "Everybody off with their clothes, we'll do this ritual skyclad."

"Isn't that sinful?" Abbot Babble Blaise asked.

When Merlin dumped his fur robe onto the ground, Parsifal gasped at it, "There's squirrels in there! It's alive!"

"But he was wearing it," Arthur reminded him. "So how is that possible?"

Merlin took his staff and drew a large circle in the dirt, the symbol of the element of fire, as he chanted, "As above, so below, by oak, ash, and thorn, I summon the Mighty Ones: fire, earth, air, and water to purify this sacred space. Guard this space. Aid our rites. So mote it be."

"I don't know if… will the magic be… "

"Don't fret," Merlin told the abbot. "We are only going to be summoning up the restless dead and ask why this curse is upon it."

"Will we be safe?" Abbot Babble Blaise asked. "It feels evil. It feels quite dangerous."

Merlin declared, "I will dance like a bear."

"Why a bear?" Abbot Babble Blaise asked.

"I'm not dancing like a squirrel, bat, or fish. I'm a decade too old to even try. It'll put out my back. Why don't you try the other animal spirits that might move a bit faster than a lumbering bear. The bear is all I can do."

Parsifal asked, "The animals will come to us? In our dancing?"

"Their spirit natures appear. We dance to create sympathetic magic to summon them, and the ones I've chosen aid with contacting the different worlds."

Parsifal crossed his arms stubbornly. "Fish don't dance. Fish are stupid."

Arthur pushed his arms down. "You haven't been where Merlin has."

Merlin instructed Arthur, "You may gape and flop as a fish, that does suit you well. Just don't do anything to hurt yourself or us. Parsifal the Hunter, though you look like a muddy worm, a squirrel will suit you, just don't flee us. Abbot Babble Blaise, the bat is how you look already. If you insist to keep your robe on to be special and modest, then flap it all like bat wings."

"But the bat is evil!"

"Don't be rude to bats; they aren't rude to you! As I chant, we dance." The wizard began in his grandest voice, "As above, so below, by oak, ash and thorn."

They danced.

"*Halt!*" Merlin screamed

"What?" Arthur asked. "I thought I was very fish-like."

"And I, like a squirrel."

"I flapped."

"Aye! Aye! Aye! And it was horrible! It was utterly undignified! A fish swims. A squirrel is squirrel-like, and any bat that flies like that will surely starve!"

"We did our best."

"It was chaos and it was horror! Anyone spying on us would think we were crazed madmen with fatal bowel difficulties!"

Abbot Babble Blaise looked sadly at his sleeves. "But we were like those animals. Really!"

"We will all dance like bears," Merlin decided. "All will follow me. We will bring on the trance in dignified unison."

Arthur exhaled, wondering why Merlin would suddenly care about dignity.

"I heard that, Arthur. When you're the King and you pause between battles to reflect on your life, you'll be glad you danced like a bear and not a fish."

Arthur reminded him, "It was your idea in the first place."

"Aye, and as with you, when I'm wrong, *I am wrong*! Now follow me and do as I do. Become what I've become."

They danced in a circle, like bears, following Merlin. "As above, so below, by oak, ash and thorn, as man and woman die and suffer and are once again born, in life after life, we rest, forgive, then try life again. I command the restless spirit of this bog to appear to earthly eyes, I command, so mote it be." He chanted this three times. Merlin smelled an odd mix of sulphur and smoke as loud sparks crackled in his ears.

"Is that cinnamon in the air?" Abbot Babble Blaise marveled. "I haven't known that since I was a boy! It makes me want to cry!"

"I just smell Parsifal," Arthur admitted. "Fresh mud."

"Hush!" Merlin bellowed back at them. "Be bears!"

"It's her!" Parsifal pointed.

They stopped their deasil dancing behind Merlin and noticed a ghostly woman floating near them. "Blessed be," Merlin said. He had a small owl on one shoulder and a raven, not Opie, on the other. But then the two creatures weren't there as if they had never been, and a mouse was on one shoulder and a quail on the other.

The muddy ghost asked, "Blessed be. Why must I speak with you?"

"Because you've been summoned by a mighty wizard's spell and you've no choice."

She slipped back under the bog but came right back up. "Stop that. I hate you."

"I don't care," Merlin told her. "Hate me. I'm not here to marry you."

"Who are you?" she asked.

"You've been summoned," Merlin said, "to explain a few things to us."

"I'm the great and fearful Boadicea, the great warrior who drove out the Romans for a time." The ghost's head glowed green.

"That's a lie," Merlin said.

"How would you know if a ghost lies or does not lie?"

"I'm a great wizard. My spell has trapped you in my world and also trapped you into the truth of my world. I know when you lie." As Merlin said this, he had a spider on one shoulder and a squirrel on the other.

"I was a Druid long before this time." The ghost's head glowed pink and she floated a bit off the ground.

Merlin praised her. "That was a great honor. Why would you bother lying about that?"

"I'm angry."

"Is that why you're a ghost? Why don't you leave this place and go rest in Summerland? Why scare Parsifal the Hunter so much?" As Merlin said that, he had a rat on one shoulder and a hummingbird on the other.

"*Him?*" the floating ghost scoffed. "Children are so easy to snare in this feral grave. They're so headstrong."

"Why do that?" Merlin asked. "That's ill tempered."

"I'm angry."

"Are you pretending to be alive somewhere under the earth?"

"Nay. I can't breathe and my soul won't stay in that place."

"Curse you vile spirit!" Abbot Babble Blaise cried. "Curse you to the Virgin's Hell! This is evil! I can feel it!"

Merlin ignored him, with a grasshopper on one shoulder and a bee on the other. "Why would an honorable druid priestess play such a petty trick as to try and stay on this earth when you know better?"

"Petty?"

"Aye," Merlin stepped closer to her. "Unworthy of a priestess, unless you were educated by cretins who only believed in a dreary dark cave for the dead."

"My honor has been stripped from me," the floating ghost admitted, her head glowing a very bright pink.

"How?" Merlin asked.

"I was a Druid priestess. It was the top status of my clan. I was in charge of warcraft and mediation in disputes. I performed many powerful rituals. So I read the entrails of a sacrifice of a fair maiden, as the ovate witches did, and when the other druid priests saw me do this, angry men from another clan accused me of being out of place. And so they executed me. This great, great indignity against me has made me wander from bog to bog in search of revenge."

"So what. Just listen to yourself. So you were put to death. That's nothing new. Go reincarnate and forget about it!"

"I'm angry!"

"You aren't now any more angry than the day you were born. I bet you were always this way. Admit it. You're just a spitfire and that is the true reason why you're still here."

The ghost was shocked. The ghost thought about that and finally admitted, "Maybe so."

Merlin suggested, "If it's possible for you to reincarnate into a kinder soul, that'd be a blessing."

"A blessing!" Abbot Babble Blaise prayed. "O' Virgin!"

"I'm mad now and that's all I see!"

"And attacking poor Parsifal the Hunter made anything right? You ripped off his fine sleeves. You soiled his pants, you brigand!"

"I'm vengeful, that's all. I'd have killed him but he has too much life in him and while I grabbed both his arms, he still got away. He kicked me in the head! Ah such boots!"

"Then we'll send *you* out of this world." Merlin angrily poked his staff at her, disturbing the dragonfly and butterfly from his shoulders.

The ghost bluffed. "You have no such power."

"I do too. And it's easy. For the dead to leave this world is within the currents of nature. The magic will flush you away faster than a waterfall."

"You wouldn't dare. I was a Druid priestess."

"You *were*."

"I still am!"

"Nay. Sorry. You're dead."

"I'll strike you dead with fear!" Her head floated up away from her shoulders and two bleeding eyes bulged out of her skull sockets.

"There's nothing fearful about the dead." Merlin yawned. "It's so natural for the dead to leave this world that a child could have cast you away with a babbling spell missed and meant for piss pot training!"

"You're not to speak to me like that!" The ghost ominously raised her arms to look menacing. She grew long claws. "I am a fright!"

"O' Virgin!" Abbot Babble Blaise cowered.

"You're dead!" Merlin angrily poked his staff again at the ghost. "Shame on you, you Druid of old! You know the cycle of life yet you hide from it like a coward! And cowards bore me!"

"I'm not a shameful coward!"

"Shame on you, shame on you, as above, as below, shame shame shame *shame*!"

The ghost said, "Don't talk to me that way! I still have power!" A mud-dripping skeleton jerked up from the bog and staggered toward them.

"Catapults!"

"O' Virgin!"

"Hush, don't worry," Arthur assured them both. "Can't you see it's dead?"

"Aye."

"And rotting," Arthur reminded them. "It's a living Saxon with muscles that you should fear."

"You're a shameful wench!" Merlin loudly pronounced, while Arthur packed a mud ball and threw it at her.

The bog-mummy's bony hands reached out to strangle Merlin as he pulled a cord from the hem of his sleeve and quickly wrapped her wrists together. The Mummy's jaw flew off, she was so shocked, knowing he'd gotten her. She realized she had let herself be so hotheaded and reckless. Merlin chuckled. "You're dead and caught and exposed and made small! And you weren't even very tall when you were alive."

"Let me go!" she screamed, trying to sink back into the bog, but Merlin impatiently shook her until her bones rattled.

"Shame on you! Shame on you! Shame on you! Shame shame *shame*!"

Lights flashed from the ether above their heads, and the smell around them became light and clean as a cool floral breeze. A gash tore down to earth like a warrior's wound, and as it widened, they saw a beautiful woman with skin as white as milk. She slowly and leisurely came down like a cloud and out of the cloud walked many ghosts upon the breeze. They gathered and took the floating ghost with a sorry glowing blue head in their hands. Then the white blinding cloud floated away and all were gone. The gash in the charged ether went with it. The skeleton fell lifeless, *dead* dead. Merlin gingerly stomped and poked at the bones until they were all below the surface of the mud. "There. You're buried. Rest in peace. Now rot like a good girl."

Abbot Babble Blaise asked Merlin, "Is she able to come back?"

"This won't be trying to act beyond its station anymore, the impertinent harpy. So mote it be."

"Did… did you see that?" Abbot Babble Blaise stammered, "Am… am I the only one who saw the goodly Virgin just now?"

Arthur corrected him, "I think it was the Goddess Summer."

"The *Virgin*!"

"As you please."

"A miracle… but," Abbot Babble Blaise complained, "the Virgin took the ghost away. I'd have thought such a murderous ghost would have gone to the Devil!"

Merlin pulled his beard. "Maybe that's where the goodly Virgin will deposit her after a good scolding. If that's what you believe then that's what your world is, a world with a Hell."

"So it *was* the goodly Virgin!"

Merlin shrugged. "If that's what you saw."

Parsifal complained, "But all the other ghosts seemed to carry her away with such care. *I* would have kicked it in the teeth."

Abbot Babble Blaise corrected Parsifal, "The goodly Virgin has too much power to act so spiteful. Only those feeling weak kick in teeth." He turned to Merlin, "The goodly Virgin was here and was like a calming mother to us all. We'll never know the mysteries of the Virgin."

"*If* it was the Virgin," Arthur argued.

Abbot Babble Blaise said, "Who else could such a sight be?"

"The old religion is better," Arthur smugly stated. "Isn't it Merlin?"

"Why?" Merlin asked Arthur.

"You know." Arthur winked. "*You* know."

Merlin said, "If you can't tell me in words, then why is it better? Your tongue is supposed to be tied fast to your mind."

"Yeah!" Abbot Babble Blaise chimed in.

"The trees," Arthur thought fast. "We notice the trees. And we think as the animals, take on their spirits."

"The Christ of Christendom," Merlin remarked, "was called The Lamb of God. The last time I poked at one, a lamb was an animal."

Abbot Babble Blaise added, "And the Christ took on a lamb's nature for a final sacrifice,"

"And before then," Merlin continued, "He told a tale using the mustard tree as a symbol."

"And branches and vines!" Abbot Babble Blaise added. "The Christ said that He was the vine and we are the branches."

"So," Arthur pondered, "The Christ was a Druid and bard?"

Abbot Babble Blaise corrected him, "We don't use those words, they're not of Rome. Christendom would like to be Roman."

"Aye, I love Rome, too. But if you were to use the words of *this* land, you would say that? Bard and druid?"

Merlin pointed out, "The Christ wasn't involved in warcraft, like a Druid. Although nowtimes men would have you think that to be virtuous you must be a warmonger. But such men actually worship kings, not Gods." Merlin paused to think, then added, "Jesus was like an ovate also."

"He presided over sacrifice?" Arthur asked.

Abbot Babble Blaise finished for Merlin, "He sacrificed himself as a lamb, so there'd never need to be any other sacrifice ever again. No one else was good enough to do this, so he was the only ovate and sacrifice, both, who could carry out this great magic to make His Father be nice to people again. The Christ came to save God from man."

Arthur looked to Merlin. "If the Christ was Druid, bard, and ovate all in one, then he's like our old religion of this land. It's the same ageless Holy Trinity."

Merlin admitted, "There's many paths to the golden bough. They all tread very much alike. There are differences though. Christendom seems to want to shy from magic."

"Why is that?" Arthur asked Abbot Babble Blaise.

Abbot Babble Blaise asked Merlin, "Aye. Why's that? You recall? I don't. Did the Christ not perform magic to show compassion?"

Parsifal finally joined in. "Christendom calls them miracles."

"Aye," Merlin agreed, "and Christendom would be nervous if those miracles happened in nowtimes. But if the abbot made water into wine for me now, I'd think very kindly of him. I would drink it all without complaint."

Arthur asked, "What's the difference between a miracle and magic?"

Merlin said, "A miracle is what's given. Magic is what's taken."

Abbot Babble Blaise declared, "*That's* the difference between the religions. I just knew that the different names for God couldn't be reason enough to make them different. Names are only names, but the difference really lies in *attitude*. Christendom is humble before God, on its knees with hands folded and head bowed, and the old religion is proud, up on its feet with boisterous songs and its hands in the air as if to grab a bit of Heaven. Christendom waits humbly to receive. Paganism arrogantly takes."

"Can we be both?" Parsifal asked.

Arthur announced, "When I'm the King, there'll be both and we'll be humble and proud. We'll help the destitute while not bowing down to anyone! The land will be filled with charity."

Abbot Babble Blaise laughed, "The man who gives out pig's feet for alms has stolen many pigs."

Arthur maintained, "It'll be a new Golden Dawn!"

Abbot Babble Blaise warned, still chuckling, "That might confuse some people."

"Confuse them? Or make them stretch their idea of what it is to be a man and a woman on earth?"

Parsifal warned him, "A king wouldn't want that. A king and Church need loyalty and nothing more. Your ideas are too liberal and someday will be your own gravedigger. Peasants should bow."

Abbot Babble Blaise assured Arthur. "You're young and naive. Once you've sat on the throne for a week, you'll know that the iron Roman way of ruling is the best. The Saxons will only be crushed by force alone. Your subjects must have true fear in them of you, that's what they want, they only want a strong ruler. If you aren't strong and fertile, they'll look elsewhere for it."

"And if I try to wage war and peace, both, when each is fitting?"

Abbot Babble Blaise smiled. "Someday when we're old, we'll drink ale together and remember this day and laugh very hard at the many frivolous ideas of youth."

"It is?" Arthur questioned.

Abbot Babble Blaise assured him, "When you become a grown hoary man with a few good scars, you'll learn that excessive talk is profitable with your women only."

Arthur sat silently, frowning. "And one more thing. There *is* a big difference between religions. Their Gods. The Gods and Goddesses of this land are shown to us in nature, and the God of Roman Christendom is an angry faced old man up on a cloud with a long white beard and impatient cold eyes, throwing lightning bolts at those who pique him, scaring children, making grown men sorry, burning a town here and there—a lot like you, Merlin. Aye! Just like you!"

A spider ran out of his beard. "That's enough of your imagination!"

Chapter Eleven

After a long roundabout hike skirting the lands of greedy knight Palamedes who'd enslave them all if they were caught, Arthur asked, "What does one do with a knight so greedy?"

"Catapult him," Parsifal said. "Fling him until he's found in four shires."

"O' Virgin, pray, just pray. Such greed is pure evil!"

"Tax him," Merlin said.

"How does one get close enough to tax him?"

Merlin said, "Start burning his barns. I always said that, that gets one's attention."

Arthur complained, "That was nonsense."

"*Okay!*" Merlin angrily agreed. "You have a land here of men who have horses so they use this power to take as they can, and holding onto it as they can. A king's job is to unite it all somehow, as big of a piece as a king can. Other kings will pick up at the borders and you'll fight without and within your entire life. How you do that is your task."

"You'll not tell me?"

Merlin stuck his tongue out and blew a loud raspberry.

"*What!*"

"My job as a grand wizard is to first and foremost give your role its legitimacy by blessing you with the favors of the Lady of the Lake and Excalibur with what influence it has. And I have. It may have some influence to all the stupid people but we can't be sure it'll go far. I'll also try to encourage a bit of old religion in you to compete with all the Roman ideas in you. What you do beyond that is your problem."

Arthur said, "But in addition to being my wizard, you're also my tutor. And I've many questions."

"I've taught you Latin and penmanship. I've told you the histories of other kings and emperors, so you might learn about how petty they were. I've told you the Druid secrets of warcraft and encouraged honor in battle so that you don't become loathsomely depraved at your very first victory. I've taught you shape shifting and invisibility, and a few more spells beyond those that a king shouldn't dabble in. You want more?"

"Of course."

"Be wary of an education," Merlin warned them all. "Wisdom and learning are two different things. True thinking can't be done from the old stories of others."

"What else is there?" Arthur asked.

"There's also great wise lessons to be learned from watching a stupid man who'll not believe other's stories."

"So what's your point?" Arthur asked.

"That to be a tutor is a tutor's waste of time. All you really have to do, to be wise, is to watch the stags for a season to learn how to mate, fight, and eat."

"You're just being a toad."

Merlin rubbed his eyes. "Aye, I'm tired. Earth is tiring, and finding the grail to heal it is more tiring still."

Parsifal said, "I know what to do about the knights. What makes a knight? A horse. Aye?"

Arthur asked, "We can't take the horses from them, can we?" They stepped into a sprawling grove of balding poplar trees.

"Nay," Parsifal explained, bending to pass under a branch. "But as the king, you'll have the ability to build many breeding stables all over your lands so that many barons and lords and abbots can also have their own horses. They'll pay gladly for them so you'll also have a share of their wealth. Then the knights won't have this power of cavalry all to themselves."

"Aye!" Abbot Babble Blaise smiled. "The knights will be eventually forced to associate with the upper classes, and not disregard them. Then they stop all their mayhem and grief!"

Arthur asked Merlin, "Will a land of horses be what I'm forever remembered for? Will I be called the *Horse King*?"

Merlin shrugged, startled, then looked up in alarm, "Nimm? Nimm!"

Arthur looked up but only saw sky and the trembling rustling leaves of the tall poplar trees. "No one's there."

Parsifal asked, "Isn't she the one who keeps falling down the well? What is she doing up in the trees then?"

Arthur asked, "But don't the poplar trees read to us the messengers of the wind? Aye?"

"This wasn't a message on the wind. Nimm really was floating over my head for just a brief moment."

"O' Virgin. It's evil!"

"Is not," Arthur interrupted the abbot. "She was a nice person." He turned to Merlin and asked, "What was she doing that to you for? What was she doing up there. Up there isn't where the Realm of Dragons is, is it?"

"She was staring at me like she'd kill me."

"Is she dead?" Parsifal asked, crossing himself. "Is her spirit passing on to Heaven, or Heaven forbid, *Hell*?"

Merlin poked at some leaves with his stick. "Maybe. Or maybe she's finally flinging out of the Realm of the Dragons, where she belongs as much as a codfish belongs riding a donkey through a Samhain purging."

"She's above us?" Arthur asked, trying to see her.

"She *was*. As clear as candle smoke in a gale."

Parsifal repeated, "We pray she isn't dead."

"I never met her," Abbot Babble Blaise admitted. "But bless her soul." As they walked just past the screen of poplar trees, he exclaimed, "Ahead! There yonder and how glorious! A bridge!"

Arthur agreed, "I *love* bridges! When I'm the king I'll have bridges built everywhere just so that I can cross them!"

"Catapults!" Parsifal excitedly agreed.

"Aye, catapults," Merlin pretended to humor them. "Arthur must build many of those to get to the Saxons quickly."

Arthur asked, "Could a dead Saxon someday reincarnate and become one of my sons that I love with all my heart?" Merlin nodded. Arthur shuddered.

They stepped up to the edge of a ravine and as Merlin looked down at the stream, he smiled. "Bless all the toads there's a bridge here. That water looks enough to get us wet."

"But…" Arthur pointed at three lizards that lay in the center of the bridge that were so dead they were only skin and bones.

"O' Virgin."

"If you don't like dead lizards," Parsifal scoffed, "then kick them into the water as we pass." He stepped onto the split log planks of the bridge and began to cross but instantly lost his balance and fell backwards into their arms.

Arthur laughed. "What happened to you?"

"Something pushed me! Nay, it was nothing pushing, but I began to spin and I couldn't keep my head steady." Parsifal walked onto the bridge again, and his arms flailed in his loss of balance and he fell to the ground. He crawled painfully away. He coughed and gagged. "I feel too dizzy to cross it."

Arthur asked Merlin, "Is there a spell on this bridge?"

Merlin put out his staff and it seemed to him like he was poking at an invisible force. He finally said, "Aye, it seems so. And it stinks."

"A ghost?" Abbot Babble Blaise asked.

"Nay. A curse left by someone still alive. An old crone."

Abbot Babble Blaise warned them all, "There's a great evil all about us! I feel it; it's everywhere! I can *feel* it!"

"Then uncross the spell so we can cross the water," Arthur ordered Merlin, ignoring the abbot.

Merlin became frustrated. "I've no idea what the spell is or who cast it."

Arthur's eyes grew wide. "It was the Pict witch!"

"Perhaps, aye," Merlin agreed but then changed his mind, "but this land is ripe with witches and there's as many reasons to curse as many bridges."

Arthur asked, "It isn't a common spell?"

Merlin carefully crept close to the first wood plank of the bridge and put his hand on it. The wood vibrated. "Nay, it's not a common spell. Maybe, indeed, it was the Pict witch. I smell her breath. Toads."

"You can't uncross it?"

"Nay, not if I don't know why or what it is. A wizard as old as me doesn't know that many varieties of bridge spells. I used to leave all that to the trolls. Bridges without trolls are rather modern, methinks. I miss the old days."

Two men came running to them from a small cave in the steep hillside, swinging sharp but wooden swords. "Stop! You can't cross the bridge without paying us!"

"Blessed be," Arthur said to them. They didn't respond in kind, so under his breath he commented to Merlin, *"They've been Romanized."*

Merlin asked the two men, "You have put this curse on this bridge?"

They smiled in embarrassment. "Oh, you've already tried."

"Did you curse this bridge?"

"Nay," they admitted.

Merlin angrily asked them, "You'd have us pay you a toll to cross this bridge and then send us to our failure in trying, knowing it can't be done?"

"A toll can be arranged in many ways," one bridge keeper said.

Merlin asked, "Why are you trying to take tolls you haven't earned?"

"Ever since our bridge has been under a spell and can't be crossed, we haven't been able to collect many tolls. It has been like this for many, many months. But we still need tolls!"

Parsifal grumbled, finally sitting upright on the grass but still holding his woozy head.

Merlin asked them, "How has your bridge come to be so cursed?"

"A while ago an old woman who was most odd crossed our bridge and that was the end of our livelihood."

"Explain it," Merlin ordered them. "How was she odd? How did she put a spell on the bridge? What was the spell?"

"I remember it well. She was bald and her skin was blue. She pushed a cart piled high with straw and grass and she seemed to struggle with it mightily, as if it was piled high with heavy gold."

Merlin asked, "Did she have tattoos like a Pict?"

"Aye, and every time I looked at her, they seemed to be of a different picture."

Merlin tugged on his moustache. "What happened when you asked a toll of her to cross?"

"She said she was old and we should have mercy on her. She said she'd nothing in her cart but straw and grass to sell to farmers and she'd nothing more. But I thought the straw might be hiding something of weight and value, since the wheels sunk so deep in the soil."

Arthur said, "Ah! Perhaps it was hiding the cauldron. When was this?"

"A long while ago."

Merlin agreed. "It could have been the cauldron that gave the cart such weight."

Arthur asked them, "Has she been by again in the last few hours?"

"Nay."

Merlin reminded Arthur, "With her cart now empty of even a trunk of parchments, she surely flew overhead in it and had no need of a bridge. But when she had something as heavy as a cauldron, she certainly could not fly."

"I never saw what was so heavy under the straw, but I did offer to sell her a pony to help pull her cart."

Merlin told them, "She doesn't abide well with ponies."

"Aye, how'd you know? She screamed. Many leaves fell out of the trees. Then when she calmed, she insisted that her cart had nothing but straw and grass, and told me to go away and leave her be. I told the old hag she was a liar. I told her she had to pay a toll like any other, or to cross the stream elsewhere. She grumbled as she gave me a Roman coin, and then heaved and cursed and pushed her cart across to the other side without the aid of a pony."

Merlin asked, "What was the curse? Did you hear the words?"

"Nay."

"Oh rot. And that was the last time the bridge was crossed?"

"Aye. That was the last anyone has been able to cross. As you can see, the lizards who can otherwise go anywhere they put their clever minds to, even they can't scamper to and fro without falling sick and rotting in plain sight."

Merlin broke into a wry smile. "Good."

"Good?"

"Good. The witch is vengeful and petty. She is so petty she would even do this to a bridge. Pettiness may be her undoing."

"But what do we do in the meantime for a bridge?" the bridge keepers asked. "We'd like to collect our tolls again. Tolls in coins! They say coins will be used again someday and we want to be ready."

Parsifal insisted, "The only thing that'll be used in this land of any worth is a good long sword of sharpness and all other sorts of weapons!" He glared at their wooden swords in snobbery.

Merlin turned to Arthur and asked him, "Should we burn the bridge?"

"Is it that hopeless? Just do an uncrossing spell and let's be on our un-merry way."

Merlin smiled wickedly. "I don't know, but wouldn't it be grand to see such a long tall bridge burn and fall into that water? Think of all the flames! Think of all the sparks!"

"But it was built so grandly," Arthur pointed out. "And it now seems like it belongs here."

"Toads and warts, you're always so bothered by the impermanence of things. You *did* burn down an entire village to find me a wife. A deed done once is a deed double again?"

"*Merlin*, why must you always speak to me in dumb riddles!"

"You must save our bridge," the bridge keepers begged. "Don't burn it!" They stood between Merlin and the bridge with their swords swinging.

Arthur accused them, "But you'd have charged us a toll even though we wouldn't have been able to cross. And we have no coins anyway, since we don't live among such shops that would trade with them."

"We could have taken one of that young lord's buttons," they admitted. "That would be as fine as any coin."

Parsifal asked angrily, "And then you would've left me in this sorry state? Missing a button and sick in the grass?"

"Toads and warts on both of you scoundrels." Merlin swung his staff and struck them, breaking both of their swinging wooden swords into hot steaming splinters.

"More cursed magic! Now we have no swords!" The two bridge keepers ran back to their hillside cave.

"May I burn the bridge now?" Merlin asked Arthur. "I'd love to see the sight of it blazing and flashing, billowing and crashing."

Arthur rubbed his lips and thought. "A bridge is a handy thing for any king to have in his kingdom, and I'll soon be the King. Did you not already say that a road should go from London to the western sea?"

Parsifal spit at it. "Stinking like death. Dirty as rot!"

"Then," Arthur suggested, "perhaps all it needs is a good cleaning spell and a good rain from heaven to wash it clean."

Merlin reminded him, "It won't rain in this shire until the holy grail is found and returned to its rightful place."

Arthur decided, "Then we'll cross the stream without a bridge, and leave the problem of it for another day."

Merlin tempted him, "I could burn it now and it'll be a great entertainment."

"Or I could have a bridge here when I'm the King, and the tolls those two men so boldly collect will be just as boldly taxed for the commonwealth."

Parsifal crawled to the edge of the ravine and looked deep within. "Going down will be easy. If you aren't afraid of a cold bath; crossing will be just as simple. Coming back out is the puzzle."

"That tree." Arthur pointed downstream to roots that had been left washed clear and exposed. "We can climb up those."

Merlin agreed, "You'd think that was the only reason they were there. A princely ladder."

"O' Virgin!" Abbot Babble Blaise cried out as he lost his footing, slipped over the edge and slid to the bottom. The others followed after, but in a more controlled manner. They bathed well while crossing the stream, whether they wanted to or not, then climbed back out the other side.

They cautiously entered a thick patch of woodland. Most of the branches seemed twisted and bent as if they were being pushed down upon by a great unseen hand.

"Are they sick?" Arthur asked. "The trees look in agony."

Merlin sadly guessed, "They may not have long to live. Or they may live long in this great pain."

"Don't you know?"

"Who am I to tell them what to do?"

"It's cursed," Abbot Babble Blaise agreed. "O' Virgin!"

"What causes it?" Parsifal touched a dead branch. A piece of bark fell. "Does the wasteland reach all the way to here?"

Merlin tasted the air. "Aye, we're coming close to its source, I would guess."

"Oh toad. I'm dizzy," Arthur complained.

Merlin said, "I am too."

"I'm so tired," Abbot Babble Blaise said with a moan. "Is it a curse?"

Merlin poked his staff into the air, testing it here and there with care, reaching a diagnosis. "Nay."

"Nay?" Abbot Babble Blaise sat down. "Then what is it?"

Merlin said, "We are so tired because we've just been walking too much. That's all."

"Aye!"

"We've pushed too far for one day." Merlin plopped down onto the ground next to the abbot. "Now, where's my fine yard of ale."

"I'm not tired," Parsifal bragged. "I'll go hunting and bring back some meat for us. I'm growing annoyed by these nuts and berries we've been splitting between us, and I'm a very skilled hunter. So skilled that someday I'll be known for it."

Merlin agreed. "I can see it. Parsifal, the Grail Hunter."

"I was presently thinking of hunting a fat squirrel."

Arthur smiled. "I'll go with you, and you can show me your hunting tricks!"

Parsifal frowned. "Nay, you'll frighten away all of creation. Stay with Merlin and the abbot and nap to save your strength until my return."

"Don't get lost," Merlin warned him.

"Nay, my father taught me hunting well enough."

Abbot Babble Blaise ordered him, "Pray to the goodly Virgin while you're gone! To be alone can invite the Devil! Are you sure you really are off alone to hunt, and not to invite the Devil."

"Nay!"

"In his solitude a young man may invite the Devil and not even mean to. It's just a failure of flesh. The flesh is evil. It is full of urges. It must be birched of sin."

"Aye." Parsifal nodded. "Sin."

"If you would ever like me to birch you of your sin, just drop your pants and I'll find a hearty stick to beat all that sin away."

Merlin started to chuckle.

"Nay, not today." Parsifal looked confused, then cautiously left them. He took a look backwards every few steps so he could see what the forest looked like to help his return. He saw Opie the raven watching him. Parsifal majestically held up his hand and said, "Opie, I know you love me. You follow me everywhere. Come to me and let's be more friendly. Help me hunt."

The bird just looked at him from a very safe distance.

"Opie! Come! Be my friend! *Now!*"

At that tone of voice, Opie flew to a higher branch. Choosing to ignore the bird, Parsifal crept further through the trees. He spotted a sparrow singing on a branch, so he picked up a stone and flung it at it, striking it. The sparrow dropped to the ground between clumps of dead brown fern fronds.

"A few tough bites you'll make." He set the small dead body on a rock and stared at it, taking in the detail of the feathers, feet, and beak. Opie the raven flew down, and quickly snatched the game away and was gone with it. "Opie! You thief!"

Parsifal began to weep, then bawl, letting all sorts of feelings out in the privacy of the cloak of trees. Then, as if his father really was before him, he heard, "You're too old now for tears, stop crying like a child and be a man! Any son of mine doesn't cry!"

Parsifal sat on the dusty moss and wiped his eyes, feeling bad for even a private outburst. "Forgive me Virgin, I didn't mean to let myself go to the Devil. Please don't tell the abbot. I don't want him birching me for this." When he leaned against a tree and his ear pressed against the hard bark, he wondered if it was his heartbeat he heard, or the tree's.

* * * * *

Prince Arthur awoke from his nap and sat up, alarmed. "My dreams will ruin my soul."

Merlin asked, "Which dream did you just have?"

"How I was born of black magic and no good can come from my soul, and my father never taught me how to hunt. My father never even looked upon me. A father should look at his son!"

Abbot Babble Blaise warned him, "This wildwood is sinister and causes bad dreams."

"Nay," Arthur argued, "I dream horrible things all the time."

Merlin said, "Caution. Dreams can lie to us if we have no wisdom."

Abbot Babble Blaise promised him, "Bad dreams are taken away by the Virgin. She catches them in her robes, and there she turns them into blessings."

Merlin frowned. "Do you actually tell that to your poor monks?"

"Aye. I have to tell them something. They dream so horribly of the demon bell."

"But I *was* born of black magic!" Arthur reminded them. "I can't boast of my ancestry. I've no forefather to happily own. Uther was a disgrace. I can't stop dreaming of this disgrace."

"Don't think about family," Merlin said. "It'll ruin all your self-esteem. And that's the fate of most mortals."

Abbot Babble Blaise said, "The goodly Virgin is your mother."

Arthur questioned Merlin, "I'm not to think about family? Everybody thinks about family! Everybody! Parsifal boasts of his ancestry with great praise. And his pride stays intact for thinking of his father. I'm jealous of his pride."

Merlin said, "Birth, ancestry, and that which you yourself have not personally achieved can never be called our own."

Abbot Babble Blaise said, "But every man wants to come from a great vine."

"Arthur, you'll be known for your own achievements, as all kings are judged. He who boasts of his descent is only praising the accomplishments of others."

"And what'll I do sitting upon a throne? Can you see that? I worry."

"You're to look regal," Abbot Babble Blaise said. "That's all."

"Throne sitting?" Merlin scoffed. "Toads. *Adventure* is the only thing that creates the next generation's tales, not throne sitting. The world is divided into two classes of people, those who do things and those who get the credit."

Arthur rubbed his lips in confusion. "So… a king can take credit for the great deeds of his army while throne sitting? Are you trying to teach me, again, with contradiction?"

Merlin declared, "Every man with a great mind must be able to hold two opposing thoughts in his head at the same time and believe both to be true."

Abbot Babble Blaise warned, "That sounds like playing with evil. I can feel that like my own heartbeat. O' Virgin."

"Evil?" Arthur asked the abbot.

"The Virgin's truth is the Virgin's truth and there's only one of those!"

"Don't be irritating," Merlin hushed him.

"I'm not! I'm instructing the young prince in Godly ways of the new God of Christendom. It's important! It's the new God of Rome, and Arthur will be an important king to keep Rome's ways alive! That's why I'm here. Otherwise the prince's only word would come from a pagan old wizard of an old dead time, and that's evil. I can just feel it!"

Merlin waved his hands three times before Abbot Babble Blaise's eyes, saying, "Sand in your eyes, your mind dense with a very long day, drop where you cede, sleep where fall."

"What? I'll not have a spell put on me."

"You'll sleep as if you just ate a feast. Your belly is heavy and your mind is at peace. By oak, ash, and thorn tree—so mote it be." He blew in his face.

"I'll not fall asleep for you!"

"A sleeping spell is easy when you're already so tired, so dead tired that I can't take any credit for your sleeping."

The monk yawned to fight his exhaustion, then crumpled, coughed, sighed, and fell fast asleep.

Arthur asked, "Did you just knock him out? That was wayward of you."

"He was tired. Tired men fall asleep easily and I didn't have a long time to waste on a long boring tale of how Arthur pulled Excalibur from the Coronation Stone, or some other such foggy Arthurian wind just to put him to sleep."

Arthur was glad the abbot wasn't listening. "Can you help me with my sad dreams with a clever spell?"

"Sad dreams are for you to live under until you learn from them, or at least learn to ignore them."

"Help me!"

Merlin warned him, "You can help too much. It's like throwing both ends of the rope to a drowning man."

"Can you help me a little? What do you do when *your* dreams are sad?"

Merlin pulled out the side of his moustache. "We're all born of some sadness. All of it comes from magic, most fall into a most common sex magic. But we are all somehow born. The odd part about being born is that it's such an important event in our life. It *is* our life. Yet we have no memory of it."

"Not even you, a mighty wizard?"

"I can't even conjure it up in a spell across the face of the waters where the Lady of the Lake rests. It's dark. And my mother is nowhere to tell me, if I even had a mortal one. But there's tales and rumors. I have tried to find what is true in them. I have charged the darkness like a yelling warrior and only found more darkness."

Arthur asked, "What do the rumors say about you?"

"The tales are magnificent. In one tale I was born of a demon and a virgin at the same time the Nazareth Christ was born, and I was intended to be the anti-Christ, but I was accidentally shuffled off on the wrong wagon and was baptized by the Church, so the evil intention was broken. But that is not a true tale."

"That's a marvelous story. Why can't it be true?"

"It's stupid," Merlin stated.

"It is?"

"They didn't baptize infants into Christendom at the very moment in time that the Nazareth Christ was born."

"Of course they did," Arthur argued. "The men of Christendom have always done such a thing."

Merlin gave Arthur an exasperated glare. "You're daft."
"How do those of us who were born from black magic escape the pain of it, the pain of how it crumbles our dreams at night. There's no pain greater than knowing you were abused by your own clan."

Merlin poked his staff into the air to test it again. "*Hmm.* Let me try a dream chasing spell."

"That sounds wonderful. I've never heard of such a marvelous thing."

"Aye, that's because I've never done it before." Merlin waved his staff and bellowed, "Spirit hounds will guard your dreams and they chase all prey with such joy."

"Are you making this up?"

"Always."

"Does that mean it'll work?"

Merlin just looked at Arthur like he was stupid. "I always make things up. I'll be intuitive with my magic and do a cunning trick that may cure you of such pointless and unproductive sadness. And nay, it may not work at all."

"It better not make me worse. You know how magic can come back three-fold."

"It's my spell, not yours, don't worry. And besides, the worry of accidentally cursing oneself is for scaring the peasants anyway. I'm a great wizard with better aim. But regardless, I'll keep the spell innocent and simple so we don't risk a curse." Merlin thought a moment and then ordered. "Find me a small rock that can be swallowed."

"And swallow it?"

"*Nay!* Give it to me."

Arthur kicked through the dirt for a while and then found a strange blue stone. "If this isn't good luck…" He gave it to Merlin.

"Nay, nay. I've changed my mind. You keep it. You hold the stone against your forehead."

"Merlin! Don't you know what you're doing?"

"Nay! Of course not. I'm not young enough to know everything! Now do as I tell you to—as I invent with my doubts—and put the stone against your forehead."

"Until you change your mind and then I've only looked stupid for you?"

"You look that in clover without my spells, now just do it. Good. Now think of all the bad things you want to think about that you dream about that you don't want to dream, that has no purpose other than to sap your joy and confidence."

With the stone on his forehead, Arthur thought of all the times he dreamt he was being carried through poisoned waters by his mother's husband, wrestling with the mad King Uther who sired him from black magic, wrestling with Merlin for custody, and Merlin chanting more and more spells until the water became black. Then

Igraine, his mother, would look at him in surprise and realize time and time again that Arthur didn't look like her real husband at all. He looked like the trickster who came to her pretending to be her husband. Then Arthur would wake cold as a stone tomb, with his arms and legs numb, all the while his father would try to drown him. But it'd be his father's murderer also, trying to kill him, looking just like his father, as his mother told him he was a mistake and should not have been born, that Merlin had made all this deceit possible, that a mother was a king's only true friend and he'd been torn from her by Merlin. Arthur wondered if it was Merlin who was a king's true enemy.

"I made sure you didn't starve," Merlin defended himself before Arthur could open his mouth.

"But there were times I *did* starve!"

"That's not my fault that you were so ridiculously bad at trapping game. I tried to teach you."

Arthur yelled, "You did *not* try to teach me! You said that I should learn how to find my own food. You ordered me to be a clever man and you went away for many days on end. I couldn't find berries or anything! I starved! I ate only dandelions and pig weed that had gone bitter. You did that to me several times! I was little! I was scared! You're an evil wizard!"

"I was just trying to toughen you up!"

"You only taught me fear. You've always ruined everything by taking me away from my father, as horrible as he was! You made me a bastard! You're the one who's ruined my life! You made me be born when I shouldn't have been! You made me grow up without a mother when all boys need a mother. I don't even know what she looked like! You're a wicked wizard! You're wicked and evil and mean! I hate you! You are worthless to me! I would have been better off raised in a Saxon privy, or a convent in Normandy! I hate you!"

"So I meddle." Then Merlin chanted in a powerful voice, "Stone so blue and pure and good, match the dreams my brother could. Find the memories in his mind that haunt him when he wearily reclines. Come out when he awakes so fresh. Come out from his mortal flesh, but let the memories so thick, to your color blue fast stick. As above so below by oak, ash and thorn, by fur, feather and fin, by earth fire water and air, let it be so, aye aye aye. So mote it be, and a Holy Roman amen."

Arthur looked around. "That's it?"

"Now swallow it."

"But you've already told me not to!"

"Aye," Merlin admitted. "But I'm making this up as I go along. Now swallow the stone."

Arthur did. "Now what? Have Goddesses and Gods and wood and water noticed this act? Are they impressed?"

Merlin said, "You should remember that spell if this works. There are many *many* people in this sorry *sorry* world who'd like to not dream at night. Many folk dream of the wrongs their mothers and fathers did to them, or the pain of working the field, or whatever keeps them crying all day long."

"The simple folk don't already have their spells?"

"I have no idea what the simple folk do, but they don't do much other than cry about it, drink a lot, and dance in circles around fires singing superstitious songs. Such folly. So remember that spell for them all."

Arthur was surprised. "But, didn't *you* remember the spell you just said?"

"Nay."

Arthur let out a loud exasperation. "Neither did I."

Merlin shrugged. "Then that was the end of that. Let your troubled peasants suffer."

"How can you not remember the spell you just put upon me? You're a great wizard."

"I was distracted," Merlin admitted, pulling hard on his beard. "I had a memory of the future. Your future."

Arthur perked up. "It must be because I'll be a great man! Only greatness comes at you out of time. Nay?"

"Many men who are great aren't remembered. You'll not be a great man. But you'll be remembered. And so for that, you'll be a very great man."

"That's a riddle," Arthur protested. "What makes a great man?"

"A great man is always a step ahead of the times. A great man does the wrong thing at the right time or the right thing at the right time. It's all about the times. A great man isn't destroyed by domestic difficulty or a new set of new enemies that are very different from the old known ones he was so familiar with from childhood. A great man builds an empire and doesn't see it slip through his own hands, but is able to pass it on to ungrateful children so they can be the ones who squander it."

Arthur became irritated. "I've chased my bad dreams away. Now, to have a calm peace of mind, I'll need to chase you and your sad waking conversation away, a conversation that would put any child into despair."

Merlin feigned that he was inculpable. "What could you possibly mean by that? I'm only acting as a tutor."

Abbot Babble Blaise began to snore loudly. It embarrassed them. So they stopped talking.

Chapter Twelve

In the celestial cardinal glow of a new fresh sunrise, Priest Owen staggered back to his village with both his eyes completely ripped out of his head. His robe was gone. He was only wearing his rosary around his neck. "What in your sorry Virgin's name have you been up to?" Mother Hubbard asked, horrified. "Rotten eggs, you've lost your robe and nay I've not a spare one to lend you."

"I've no clothes?" He grabbed his naked belly in alarm. "What?"

"Why can't you behave? Where are your eyes?"

"The bell." The orphan children from the barn ran to him and helped hold him up. "Nay blessings on me—nay—blessings on me. I need blessings!"

Rafe asked, "Was it the same demon bell that tried to take Mum?"

"The bell."

"Where? We heard no bell?"

"From the tree, the evil tree!"

"Trees are not evil!" Mother Hubbard insisted. "You always tell us that but it's just not so."

"In the tree, the grove. Evil. The bell! It rang in the night! It made me come to it!"

Mother Hubbard asked, "The sacred grove is *not* evil. And what of your poor eyes?"

Priest Owen sobbed. "Taken for the trees, so the branches could see! Oh blessings on me, blessings on me, I can't see!"

"Who took them?"

"The tree witch," Priest Owen answered.

The children cried in confusion, "A tree witch?"

"Nonsense," Mother Hubbard said. "A tree witch is in a tree and there isn't much to do in there. This man of God has been cursed and is confused. I'll take him to bed and you all leave me alone while I do it."

"Will he be all right?" Rafe asked.

Mother Hubbard ordered the children, "Go to the barn and play a naughty game that reminds you of the old ways. Just don't burn the place down. I'll be with you when I can."

Mother Hubbard shooed the children away and led Priest Owen into an empty hovel and pushed him onto a bed. He venerated her for it, "Blessings on you as me. Many blessings on me."

"All right, you stupid priest," she yelled at him. "Why are you saying what you're saying?"

"It's true," he insisted, sadly touching at his sunken eyelids.

"What happened?"

He took a deep slow breath before he began again. "The same bell. Nimm heard the same bell too. Only it called me all the way across the waters to an island that was a giant turtle's back. There were men and women's eyes everywhere in the branches of the tree, guarding. The tree witch didn't know who I was. I remember now! I remember now!"

"Then tell me if you remember now."

"The tree witch took my eyes for the tree and then ripped off my cloth. Then she must have been surprised by the sight of my cross that had been underneath. She gasped, she screamed so that leaves fell out of the trees. I said a loud prayer and found myself guided by the Blessed Virgin, or angels that sounded like swans, and I was guided home."

"A tree witch?" Mother Hubbard wondered, confused. "But they're just *tree* witches, not the monsters you speak of. A tree witch is just a witch stuck fast away inside a tree!"

"They're evil. She was blue. She was covered in tattoos that changed from one picture to another."

Mother Hubbard said, "I doubt that."

"It's true!"

"Sleep now and we'll argue on this later."

"I can't see."

"I know, you fool."

"Tell me a story," the priest asked, "gather the children and tell us all a cautionary tale that will frighten them into being good."

"You're tired. You're injured. Sleep first."

After Priest Owen slipped away into a deep rattled breathing, Mother Hubbard raised an ax and violently struck him, chopping off his head. As his feet kicked, blood sprayed all over the wall.

"Eee-*ucht*! Blessings on you!" She stuffed him into a bag, dragged him to a defensive ditch to the west of the village and indelicately kicked him in. "Enjoy the meat you profane wolves." Mother Hubbard kissed a small handful of dirt and tossed it down onto him, and then she went back to the barn and gathered the children. "Listen, all you poor orphans! Come sit here. I've a tale for you. Aye, it's tale time. This one is called, 'Tom Thumb Goes to Hell.' "

The children frowned. Rafe asked, "May we hear the tale of the giant and the princess with two heads?"

"Don't look at me like that. Your evil eye isn't nice. Now listen and be glad. This'll be a wonderful story of bravery and the joys of being small." She went on to tell a frightful tale, then concluded, "Be wary little dear children. The Hounds of Hell are now still out there roaming the earth, searching for a thumb-sized morsel to gobble down, and that could be your fingers or toes or other little tender things, so stay fast in your bed at night, high up in the loft of the barn where vicious mad dogs can't climb, and you might be safe. Maybe. You might. Maybe."

The children had horrible looks on their faces. Rafe asked, "Will dogs *ever* learn how to climb into our loft?"

Mother Hubbard looked at them all like she may never see them again. "Maybe. Everything out there is pushing harder and harder to survive. If you aren't strong and clever, you're eaten right down by something that *is* stronger and more clever than you. It's a dangerous world, my dear little ones, and don't you ever forget it! Don't ever wander off at night so that come morning time it's just your eyeballs hanging off some tree. We've had a restful story, now it's time for a chore. I want you all to go to the frog pond and catch me as many as you can. And don't fall into the drowning pool. Just stay at the other end where you can clearly see the bottom."

Rafe asked, "Is the pond ready for frogs again?"

"I believe so, but how can I know for sure unless you first go see. If the frogs are back in proper numbers, there'll be no missing them. Just stay away from the drowning pool! It goes all the way to the Realm of the Dragons, they say, and drowning into death is no proper way to get there."

Rafe promised her, "We'll catch you a fine supper!"

* * * * *

The children sang songs as they paraded over the dry fields until they came to the thick marshland of tall orange rushes. They carefully pushed their way through in a single file, to flatten a narrow discrete path through the plants. They sang, "Merlin is the name of the land. He became an owl to sit on the tree. The men hunted him so he flew to the moon. He became man in the lusty month of June. Merlin is the name of the land."

As they reached the water's edge, they saw the shore alive with frogs, anew. Rafe proclaimed, "Enough to eat for a week!"

As the children splashed forward, the frogs did likewise and not many were caught. As the children rested a moment before resuming their hunt, the water began to bubble and then hundreds of frogs shot out of the water as if from sling-shots. They struck the trees so hard the little creatures were dazed or killed outright.

"Frogs! A miracle of frogs!" After they had stuffed their pockets and bags and were ready to leave for the village, Rafe noticed the rushes parting on the far side of the water. "A beast! From the drowning pool!"

A giant dead black dragon was pulled forward from the muddy depths by dozens of white swans. The children watched in shocked amazement as the dragon finally burst forth into flames from the light of the sun. The tremendous black chamber of its chest split open and through the smoke, Rafe saw his mum, Nimm, fall out. The swans pulled her away from the fire and pushed her to shore, gently using their heads to keep her mouth above water. "Mum!

Blessed be! I thought you were dead, again. And now you're back again. Are you back to stay? Or are you dead and gone again? How did you survive falling down the well?"

She finally opened her eyes. "What is this?"

"Mum! It's me! Rafe!"

"My child?"

"Mum!"

"Where am I?"

Rafe pulled on her. "Where are you? You're right here!"

Nimm coughed. "Where's that?"

"*Here!*" You're right *here*! Where else?"

"I've always been somewhere."

Rafe assured her, "*Here!*"

"Oh! Blessed be! Earth?" She coughed again. She pinched herself. She slapped her face. "Aye, I see we are… I'm not dead… I've been blessed to be returned to my son!" They helped her up out of the water and a few pieces of straw that were fashioned out of gold fell from her hair. As it hit the sunlit ground, it burst into flames and was gone.

"What was that?" Rafe asked.

"I can't remember."

They all returned to the square, joyous for all the miracles, singing more of the old songs in joy.

* * * * *

A tall tower of blood violently shot out of the town well, and there was much dragon roaring until the thatch fell off all the roofs. Then Arthur realized he was dreaming and awoke with a puzzled scowl.

"You dreamt something bizarre," Merlin said. "I can tell. You wear the memory of your dream like a wet blanket. Didn't my dream chasing spell work at all?"

"Aye. Maybe too good. It was a most fantastic dream and my false father didn't step in to ruin it, not once!"

Merlin asked, "How was the dream too good? What was it of?"

"Maybe the curse of the spell is that it takes out the mundane dreams leaving room for the magical ones."

"What did you dream?"

"First, at the very beginning of the dream, a tree was chasing you."

Merlin chuckled. "Me? Is that what your mind thinks of me when your good manners have fallen asleep? Was that an important dream or just one to amuse you. We all have dreams only to amuse our mind as our body lays as if dead at night, and the dream chasing spell may leave you with only such diversion and folly."

Arthur shook his head. "Nay, this seems more than that. The tree was from a sacred grove and it wanted you for a sacrifice."

"*Oh*! Did it catch me?"

"Aye and nay. For some reason you were then climbing it. It took hours to climb it. You were not alone but with a shadow of yourself and you called her a *witch*. Then you fell and the branches were like knives slicing you into red ribbons. I realized I was falling too. I was about to be cut in ribbons by all the sharp branches. I woke up with a terror. But then I realized I had not yet woken up, and blood shot out of the village well. Dragons!"

"Frights. That was a ghastly dream. I hope my spell didn't put that in you." Merlin quizzed Arthur, "Where were *you* this entire dream?"

"Most the time I was just watching."

"From where?"

"I was merely two eyeballs watching from afar."

"Only your eyes? Where was the rest of your precious face and body?"

Arthur said, "Dreams don't have to make sense."

"Aye," Merlin agreed.

"And *you* had no eyes!" Arthur recalled. "The tree that was chasing you had stolen them from you and was wearing them, so it could see you no matter where you tried to hide in the wood, as you stumbled and cowered blindly. Why must I dream so horribly of eyes apart from their master?"

Merlin doubted that. "If cowering is what occurred, are you sure the dream wasn't about you rather than me?"

A cluster of bushes cracked and parted as Parsifal stomped forward, frowning, holding forth a squirrel.

"Blessed be."

"Ah, a banquet!" Merlin praised him. "Blessed be! You were gone so long we feared you had found a brothel, or at least had become a brothel of one."

"*Merlin!*" Arthur admonished. "Don't be impertinent!"

"Why not?"

"Don't be bawdy."

"If you have a body," Merlin said, "you should be bawdy. I was only joking anyway. A joke thrown at one is like salt. It doesn't hurt unless you have sore spots."

Parsifal wasn't listening. "The forest isn't thick with game, or else I've utterly lost my skill as a hunter."

Arthur pointed. "You have a squirrel. That's something far better than nothing when men are hungry."

"And I saw a horrible sight getting it. I saw where we are going and it's so evil it can't be seen."

"Can't be seen?" Arthur asked.

Merlin ordered him, "Make yourself clear."

Parsifal waved his hand about. "It's like a smear of black soot over a spot on the land and sky and everything. The sight of it made all the hairs on my body feel like they were sizzling with hot fire."

Arthur asked, "How did you come to see this?"

"I saw a squirrel up a tree so I took out my dagger and flung it up at it. The dagger went clear through the squirrel and its tip sank deep enough into the wood to stick it there. So I climbed the tree to fetch them both and as I got high enough, I could see there was a valley in the distance. So I climbed higher and higher still until I was at the very top and I could see for a great distance over the valley and beyond. And as I looked about, I could see that at the spot of our destination, at the western sea, I couldn't see it! No image shows up for the eye to behold. There's a black sooty smear that blots out the ground and sky, both, at just that one faraway spot."

"What's that mean?" Arthur asked Merlin.

Merlin chuckled. "If the Pict witch would disguise herself, she seems to have bumbled badly. Nothing will show up just as greatly as something, it seems."

Parsifal nodded. "To see nothing is very alarming."

Merlin said, "You have a look on your face as if you then fell out of that tree. You've torn the seat of your trousers. Now you know why common sense would have it that pant legs always be kept separate."

Parsifal sadly rubbed his arms where he'd long lost his sleeves. "Aye, and though no one was there to see, it was a great embarrassment."

"Did you fall far?"

"A bit," Parsifal admitted. "But the hard soles of my boots saved me." He kicked his leg high up and showed them the strong metal heels.

Chapter Thirteen

"Nimm!" Mother Hubbard greeted the victorious children's procession back in the square. "You're back and look as though you've seen a ghost!"

All the children joined in. "She's back, she's back, she's back, hooray!"

"How did you go away," Mother Hubbard shouted over the shouting. "And how did you come back? Tell me your spell for traveling into the beyond. Tell me! Tell me so I can do it too!"

"She's back, she's back, she's back, hooray!"

Mother Hubbard yelled, "Hush all you mad spinning creatures. I've work to do!" She gently shook Nimm. "Did you go to the Realm of Dragons? How did you get past the gates? How did you come back in one piece? Tell me so I can know!"

"I don't remember a spell."

"Aye you do!"

"Nay."

Mother Hubbard shook Nimm. "Eee-*ucht*!" Then she shook her even harder. "Don't be such a rotten egg. Of course you remember the spell, you've used it twice now. Two times! Did you go to the Realm of the Dragons? All the way in? How did you do this? What's your spell?"

Nimm pulled herself away. "Ouch. I don't remember that."

"And don't give me such an evil eye. I can't abide by that!"

"I'm not trying to look at you in any certain way. I'm just trying to remember." Nimm rubbed her forehead. "I was with the dragons, but on my way back to middle earth I saw the demon bell! The one that causes our blight."

"How?" Mother Hubbard asked. "You sure it wasn't from confusion? To be so far under the earth is to be so far away."

"I wasn't in Hades or Summerland. I was in the Realm of the Dragons, and like Avalon, it's not up or down. It's not a place like a place is a place—soil, sky, trees or creeks"

Mother Hubbard said, "Tell me what you can and don't worry about how it sounds."

"But I felt like I was up on a tall mountain and I saw the unholy grove of trees that hides the demon bell. It's a grove that even the Roman army couldn't or wouldn't cut down."

"You saw this up on a mountain? What mountain?"

Nimm nodded. "It was like a mountain. Very tall, very purple, and crystal. I could see the bottom through the top; it was an odd purple crystal."

Mother Hubbard shook her again. "Go on! Go on!"

"I saw Merlin and Arthur and two other men. That nice boy Parsifal with the wonderful suit of clothes. But they were so dirty and his sleeves had been misplaced, and there was some abbot. And a raven was following them—Opie the raven—like a silent banshee, not proclaiming death but thinking about it all the time. I floated over them, even the raven, for just a moment, very *very* close at some poplar trees. I did this as I passed between worlds."

Mother Hubbard asked, "What did you see them doing?"

"The leaves shook and tried to talk to the men to tell them I was there."

"Nay! Listen. What were the men doing?"

"Walking and walking. They were on their great grail quest. Merlin saw me for a moment as clearly as you see me now. He called out my name."

"What were they doing?"

"They were going to a bridge that would take them to the grail."

"But Mum," Rafe interrupted her, "We all saw you surface at the drowning pool, coming up from inside a great black dragon."

Mother Hubbard reminded him. "There are no dragons on earth. They live in their own realm. Don't be daft."

"It was dead," Rafe said, "and it burned up at the first touch of the sun leaving Mum behind from inside its bones."

Mother Hubbard turned back to Nimm. "Where is it? Where is the demon bell's grove? Think of it quickly now before it all fades from your mortal mind."

Nimm looked at the sky and turned this way and that. "The other way, the other way from the old trading post."

"London?"

"Aye."

Mother Hubbard helped her get her bearings by turning her to where the sun sets. "London? The old Roman fort is east, dearie."

"Ouch! Don't do that. I'd already said they were going to the sea."

"Don't be rough with my Mum!"

"What happened in the west?" Mother Hubbard demanded. "What's going on there?"

"Terrible. Blood. Death. Great thirst and sorrow. The holy grail. It's at the sea! They're going to the sea! The Bristol Channel!"

Mother Hubbard marveled. "The holy grail is at the sea? But that's a bit far."

"To the west!" Nimm pointed. "The demon bell is *there*! The cauldron is in and with it, the holy grail to stop the wasteland!"

"Aye, to the sunset, land of harvest." Mother Hubbard shivered and got great goose bumps. "Odd. In the old stories, the west has always been connected with the magical element of the cauldron of plenty. Are we reenacting an ancient myth, I mean *actually* reenacting it in a most literal acting out? Will we be placing our footsteps in the exact same place of those who traveled there before us?"

"We must go now and hurry," Nimm said. "I can take you. I saw it all like a map from on high. Let's go and let Priest Owen watch the children so he finally can earn his keep."

"He's kept," Mother Hubbard said. "Dead and in a ditch, his bones kept well for rotting, his mouth forever shut from all our food."

"He's dead? How?"

"He went blind. It seems blind men don't live long in these dire times."

Nimm complained, "And in a ditch? That's horrible! Why not a proper burial?"

"I've no apples and if I did I wouldn't waste any on that man's head."

Nimm protested, "But it still sounds terrible to toss him in a ditch to be picked apart by wolves and ravens."

Mother Hubbard walked to the barn. "We really should go help Merlin. Men can be so incomplete."

"Aye." Nimm looked around, worried. "But when we return, the village will be a wreck."

Rafe asked, "What do you mean?"

Nimm explained, "I don't think a village of children will end up very tidy. It's a shame they don't have a helpful brownie to help them catch up on some of the household chores."

"What's a brownie?" Rafe asked.

"A helpful little creature of magic, and when he appears for our eyes, he's shaggy from head to toe with dark wool. At night when we sleep, the brownie pops out of the hearth and helps us with our household chores, since he seems to get such satisfaction from the mundane."

Rafe scowled. "Mum, why do you tell me such silly stories as if I were a child."

Mother Hubbard defended Nimm. "Your age has nothing to do with it! A brownie is a brownie and he could utterly care less if you believe in him or not, if you are young or old."

"That's ridiculous," Rafe insisted.

Mother Hubbard stated, "You just don't understand the old ways. Before the Romans came, the land was filled with enough brownies that no one would think to question their existence. But the Romans came. They were very fastidious with an angry passion for order, and the brownies mostly all went away. They've all pushed far north into the highlands where the primitive folk are most untidy."

Mother Hubbard went to the barn loft and dug into the hay to retrieve her hidden staff and then went back outside. With every spell and blessing she could think of, she drew a hasty but prayerful circle in the dirt around the barn. Then she pointed the top of her staff, where a small crystal shard had been imbedded deep in the grain of the wood, at everyone, repeating all the blessings over again, finishing with a solid binding, "So mote it be!"

The two women trudged off toward the west, toward Glastonbury and Bristol Channel.

Chapter Fourteen

As the two women walked along a path high above a creek, Nimm groaned and jealously asked Mother Hubbard, "Your staff seems to give you strength."

"It's my *magic* staff. It was my lucky day when I found a crystal shard, a precious stone as clear as ice. That was the day I made my staff."

"I don't think I've ever come across a crystal. But I've heard of them, of course."

Mother Hubbard was proud. "They're the stars within the earth. I found it while in a trance. I'd been working with potions and I fear I only came up with poisons. Don't mix bluebells, pasque, and melilot. I fell on my face. When I awoke, my mouth was full of grass. I revived myself with my pocket of camphor and opened my eyes to see something glittering before me. A star." She paused and looked down at the creek on the ravine floor in curious recollection.

"What? What's wrong? What do you sense?" Nimm asked, cautiously sniffing the air. She only smelled the tangy green blood that pulsed through the leaves.

"We're at the kink of Kinker Creek." Mother Hubbard pointed her staff down at it.

"Is that important?"

"Aye. There's a town nearby full of healing women, young and old. We should stop in and take advantage of their hospitality."

"Nay," Nimm argued. "We mustn't stray far from our path."

"They could help us on our quest. Could you imagine an entire army of healing women taking down the demon bell from where it rings, and then giving the bell ringer a gift in return suitable of her treachery?"

"Hmmm." Nimm chuckled. "Where's this town?"

"Not far. Let's go now. They bake good bread too."

At sunset, they entered the square and saw all was quiet, not even a dog roamed the street. At the town square, they walked up to a large tree that had been used for hanging. It was full of women, dangling from the neck like drying fruit.

Nimm let out a sob. "What is this?"

"I count seven, three times over. Seven maidens, seven mothers, and seven crones."

"What? How?" Nimm shuddered.

"Odd," Mother Hubbard said. "All hanged for witchcraft and they were only trying to give the wounded some peace. But what's even more odd is that not a fly or raven has moved to consume them."

"What preserves these dead bodes like this?" Nimm moved closer. Then she saw the footprints circling around the entire tree in a thin ring of creek sand. "Dozens of footprints, and all woman's feet at that!"

"And as many sets of prints as there are hanging witches. Count them."

"Oh dread!" Nimm gasped. "Restless! Every last one of them! But how?"

"Curses."

"What kind?"

"I feel curses." Mother Hubbard shivered. "A set of curses for every hanging witch."

"As they died they cursed their executioners?"

Mother Hubbard nodded. "And they unified all their curses into one, but it still wasn't enough to break them free enough to give chase. Thank earth for that small rule."

"The dead aren't allowed to take revenge on those who killed them?"

"No, never."

"Never?"

Mother Hubbard nodded faster. "It's just one of those rules."

"Are you sure?"

Mother Hubbard rolled her eyes. "Can you imagine how many battlefields would still be filled with jousting corpses to this very day if every last soul tried to get the very last word in?"

Nimm asked, "What can we do to break this failed spell?"

"They must be allowed to rest. You know, they can't reincarnate if they're stuck in this circle. A Roman funeral might be best in this time."

"Roman? Aren't *our* ways best?"

"Find me an apple tree with three times seven plump apples to bury, or even apple cider vinegar to pour, and I'll say to you: why are we questing to restore the wasteland with such bounty already at hand?"

"Aye." Nimm smiled and grabbed her thin belly. "Sweet wet tangy tasty apples. They'd go directly into my mouth to help prevent my own premature need to reincarnate. They wouldn't go into a sympathetic magic. That would be foolish for a time like this. I agree; when the magic is to be bland and dire then the Roman way is best."

Nimm helped Mother Hubbard cut down all the hanged women from the tree, and they piled them high on a pyre of kindling and set it on fire. As the last hour of the day finished and came to its noon of night and the sky became its blackest, and as the flames grew their brightest, the dead bodies sat up and started marching a ring around the pyre.

"Be free!" Mother Hubbard yelled at them again, angrily poking her staff toward them. "Do as I say. Don't mock me, and Creation, and the circle of time, and the Goddess who keeps the spider web taut. Go to Summerland and let yourself rest!"

"We have failed." Nimm began to despair.

"Wait." Mother Hubbard said. "They've hung a long time from that tree and have had a long time to dry out from the wind. They won't march this close to a fire for long."

As the pyre grew hotter, the bodies finally lit with it and they consumed into white ashes and sparks. One by one they finally fell where they marched until there was nothing left but bone, and then, those bones also turned to white ash and blew out across the ground with the light puffs of the cool night breeze. "I smell a very strong bee's wax!" Nimm said sniffing and looking around for candles.

"I smell an entire harvest!" She scooped her hands to her mouth desperately trying to taste it. "I'm so hungry! I am so hungry!"

"It's a good smell. Their souls are free," Mother Hubbard said.

A long thin swarm of bats streamed from the side planks of shops and took to the night air. "Is that an omen?" Nimm backed away.

"How lucky for the dead witches!" Mother Hubbard smiled as a stream of bats flitted over their heads. "What luck!"

"*What?*" Nimm quacked indelicately as she ducked in panic and flapped her hands over her head. "My hair! They're all going to claw my hair."

"Don't be vain," Mother Hubbard scolded her. "They don't care about you or your pretty hair, and they don't ever fly into anything. Bats are the guides to our past lives. How lucky for these witches. Before they go on to their next life, the bats will surely show them their past ones. This may help make them wiser, to give them something to ponder as they rest in Summerland."

Nimm asked, "Will those witches all be mightier in their next life?"

"I hope. Knowledge is power." Mother Hubbard pulled on Nimm to get her back up off the ground.

"Are the bats gone?"

Mother Hubbard ordered, "Get up. Let's go."

"I hate things in my hair."

"The bats don't care about your hair."

"Are you sure?"

"Why would they? Think! Think! Eee-*ucht!*"

"Aye." Nimm ran her hand over her scarf on her head.

* * * * *

The next morning, after trudging through a damp bog to avoid the lands of lascivious knight Gustave, Nimm remembered, "We can't walk this way. There's a deep ravine that might be difficult to cross. We must head north for a day."

"But don't you remember a bridge from when you floated over Merlin?"

"Aye. That's right! Maybe we can cross there. I'll try to remember. Curses! I think it has a toll."

"A toll?" Mother Hubbard shrugged. "So? They all do. They say that one should burn all their bridges that have a toll or a troll, but I think that was being symbolic."

"But what'll we pay with?"

"A kiss?" Mother Hubbard batted her white stubby eyelashes prettily.

"Maybe we can sneak across the bridge in the night!"

Mother Hubbard stopped practicing her flirting and agreed, "That's what we'll have to try."

"What's the alternative?"

"Get our poor skirts wet."

Nimm shook her head. "That's not what we want." They came to a grove of poplar trees and Nimm remembered, "This is where I was when I looked down on Merlin. This very site. I came down on the trees like the wind and stirred all the trembling leaves."

Mother Hubbard asked, "And what did the trees say for your doing that?"

"I'm not sure anymore," Nimm admitted.

"The trembling leaves of the poplar are sensitive to the messages of the spirits of the wind. We can read them if we're wise."

"Oh. Well anyway, I'm sure that if it had anything to say to Merlin then it wouldn't be very kind. There, just beyond that, up there is the toll bridge." Past the screen of poplar trees they saw the bridge, then hid a short distance from it behind scraggly bushes, and spied. The day passed and they only spotted two bridge keepers who nervously paced before the bridge but never stepped up onto it. "Not a soul crosses this bridge much, do they? Not even the keepers."

Mother Hubbard observed, "From the quality of the path leading to the bridge, and the heartiness of the bridge itself, you can tell that it used to be a busy crossing. Not now."

"How odd."

"I wonder what happened. Did all the towns west of here fall into the sea?"

"We'll find out at nightfall."

They napped behind the bushes and when sunset turned into darkness they awoke, and Nimm smiled. "The moon is full tonight. How lucky for us."

Mother Hubbard agreed. "Nothing is better than light shining on things so we can see."

They scampered quickly to the bridge. At its edge, they felt like they had hit a wall. Both of them staggered backwards off the bridge and fell sick to the grass. At morning, they awoke to two men holding crude spears to their heads.

"Blessed be," Nimm mumbled.

The bridge keepers didn't respond in kind. "You have to pay a toll!"

"Infidels," she added.

"You have to pay a toll!"

Mother Hubbard moaned in pain. "Like those poor dead lizards in the middle of the bridge?

"Nay, we didn't mean for the bridge to kill the lizards."

"Is that what you did?" Mother Hubbard gasped. "Put a stinking curse on the bridge because you feared we might arrive? Rotten eggs on you!"

The men insisted, "Nay, we'd never curse our own bridge. But woe, it is cursed aplenty just the same."

"You didn't do it?" Mother Hubbard marveled. "So you tend a cursed bridge?"

Nimm asked, "And you'd take our tolls and then leave us to our fates?"

"Aye," the bridge keepers admitted. "We still have to live on something."

Mother Hubbard said to the bridge keepers, "My dear paramours, if you've such a stinky spell on your prized property, why don't you just wash the spell away, you lazy simpletons!"

"A wise wizard said that would do the trick, but we've had no rain."

Mother Hubbard sadly shook her head. "Leave it to men to wait for it to rain so they can say something has been washed."

The men asked, "How else would we wash a bridge?"

Mother Hubbard pointed to the stream below. "The bridge is over water, more than you need. Just haul it up in buckets and then with fat brushes of fresh sage and rosemary and mint, wash the cursed bridge of its simple stinking spell so someone can cross it."

"Mint won't grow in these parts anymore," the men said.

"Well then, hmmm" Mother Hubbard looked around. "You'll have to do without mint. What a shame, it strengthens spells. You'll just have to scrub harder, then. But rosemary and sage when added to the water will cleanse even the stink out of a man's summer bed. And that's pretty ripe."

"Clever, but wouldn't a wholesome rain be so much easier on us? Scrubbing on knees is not a man's work."

Mother Hubbard wagged her finger at them. "You two men are lazy. Now go and scrub down that bridge like you're angry at it or you'll not be able to collect a toll until the next rain."

"We'll wait." They looked at the sky.

"We're in a drought."

The bridge keepers grumbled, argued with each other, and then hauled up buckets of water and proceeded to put themselves into a woman's posture and scrub. Resting in the grass, Mother Hubbard made the men's task complete by chanting a spell under her breath, until she came to the end of her clever rhyme and shouted, "So mote it be!"

"What was the cleaning spell?" Nimm asked, lying a few yards from her. "You were so hushed about it."

"Nay."

"Tell me," Nimm begged. "I'd be wiser to know."

"It was my secret spell and my secret spell to know, alone. An old woman has to have her secrets."

"It's no concern to me; I wouldn't remember it anyway."

Mother Hubbard scolded her, "A woman has to remember her spells and keep them orderly in her book of shadows, even if that book is her heart."

"Okay, I'll be mindful," Nimm promised. "So what's the spell you just uncrossed on the bridge to clean it, and I'll try to remember."

"Nay! That's my spell. You can't take on new spells so casually. Especially not from me."

"Why not?"

Mother Hubbard bragged, "I went through great effort to be schooled in what I know. You'll not simply take my secrets from me like a thief."

"I'm not a thief. And if you wish to have secrets, that's your quiet prison."

Mother Hubbard grew angry. "When you tell me the secret spell of how to go to the Realm of Dragons, I'll tell you the cleaning spell. And stop looking at me like that! I'll not abide by the evil eye!"

"I'll look at you like you're a mad woman all I like, when you act like a mad woman. And I don't know a spell to get you into the Realm of Dragons."

"Then how did you get past the underwater gates?"

Nimm repeated, "I can't remember. It was like I was walking past the best Roman army and no one saw me, not even the gate keeper. I just walked in and no one glanced my way, not once. I walked on a path of purple stones that seemed to glow. They were so deep in their beautiful color, it humbled me to be on something so precious. And I walked past all sorts of people and plump well-fed farm animals and no one gazed upon me for even a moment."

Mother Hubbard pulled a bit of grass up and threw it at Nimm. "We know there are no Roman guards or farm animals at such gates."

Nimm impatiently moaned. "I told you I don't know."

When the two men were finished scrubbing the bridge, and they fell faint in the grass, the two women got up.

"Hey," the men called, angrily crawling back up. "You can't cross. Where's your toll!"

"We have paid with our good advice," Nimm insisted, putting her nose into the air.

"Nay!" they protested, grabbing their wood spears and poking them wildly toward the women. "Advice isn't a coin. We can't live on advice."

"What fools you two are." With a few swipes of her walking stick Mother Hubbard tripped the men so they went tumbling over the edge of the ravine and rolled all the way down to the water. "Quick," she called to Nimm. "Let's get on our way before they crawl back out and attack us all over again."

Nimm and Mother Hubbard scampered across the bridge all the while the two sodden men below, screamed up loud curses. "Damn you! Damn you! Pay us our toll!"

On the other side, Nimm paused and worried, "Where to now?"

Mother Hubbard asked, "Don't you remember the way?"

Nimm sadly shook her head. "Not after the bridge. And there are many ways from here to the sea. How will we catch up with Merlin?"

"Do we want to catch up with that horrible husband of mine? Or do we beat him to the holy grail, take it all for ourselves, and make his quest vain." She chortled.

Nimm smiled naughtily. "That might be fun."

"But I'd like his magic advice when the time comes, if we must battle evil."

Nimm agreed. "An old wizard would be helpful."

"If you're going to be so dramatic about it, then we'll see if we can find him. I agree; *much* magic is better than *some*."

"But how will we find him now?" Nimm licked her finger and put it up in the air. "Which way does the wind blow?"

"That won't help," Mother Hubbard chuckled.

Nimm prayed, "The wind, the wind, speak to me of Merlin."

"The poplar trees are far; you won't hear them."

"Wind! Help me!" Nimm repeated stubbornly.

"The wind isn't going to speak to you! You are not so clever to hear it!"

They heard a raven's caw.

"What was that? Opie!"

Mother Hubbard pointed out to Nimm where he perched on top of a far bush. "Where this bird flies, Parsifal isn't far."

Opie flew off the bush and they followed it over the edge of a ridge of dead trees.

When they spotted the black smear that hung low in the sky, Nimm halted in alarm. "*That* is certainly where we're going. The black robes of Death Himself."

"Aye," Mother Hubbard smirked. "The Pict witch is careless. Her invisibility spell is ridiculous."

"I hear water." Nimm shivered. "We must be near the sea." A sharp icy breeze that smelled like brine blew at them. They grabbed each other to keep warm.

"We're at the sea already? My staff is swift." Mother Hubbard used it to help her climb down a white rocky embankment to a sandy seashore pounded by swirling, salty water. "Lochlann Death."

The shoreline was dotted with the skeletons of many whales. "The underworld of the sea is cursed."

Mother Hubbard glared where the black smear clung to the horizon far up shore. "Some great confusion may have tricked them into trying to swim on land."

As Mother Hubbard kicked at the bones, Nimm spotted figures far up the beach, "There they are! Ahead! Do you see them almost blowing over, way up the shore? Arthur. Merlin. Two others."

"My staff is swift!" Mother Hubbard kissed it.. They ran to catch up with the men. "Blessed be!"

Chapter Fifteen

"Blessed be, more mouths to feed," Merlin grumbled at the sight of Mother Hubbard and Nimm.

"My husband!" Nimm took in the grand display of Merlin in his red cap and wildly blowing fur robe.

Mother Hubbard said, "What do you mean *my husband*! He's *my* husband!"

"I remember you now!" Nimm accused him. "I remember you, Merlin! I remember you in the Realm of Dragons! You were my husband! *Are* my husband!"

"Impossible," Mother Hubbard said to Nimm. "Marriage is merely an earthly piddling affair to keep babies of flesh coming and coming to keep the Goddess of War from growing bored with an empty battlefield."

"But we were married and lived as man and wife, as if on *this* earth."

"W… *what?*" Merlin stammered, genuinely confused. "What do you remember of such a place? You can't remember the Realm of Dragons, Nimm! That's impossible. You're but a mere mortal."

"It has changed me." Nimm smiled knowingly. "All my brushes with magic have changed me into a powerful witch, a soon to be *more* powerful witch. I've yet to truly grow into my powers."

Merlin tried to dismiss her. "That could be a danger or a blessing. Your marriage to me in the Realm of Dragon could be a trick."

"Not a trick." Nimm pointed accusingly. "You, you're the trickster and I remember parts that were more and more tricks to have me think I was in a world like this one. But I was married to you."

"So was *I!*" Mother Hubbard fumed. "Merlin! You're stuck with me for now!" Then her apron blew up against her face.

Nimm shivered. "First, we should travel up off this coast and stay deep in the trees. It's too open here. This sea is so windy and cold I can't even think or feel my fingers."

"Aye," Arthur agreed. "You can all quarrel in comfort."

Mother Hubbard nodded. "The wind has nearly torn my clothes off. Why were you men so stupid to walk along the shore? Oh, I know why, because you're stupid men. The wind has nearly torn my ears off."

"Aye, let's travel in the trees," Merlin agreed. "A man would like his woman to have her ears and lose her tongue."

"Cad."

They climbed back up the white rocky embankment and went past the scrub, deep into the weald, and there the breeze was calmer. Nimm sat on a fallen log and shivered. Arthur and Parsifal sat on each side and held her to help them warm up.

"O' Virgin," Abbot Babble Blaise prayed. "Keep us safe."

Nimm said, "I'm so cold I think I'll die."

Merlin offered, "I can set something on fire. That's one of my tricks." He looked at Mother Hubbard.

Nimm nodded off into a deep sleep, and with her eyes wide open but rolled all the way back up into her head, she began to say, "Merlin and I went down under the greensward. The banshee stood on the edge of the well and said, not yet, not yet, so it wasn't my time to die. We fell through the seven seas and seven planetary spheres of the eyeball and seven castle towers made of air, through all things known and unknown and finally rose through a great mist to a small island in a sea of stars, candles and things like glistening pebbles."

Merlin ordered, "Somebody wake her up. We don't have to hear this."

"*Eee*-ucht!" Mother Hubbard hushed Merlin. "I want to hear what a rotten egg you've been."

Nimm continued, "We lived in a cottage as young man and wife and in the center of it was a grand marriage bed. It was all proper with rose petals in the mattress. But that's only how I remember it because in the Realm of Dragons you don't use your earthly body or grow roses. But what I remember seems like I had my body, so young and everything about it seemed so new. And I lived in a strange land; it felt strange like dream."

"You're only dreaming now," Merlin insisted.

"*Shhh!*" Mother Hubbard cut him off. "You're a rotten egg. Just let her talk!"

Nimm continued, "On the west shore of the island was a long row of hundreds of old dead elephants who'd lived and served in the Roman time. They were standing, with scaffolding built inside of them, and dwarves were all busy stuffing them with straw to preserve them. On a far tall hill I noticed a bright star. I walked to it and saw it was a towering oak tree made entirely of the purest crystal. When I looked inside, I instantly began to cry and saw a deep green forest. The men were cutting a mistletoe bunch from a tall oak branch with a sickle coated in gold, and it fell onto a fine linen blanket the whole clan was holding out for it. The men piously brought it back to the village and they pounded the magic milk out of its berries and the women put their fingers in the bowl and wetted them and then ran into the gardens and wiped the juice onto the leaves of all their crops. Then they were drenched with water from buckets and this insured fertility and rain. Then the sacred sheep gave so much milk that afterwards she felt so light, she jumped over her mother, the moon."

"That's ridiculous," Merlin said. "It may be hardly a sacrilege, but I've never heard of the sheep and moon together in the same endeavor, and I know my stories!"

"*Shhh!*"

Nimm turned her head to Merlin, her eyes still rolled back and blind and glowing white. She answered him, "That's how it seemed in the Realm of Dragons. Of course there are no moons, sheep or mistletoe bunches in the Realm of Dragons; those are only earthly puddles. But my memory can only put it that way."

"Aye," Merlin agreed. "So we can't rely on it."

Mother Hubbard prompted Nimm on. "Spin your yarn and tell us what happened. Or was it all just sheep and moon oddities?"

Nimm finally closed her eyes and her head fell into Parsifal's shoulder. She kept speaking in her trance, "In our cottage, one dwarf became friendly and chatty with us and came to visit us often. The dwarf acted as the Druid, and married Merlin and me with a proper knot of rope. Caraway seeds were showered over us in such abundance that we only felt love. Through the days as Merlin bedded me in an endless dance of warmth and fulfillment, the dwarf would spin love spells. As I'd make the sheets up after he'd finished, the dwarf would spin closing spells. As I'd spin thread at the wheel, the dwarf would spin spinning spells as he banged and strummed a lovely bowed lyre crwth on his lap, until the thread I was spinning came out pure gold!"

"Toads," Merlin scoffed. "How can you do what the greatest alchemists can not?"

Mother Hubbard agreed, "It's a crying sobbing shame that it can't be done here. I'd be high in the highest castle dressed in silk, if it were so."

"Aye," Nimm agreed, nodding in her odd sleep. "But gold doesn't bring happiness. One day, the three crones of Camelot, from the old castle of King Camelis, came and busted right into the door and screamed at Merlin, *You're not to be on holiday at this time. Go back up and out and pound the Roman out of that poor boy. Give us a real king we can use. We need some order on earth, and soon.*"

Merlin marveled. "How do you remember that?"

"The dwarf was with us, as he usually was, and though he smiled, he hid under the table as if he was ashamed or afraid of the old women. Then, to my horror, the three crones of Camelot turned to me and screamed, *This cad of an old wizard has been eating your soul!* I puzzled, of course, not knowing a soul was something that could be eaten."

"I'd never do that."

"Shhh! *Eee*-ucht!"

"You did! So the three crones of Camelot explained, *Like a mother's milk, the soul comes forth without ceasing, as long as it's alive. He's been eating your soul like mother's milk.* I asked, *Is that the nature of marriage… for a husband to endlessly eat his wife's soul?* The crones of Camelot explained with much shouting, *That's the nature of a secret marriage. A proper marriage in the town square is a see-saw of much activity. Behind closed doors, where other men can't see and all is a secret is where a wife has to fear. Merlin has been a cad and will stop this abuse this very instant!* Two of the crones firmly took him by each ear, and the third held wide the door, and by his ears they pulled him and they marched him out of the room. In the very same instant that the door slammed, I finally saw the dwarf, still hiding under the table, for who he really was. He wasn't a wee charming man but a giant black dragon. The dragon had me and piles of gold that I'd spun, as his possessions. But a dragon can do nothing with a mortal woman nor do anything with piles of gold. It was pure blind greed and nothing more. As misplaced and stupid as this greed was, the dragon was hungry for more. So night and day I was his prisoner and I spun more gold. One day I heard the heavens roar again, as all the monsters in the Realm of Dragons were warring more and more. One day, all the things about me in the cottage began to shake to the floor and I heard the most violent wind. As I hurried outside, I saw my black dragon chased through the clouds by many red dragons. My black dragon had his tail bit off and it released a long trail of blood that oddly soaked into the sky and stained it in a long sickening swirling pattern. When my dragon could fly no more, he quickly swooped down and swallowed me whole where I stood watching. In the blackness inside, I came forth from the drowning pool through a veil of black smoke tenderly pushed to shore by many swans who were sent to receive me and care for me by some magic I don't understand. My son was there at the shore and I knew all was well."

Mother Hubbard said, "You were only gone a few days. Your story sounds as if it had gone on for many weeks at least."

"There really weren't any temporal things of earth that I saw. The Realm of Dragons isn't earth. And I don't think time belongs there either. I think time is only a part of the temporal ways of earth. Time needs a real dirt road to plod along. There's no real dirt or road except here on middle earth."

"I wonder why you keep going away from us in one way or another and coming back." Mother Hubbard was baffled. "To the rest of us, we leave or lose our step but only once and it's called a terrible accident and we're dead. Your terrible accidents have no grip on you. You're a most powerful witch and you don't even know it."

"Things just come at me like odd music and then pass the ear. And aye, I do feel the witching in me bubbling stronger with every dance with the Grim Reaper."

Arthur asked Merlin, "What are the three crones of Camelot? What is Camelot?"

"It's your destiny."

"But what is it?"

"It's your home," Mother Hubbard said with a gentle warm smile.

Merlin took a deep impatient breath and explained, "Nay, not so simple. For you and your future, Camelot isn't one fixed place but is whatever castle you'll be staying at. To hold so many disparate kingdoms together you must always be on your way from one stronghold to another, making brothers of all your countrymen, or at least keeping close to your enemies. Someday men will think fondly of Camelot as a new Golden Dawn, but only because it couldn't be pinned down and made literal."

Arthur asked, "What do the three crones have to do with this?"

Mother Hubbard asked, "Will they visit him and foretell fortune or death?"

"Nay," Merlin corrected her, "the three crones of Camelot are your always moving *court, conscience*, and *charity*. They're with you at whatever castle you're sleeping in. But such ideals are far too grand for anything other than when you live within a castle's strong walls, as well as having men to guard you. Outside in the wildwood you must live as a fox, bear, and hawk."

Arthur frowned. "There's no charity in the wildwood?"

"None at all, none to be found. There's only sheep or wolves."

Nimm woke up, yawned and then moaned, "Why was I sleeping at a time like this?"

Mother Hubbard asked, "Do you remember anything you said in your dreaming?"

"Nay. What'd I say?"

Mother Hubbard asked, "Do you remember the spell to get you past the gates into the Realm of Dragons yet?"

"Nay."

"Eee-*ucht*! I should have had the presence of mind to ask you that while you were babbling on in a trance so freely."

Nimm stood up too quickly and fainted.

Merlin decided, "We'll rest here for the night. We won't fight a Pict witch in this weary condition."

Parsifal asked, "How will we keep from wandering off in the night if the monster should ring her bell. We're so close now, we might even hear the monster cough."

"Aye! O' Virgin! We're so close it'll shatter our ears!"

"Your ears won't shatter, abbot," Merlin assured him. "We'll deasil our camp twice over. No evil will penetrate."

Mother Hubbard bragged, "And my staff has a crystal. Mine is strongest and best."

Merlin waved her off with his hand. "Fool. It isn't the staff that makes the magic, it's the magic."

"Men always say that. Make yourself happy," she replied, unconvinced, as they both drew their own magic circles in a wholesome clockwise direction around the camp.

"Will that be enough?" Abbot Babble Blaise asked, doubting. "I don't think so. I can just feel it. O' Virgin!"

Merlin instructed them, "We all sleep with our feet together."

Arthur asked, "Does that make magic?"

"The best kind, practical." Merlin pulled a length of cord out of his sleeve and tied their ankles all together so they couldn't try to wander off without waking all the others.

* * * * *

The next morning, after Merlin unknotted the cord that kept their ankles tied together, he took off his red cap and fur robe, stood before them all naked, and announced, "I'll leave you all now." He poked at his ribs. "This skin that I'm squeezed into has tired me out beyond endurance and I must get some rest before Arthur becomes king."

The two women's faces dropped. "You can't leave us! You're married to us!"

Arthur's face showed panic. "You can't leave me! You're teaching me!"

"The women never needed me, and you, Arthur, have always badly needed something, but for now a well-rested wizard will serve you best in the end."

Arthur protested, "You keep telling me wisdoms but I don't know anything. You can't leave, yet!"

"I'm done with you."

Parsifal asked Merlin, "But how do we find the holy grail?"

"Oh that. Just follow the song of the wren."

"What?" Arthur questioned. "Why would a poor sweet wren want anything to do with such horror?"

Merlin reminded him, "The wren is the most sacred bird to a Druid."

"Aye, but why?"

"The sound of a wren is the sound of inspiration. *That* is what you need. That's all you need. Without inspiration, your schooling's been in vain. Without inspiration, many a learned man has driven a sword through his own belly."

"Merlin," Arthur begged, "you can't leave."

"I've only one last parting wisdom. A square table is best for lovers, a round one is best for friends."

"You already said that and it makes no sense."

"Goodbye then. To the Realm of Dragons, through the holly gates of Apple and Mint Islands, Brythonic Light, Furious Host, Goddess Ceridwen awake and change forms. Boibel to Jaichim, fith fath. Branch slap. So mote it be."

"Nay!" The women screamed, grabbing at him but he ignored them and after tapping his staff on a fat tree, he left it behind and walked into the bark. With the bright sounds of crackling and odd vibrations he went deep inside. Merlin melted away with the wood, and as his skin slipped from their grip, the women were left outside empty handed and cursing.

"Eee-*ucht*! Rotten eggs!"

Nimm scratched at the long scar that his passing had left on the tree. "Merlin?"

"Eee-*uch!* Chop it down and pull the scoundrel out by his ugly little dragon! What's the spell?" Mother Hubbard yelled, trying to push her own way in, but only getting bark prints on her cheek. "How'd he just do that?"

"He said the spell! He said it aloud before he went in!"

"What was it?" Mother Hubbard asked. "I was too upset to hear a thing! "What was it? What did he say?"

"I didn't hear it either," Nimm admitted. "I was also too upset. Did you hear it Arthur?"

"Nay."

"Did you hear it?" Nimm asked Parsifal and Abbot Babble Blaise.

"Nay," Abbot Babble Blaise shuddered. "Did my eyes even see what I thought I saw? How can a man walk into a tree?"

Parsifal reminded them, "Merlin is a bit more than a man."

Mother Hubbard slapped the tree. "I'll have to cast a strong memory spell to bring his words back to my ears. It'll have to be done just right. It'll take me a while, but when I get that spell I'll tear Merlin out of the Realm of Dragons so fast he won't know what world he's in."

Arthur put Merlin's red cap and robe on himself and paraded about. "I now look like a prince. What's wrong with this robe? It's hot!"

The robe began to wobble and then fall apart and kick at him as dozens of squirrels came to life and scampered away. Then his feather cap flapped on his head and squawked. Talons scratched his scalp and then flew away.

"Yikes!" Arthur put his hands to his head. "More of Merlin's tricks! And I thought I'd have something nice from him."

At that, Mother Hubbard angrily broke Merlin's abandoned staff. "*Well, I'll* not let it be known across the land that Merlin left us, *abandoned* us in such a hasty manner! I'll not be so humiliated. I was his wife and to be abandoned by one's husband is so vulgar I could scream! I'm not common!"

Nimm suggested, "Why don't we women fib a bit and say we used our powerful witchery to imprison *him* within a tree! We'll make the final hour of the story *ours* and not his."

"But that's a lie," Arthur reminded them. "He just walked away from us at his own leisure. That's how he is."

"But he insulted us," Nimm protested.

Mother Hubbard pouted. "My pride won't have that be."

Nimm warned Arthur, "*You* say what you will of Merlin when you're the King. But *we* will spread our own tale of how we imprisoned him within a tree for our own vengeance. We'll see which story wins out through time."

"You don't need to threaten me so. I don't care how Merlin went away, only that he went."

Parsifal said, "We'd better go find the holy grail now. We may need the entire light of day."

"Aye," Abbot Babble Blaise agreed. "But I worry how it'll be done without Merlin."

"Don't worry. I will take care of everything." Mother Hubbard proudly held her staff out before her. "Mine has a crystal! Now, *I'm* in charge! I should have always been in charge. Merlin is a cad! Everybody follow me!"

As they walked, Arthur tried to find a wren's song. He heard nothing above from the indifferent rustle of dry branches, but decided he wouldn't be discouraged. He decided to find his inspiration from inside.

"Oh, you're resourceful," Merlin praised him.

"What's that?" Arthur asked. "I thought you were gone."

"I was just talking to your shadow self. Naturally."

"Will you send me a wren?" Arthur asked.

Merlin laughed in Arthur's shadow self face. "Do you think anyone can order about a wren? Not even a wizard or king."

Chapter Sixteen

"I'm worried about Rafe," Nimm admitted, stepping off a fallen tree that spanned a dried creek gully. "I pray all the children are well and still have enough to eat. Do you think those sneaky geese are still laying a pile of eggs in the greensward when no one's looking?"

Mother Hubbard asked her, "Did you have a premonition?"

"Nay." Nimm helped her down off the fat log. "I just worry about my son. I'm allowed that."

Abbot Babble Blaise clasped his hands. "I'll say a prayer for him."

"Your good intentions are appreciated," Nimm thanked him. Then she asked Mother Hubbard, "Haven't you always wondered where all those eggs came from when not a single goose could be found? Do they really fly in and fly away so fast? That's what Priest Owen would say."

"Priest Owen couldn't see when he had eyes and lost his head when he never even had one. *Think*!" Mother Hubbard poked her finger at her. "Do you really think it was geese coming and going so fast you never saw a single one? Not once? Not ever?"

"Where there's a goose egg, there's a goose."

Mother Hubbard admitted, "Nay, there wasn't a single goose. *I* laid the eggs in secret with a powerful and exhausting egg spell."

"O' Virgin! That sounds evil!"

"That's not possible," Nimm said. "Where do the eggs really come from? What magic can still create eggs without geese?"

"Why isn't it possible?"

Nimm said, "Magic is lazy and needs a path on which to roll. Magic needs the natural world. How do you make this magic?"

"I lay them!" Mother Hubbard repeated.

"*You*? But you aren't a goose! Only birds can lay eggs!"

"Aye." Mother Hubbard nodded proudly. "Everything you say about magic is true. That's why a man would never be able to do this trick, no matter how skilled a magician, powerful his blood, or clever his spells. A man just isn't going to lay an egg. There's something very feminine about laying an egg."

"*You* lay the goose eggs?" Nimm asked again.

"I said *aye*!"

"How?"

"The magic spell is one I learned in a coven in Sweden."

"A coven?" Abbot Babble Blaise gasped, quickly crossing himself. Parsifal quickly followed, feeling spooked.

"An entire coven?" Arthur marveled. "How grand to have so many friends all at the very same time!"

"Aye." Mother Hubbard nodded proudly. "Twelve of us and a leader. But don't be jealous of this coven. We were a coven devoted to learning all the tricks of women for selfish goals. We would have utterly destroyed men if we could have learned the trick. We were mad with power but really had no power and got into trouble with nature."

"O' Virgin! That sounds evil! I can just feel it!"

"Eee-*ucht*! Feeding hungry children at the cost of my own health isn't evil, you split-pea minded dolting abbot!"

Nimm asked, "What's the spell to make eggs? How do you do something so extreme and not fall sick?"

"It's my own spell!" Mother Hubbard said. "A deep egg magic."

Nimm gasped. "Any egg magic is very dangerous! So arduous, complicated and draining, I'm sure you twist the cosmic web nearly to breaking! That's almost unnatural!"

"Aye." Mother Hubbard gave Nimm a worried expression. "Almost."

Arthur said, "Merlin had said that only the greatest of witches can make egg magic, and then only the greatest can make a dozen eggs in reality before they're dead from it, because their entire bones have been sucked out from under them from the taking of minerals."

"Aye!" Mother Hubbard smiled proudly. "Such an act of creation is cheeky for a mortal woman to take on. But I'd no choice."

"How do you do it?" Nimm asked.

"I'll not tell you the spell. It's too dangerous, anyway. But I'll tell you that once the path on the web is mastered, the magic is as obvious as nature. The egg is an example of all of creation, recreated in one tiny package. The yolk is earth, the white is the Realm of Dragons which holds it, and the shell is Heaven which binds even that which holds us. The egg. The divine egg. Witchcraft sees the cosmos in every detail of its creation but the egg is its most perfect, complete, and whole example. And witchcraft can create copies of that if it follows easily enough down the threads of the cosmic web. That's why men can't do it. Men have other uses in the fertility of the cosmos."

Nimm asked, "Tell about the coven you learned your spells in? You can tell me more about that, can't you?"

Mother Hubbard raised her eyebrows. "What do you want to know?"

"You'd said that you were mad with power and that it got you into trouble."

"Aye. In those days we were all young and arrogant and just mad with our own beauty. We even grew to hate the men because they were so weak compared to us, or so we'd come to think. We let our hatred and arrogance poison our rituals. One noon of night while in the sacred circle in the woods we loudly blasphemed to the Goddess to serve us and our selfish goals. We demanded that She reward us. Think of our folly, to ask her to reward our lack of wisdom. An army of stags attacked us and carried us away on their great horns, surely sent by Pan. I woke up inside a fat living tree, the tree of life. I couldn't move. I was bound there day and night."

Nimm gasped. "You became a tree witch? But how are you *here*, now?"

"One day the Viking Swedish God, Oden, walked by in a glum and decided to crucify himself on the tree. He said he'd see if any mortal would pity him. As he hung, many men and women passed and barely gave him a glance since they were so busy worrying about their own sorry fates. For the first time in my life I began to feel compassion. At least enough compassion to feel sorry for a neglected

God. So from where I was warmly and safely wrapped inside my tree, I sang, *I know you have hung from the windy tree with spears in your side, a sacrifice to yourself, oh God. Who would care.* And he grumbled back to me, *then why did I do it?* And I suggested that to face death, God can feel the fate of the mortal and his heart will grow with it and his knowledge will grow with it since death is something Gods otherwise don't know. The shadow of death worries people from peasant to king all the days of their lives. I told him that knowing the fear of death is forbidden wisdom for a God. He thought about it. Then He argued with me that humans don't fear death, that death is as easy as lying down. He said that men and women fear life and fear how to feel alive, as they walk through their dangerous lives where only the strong survive. He said that when it comes time to die, mortals are finally released from the responsibility of always having to be strong enough. So at that, I asked to feel alive."

Arthur doubted, "You really had this chat with a God? Like that?"

"Maybe I dreamed it," Mother Hubbard admitted. "But stuck inside a tree as if I'd been grown there, the dreams are vivid. And they are many."

"How are you here then," Nimm asked, "if you were so imprisoned in a tree by an angry Pan?"

"A knave who was defying the king's forest law was stealing wood to sell. He chopped me down and when I stood up, standing for the first time in tens of years, He smiled, thinking I was an answered prayer for his pleasure. I wasn't. I walked away."

"And you left Sweden?"

"I wandered," Mother Hubbard answered, "wondering what a free tree witch is to do with her magic. When I sailed across the ocean and then finally came here, I saw all the grown men and women taken in the night by the sound of a new mysterious bell. I didn't hear it myself, but one woman did make it back alive, and she told me of it. Our dear blessed Nimm."

Nimm smiled. "I came within hearing the demon bell and yet I lived. Then I went into the well and yet I lived."

"The goblins of Hades don't want you, methinks," Mother Hubbard chuckled. "You're rotten eggs!"

Arthur asked her, "Do you have any idea what's going on with Nimm's amazing newfound abilities?"

"Aye," Nimm also queried, "what's going on with me! Why am I this way?"

Mother Hubbard swung her staff forcefully against a few hanging vines to part them. "*Eee*-ucht! I have no idea."

Suddenly the forest was pitch black. "My eyes!" Mother Hubbard cried. "I've been cursed *already*! Something has taken my eyes! Rotten eggs!"

"I can't see either!" Abbot Babble Blaise joined in. "O' Virgin! Help us!"

Arthur called out, "I can't see anything!"

"Nay," Parsifal said. "It's not your eyes. It's fallen dark for all of us."

"Eee-*ucht!*"

"A small relief," Arthur said, waving his arms out before himself, not able to see his hands. "I feared you were all fine and it was just me, and you were all about to get a blind king. But if it's dark for everybody, then this is something else."

"Nay, it's not just you." Nimm moaned. "My hair! I fear something might claw into my hair!"

"You're fine," Mother Hubbard assured her. "The only thing that claws into your hair is your own nervous fingers."

Parsifal said, "We've stepped into the blackest night. How?"

"Nay it's not our eyes; we're inside the black smear," Nimm explained. "We're in the middle of a powerful spell! My hair! Something has grabbed my hair!"

Mother Hubbard reached out to find her to help her get unstuck. "It's just a twiggy branch you walked into. And that's no fault of the branch."

"My scarf is gone! I can't find it! I can't stand things in my hair!"

"I know. It's rotten eggs on you. Hush and I'll rip it out and you won't have to worry about it anymore."

"Don't rip her hair out!" Abbot Babble Blaise ordered her.

"Nay! I'm ripping out the twig, you fool!"

Parsifal asked, "What's causing this complete lack of light?"

Mother Hubbard griped, "That wheedling Pict witch's blind spot has blinded us now that we have walked into it! For all the stars, I *hate* her!"

Abbot Babble Blaise whimpered, "How can we proceed without God's precious gift of sight? This is just evil! O Virgin! Make the sun rise again! Beseech your Son to do it!"

"The sun out there is fine," Mother Hubbard said. "It's as if we're in a deep cave. We must find the end."

"We'll have to feel our way," Arthur said. "Take care you don't trip. We'll take each other's hands so no one's left behind, and we'll push onward and see if this blind place has an end."

"It's just evil, I can feel it. O' Virgin. Evil!"

Parsifal tripped. "How do we know if it has an end?"

Abbot Babble Blaise added, "We could be walking to the edge of the world. We could step right off and fall into oblivion! I say we turn back!"

"Nay!" Arthur said. "Hush! Listen!"

"What?" Abbot Babble Blaise asked. "What!"

"Hush! Listen! I hear a bird. A wren! Listen! Do you hear its golden warbling! It's a wren, I'm sure of it!"

"Maybe it's just a warbler," Nimm offered.

"It's a wren," Parsifal agreed with Arthur. "Why would such a tiny bird be singing in such blackness?"

Arthur said, "It wouldn't sing in the dark. It's certainly singing in the sunshine, certainly it's bright again just on the other side of this black cloud we're in, and it's not far."

"Lower your head for a moment," Merlin told Arthur, "or a branch will scar your forehead."

"Merlin? You're here? You *do* care for me!"

"Not in a genuine way."

Arthur argued, "And what's genuine? What's that?"

Merlin explained, "When two people are stuck in the greenwood together, lost or for tutoring, they certainly bond with each other even if they're not otherwise compatible."

"So you at least admit you've bonded with me!"

"Barely."

The wren sang, *"In ancient times, in the land called Merlin, blood was offered to the soil. One day an owl sprung forth. Man had never seen such a creature before. They tried to eat the owl so the owl hid in the wood. In a thousand years passing the owl learned to disguise himself as a man, and his name was Merlin, the name of the land."*

"The wren is singing the hunter's song," Arthur announced. "Do you hear it, hear the words? Merlin is the name of the land!"

"I only hear a bird song," Mother Hubbard admitted.

"A warbler," Nimm stated.

"It's getting louder," Parsifal said. "We're almost there."

"I see my hands!" Nimm cried.

"O' Virgin! I love you!"

Adjusting to its harsh glare, Parsifal finally saw that they were at the edge of the seashore. He held out his arms to stop everyone so they wouldn't step into the water. "Halt. We're here."

"O' Virgin! You're naked!" Abbot Babble Blaise said to Nimm. "Your head!"

She reached up and felt that her hair was all falling about and exposed and indecent without her scarf. "I'm not going back in that cloud to look for it."

"Eee-*ucht*!"

"Can we survive that?" Arthur asked, looking at the other side of the strait where there was an island partially covered in an ugly green mist that wasn't drifting about at all, but hanging low, thick, and chokingly still.

"Rotten eggs. The Island of Ys!" Mother Hubbard frowned. "I'm certain of it."

"Merlin mentioned it once."

Parsifal asked Arthur, "What did he say of it?"

"That it'd never be a part of my kingdom."

"What nonsense!" Parsifal made a fist. "If we can cross the waters, we'll conquer it now."

"How. With what?" Arthur asked.

Mother Hubbard's eyes narrowed. She waved her staff side to side, pointing it at the width of the island. "With that, we'll see."

"How do we even cross such a frightful water?" Nimm looked into the depths crowded with great monstrous eels swimming back and forth, touching noses calmly or touching noses and then fighting.

"There!" Arthur pointed up the shore to where a white stag was casually walking across the water to the island, completely disregarding them.

"A ghost?" Abbot Babble Blaise worried. "O' Virgin!"

"It's a miracle or a curse," Nimm presumed. "Is he coming from an otherworld or going to it?"

Mother Hubbard suggested, "Maybe the white stag is just walking across a shallow part in the strait, and there's no magic in that."

They hurried down to the spot to see for themselves, and it was, indeed, as shallow as a brook where the white stag had crossed. They followed in his path, only getting the very bottoms of their feet wet. At the other side at the island, they saw large hollow turtle shells littering the shore. Arthur asked, "What odd rocks are these?"

"Turtles." Parsifal kicked at one. "Just their shells. I think these kind are accustomed to living in warmer waters than these. I wonder what brought them here to die?"

"For stew?" Arthur wondered.

"Or just more senseless lost death." Mother Hubbard kicked gently at one, noticing how large they were, four times the length of her own foot. "The bottom part of the shells haven't been removed so this wasn't eaten by anything other than worms. Rotten eggs."

They silently walked up the bank of the island and deep into the green mist. Arthur smelled a spicy dried lavender incense and then his legs fell off. He crashed onto his face in great pain. "*Aaaaah!*"

"Oh my dear warts and toads what curse is this on you?" Merlin cried.

"The grove is cursed," Arthur answered.

Nimm's arms fell off, plopping heavily and absurdly at her sides. "What do we do?"

"Wake up," Merlin ordered.

"Wake up! Wake up!" Arthur awoke where he stood and saw that no one had fallen apart.

"Are you ready to faint?" Nimm asked Arthur. "Is this cloud too thick?"

Arthur tried to shake away his horrible feeling. "I'll be fine." The mist thinned and they saw that they'd come to the outside edge of the terrible sacred grove fenced by many thick braided garlands of yellow vines that wove all the outside trees together in a great irregular basket-sized coliseum. At the sight of it, Nimm crumpled and fell to the ground.

"Eee-*ucht*!"

"Catapults!"

"Are you well?" Abbot Babble Blaise asked her. "O' Virgin!"

"Nay, I fainted."

"Just be quiet and don't dare pray for me; let me lie here a moment."

Abbot Babble Blaise said, "But we were so terrified that you'd died!"

"I'm honored by your tears. It isn't everyday a mother gets to attend her own funeral." Nimm got up but then fell again. "I'm just a bit breathless. Give me a moment to rest and I'll be ready to travel on."

Abbot Babble Blaise sat heavily onto the ground and joined her. "Just a wee rest, before we go into *that* Virgin forsaken place."

As they all sat, Parsifal asked Arthur, "What if the grail quest comes to the point where it demands an answer of you?"

"Like what?" Arthur asked.

"Who's your master? Who do you serve? Great questions."

"All I know is that I'm to be the King and I take what I want."

Mother Hubbard questioned, "You'll just take it because you'll be king?"

"Aye," Arthur nodded. "That's my authority."

"Whose authority?"

"I don't know," Arthur admitted to her. "But I do have a great wizard and the Lady of the Lake on my side."

"Not all will recognize that," Abbot Babble Blaise warned him.

Arthur winced. "Isn't that what battles are all about, and all I'll be doing? I take what I want, and if they won't give it to me, I take it some more. *There*! Didn't I say that in a manner as cumbersome as Merlin would."

Mother Hubbard warned him, "There's a cautionary tale about such kings who think they can always simply take what they want."

"Then why be king? If the king doesn't tax, and taxing isn't taking, then why have the king at all?"

Mother Hubbard shrugged. "Having come from a coven, I thought I knew all there was to know. I'm lacking in many spells. I feel like a sheep." She gave Nimm a jealous glare. "I'm lacking the spell to pass through the gates of the Realm of Dragons. But I'll remember Merlin's words when my memory spell decides when it wants to begin. I'll remember and repeat his words! Then I'll show you all how powerful I am! And then I'll go to the Realm of Dragons and there is a place where there is no king at all, I'm sure of it."

Nimm asked, "Why can't you control the timing of a memory spell?"

"It's hard to force the timing of any spell, but a memory spell is the worse, since you're intruding back into time."

"Then you'll *share* the spell of how to willfully access the Realm of Dragons?"

"Nay, you seem powerful enough to have done it without a spell."

"I don't feel powerful." Nimm frowned. "Maybe we women should wait here for you men to go get the cauldron and bring it back here. Then we all won't be killed at once."

"We won't be killed," Parsifal said.

Nimm shrugged, unconvinced. "Look at us women. Warriors?" She gave Parsifal a pitiful expression. "You *men* go and take care of the cauldron and leave us women behind to build the great Roman funeral pyres made for heroes. Somebody has to burn you up after you've failed."

"We *all* go," Arthur insisted. "We stick together. We won't fail. It's only a demon bell. It can't be as awful as Merlin." He stood up.

Nimm looked up at him and asked, "We're an army of a few wolves and a few sheep."

"Merlin once told me that an army of sheep led by a wolf will always conquer an army of wolves led by a sheep."

Chapter Seventeen

"Time to go!" Nimm jumped up when a few gnats swarmed in her hair.

Arthur cautiously led them onward. "Am I to be humble or am I to be brave. Oh toad, Merlin taught me both, so much so, that I'm lost. Do I win feeling arrogant, which gives me strength, or do I win feeling danger, which gives me pause? I wish Merlin had made more sense to me."

Mother Hubbard said, "Maybe he didn't know what he was talking about."

Arthur reminded her, "But he's a great wizard."

"Rotten eggs."

They stepped through the thick woven garlands of yellow vines of the Pict witch's grand enclosure and entered a meadow of thin trees and fat ferns until they were near the center of the grove where it cleared even moreso into a grassy marsh. In the center of the marsh was a lone fat gigantic tree that towered far taller than all the others, almost reaching the clouds.

"There it is as you said!" Arthur pointed. "Way up there. See it? *There*! The cauldron!"

"Where? I don't see it." Abbot Babble Blaise squinted.

"Right where I'm pointing. Hanging upside-down like a bell. It's near the very top. See it?"

"It's so high up it's hard to see," Mother Hubbard said, "but aye, there it is!"

"I see it!" Nimm joined in. "Upside-down! What disrespect! The sight of it like that makes me sick! *Our cauldron*!"

"Aye," Mother Hubbard agreed. "A blessed cauldron inverted into an unholy bell. How diabolical. That's just wrong."

"And so high up," Arthur frowned, "How did it get so high?"

Nimm grumbled, "Some sinister magic for sure. It's too heavy to fly."

"Unless maybe an ox could fly." Parsifal asked, "Do you think that's possible?"

Mother Hubbard frowned. "If that's possible then anything's possible. Anything is *not* possible. Eee-*ucht*! Rotten eggs."

Abbot Babble Blaise frowned. "It's evil."

Mother Hubbard agreed, "Unnaturally, it's a witching tree, naturally."

"I can climb the tallest tree," Parsifal bragged, "and like a squirrel! And I've the nature of a squirrel; I can move quickly from danger."

"Nay," Mother Hubbard repeated. "This tree has a spell and much worse than a stinking bridge spell."

Arthur asked, "What else can be thrown at us?"

"We would be treed?" Parsifal asked. "Like dogs tree a bear?"

Nimm asked, "Is it a one way trip up into the afterworld? Maybe we womenfolk should wait down here at the bottom and you menfolk can go up and drop the cauldron down to us. If you find it before you're killed."

"We must *all* be brave," Arthur commanded. "We stick together."

They cautiously walked forward, then heard deep belching sounds. The ground opened up in pockets and bubbled here and there as if it were a thick boiling oatmeal. They began to sink. "Another cursed bog!" Arthur yelled at it in anger. "Another one!"

"Rotten eggs!"

"My footing! I'm getting all muddy! My boots! My pants!"

"A curse! O' Virgin!"

"A trick of the ground!" Nimm cried.

"Eee-*ucht*!"

Parsifal scrambled backwards and freed himself first, and then helped pull the others back to where the ground was solid again. Abbot Babble Blaise slapped at the mud on his robe. "What a place for a cursed bog. This Pict witch has certainly guarded herself."

"But," Mother Hubbard said, "that wheedling Pict managed to get a heavy cauldron and her victims across this sinking swamp. So we'll be clever and do the same."

"Fly?" Arthur guessed. "Or walk on turtle shells."

"What a *brilliant* idea!" Mother Hubbard said. "Let's all go back to the shore and carry as many as we can. When I'd kicked one I noticed that many were about three or four feet long. That should make a sturdy enough bridge of stepping stones, just long enough for us to cross."

Parsifal added, "If we cross very quickly perhaps."

They backtracked over the vine fence and returned to the island's shore to gather turtle shells and could only carry two apiece, they were so fat and unwieldy. Returning into the green mist, they wandered astray from their previous path. "This is confusing me! Rotten eggs!"

"Are we lost?" Parsifal asked. "I can't decide." He jolted with the sudden horror of the realization that he'd never been out hunting and gotten lost before.

Nimm asked, "Why do I smell lavender incense?"

"Nay," Abbot Babble Blaise sniffed. "Only dry straw. Why?"

Arthur was horrified that his arms and legs were falling off. "I'm sorry I can't go on this way."

"What are you talking about?" Abbot Babble Blaise asked. "Are your turtle shells too heavy for you?"

"No, my arms and legs have fallen off."

"Wake up!" Mother Hubbard hollered at him. "You're dream walking again. What are you dreaming?"

"Is it a premonition?" Nimm feared. "A bad inkling? Aye! Our arms and legs are all about to be cut off!"

"My body is small," Arthur apologized. "My know-nothing mind seems to be trying to compensate. My mind is always jumping ahead of the hunter's killing arrow of time. The hunter's arrow is too fast until it's too late and has killed."

"Wake up!"

Nimm asked, "How does it do this trick? I smell lavender everywhere. It's been dried and burned. I see no flower. Am I in Summerland?"

Abbot Babble Blaise argued, sniffing in the dry grassy fragrance, "It's just piles and piles and piles of straw I smell."

Mother Hubbard yelled, "Wake up, all of you!"

Nimm said, "I'd like to think somebody can outsmart a tree. Our dreaming may be trying to tell us the trick."

Parsifal said, "I've outsmarted trees all my life. You just climb up them and know where the branches are so that if one should break beneath you, you can quickly step over to another."

Nimm said, "Sometimes death is inevitable. And it smells like incense. Am I on fire? No, it's all coming down from the tops of the dead trees."

"When you say death is so inevitable," Arthur said, "it sounds so inevitable. We all know it can be outsmarted."

"Are you awake now?" Mother Hubbard poked him.

"Aye."

"How do you know?"

"I've my arms and legs."

"Arthur," Nimm said. "You know what you were dreaming and it can help us. Prod into your memory of your dreams. Prod!"

"It makes no sense," Arthur answered. "Sometimes dreams make no sense."

"Tell us anyway," Nimm continued. "We're patient."

"Patient!" Abbot Babble Blaise said. "O' Virgin, I'm not patient! But I *am* willing to help a few rapidly aging witches and a short-lived prince outsmart a tree."

Arthur quailed and admitted, "I see bodies chopping into bits."

"Knives?" Nimm asked, "Axes? What? There's no weapons on that tree. Not that I saw. Was there? I didn't notice any but I've an odd feeling the branches won't let you come back down. It's just a one way tree."

"Don't be like a dumb cat," Mother Hubbard shamed her. "And even then, trees aren't filled with cat bones for a reason. No matter how they cry and cry up in the tree, cats do eventually surmount their fear and come back down."

Arthur continued, "I've been getting strange dreams about bodies falling apart. It may be nothing more than my own insecurity about soon being the King."

"Nay," Nimm said. "It's the tree. It'll cut us to bits. I think the womenfolk should stay and wait on the ground in case that's so. You can just toss the cauldron down to Mother Hubbard. Then we can run off with it from there before your body parts start raining down on us." She imagined men's body parts raining down on her and she shuddered.

Arthur said, "I see branches, not knives. I'm confused."

The green mist lifted. Parsifal smiled. "I see the woven vines! I wasn't all that lost after all!"

Mother Hubbard loudly huffed in relief. "Thank all your mighty warts and toads. I was growing mighty tired of lugging these turtle shells around in circles."

Arthur said, "You're beginning to sound like Merlin."

"Eee-*ucht*! But he was a cad!"

They stepped through the great yellow woven basket and entered the grove again and came back to the spongy sinking bog. "How should we do this?" Nimm questioned, holding her shell out over the spot where they'd gone down, spots that were now holes of black, shimmering breathing muck.

"I'll go first," Arthur volunteered. "I'm the lightest. I'll put down my shell and you can hand me yours and I'll see how far in I can get. I pray all the way to the other side."

"Very well," Mother Hubbard agreed, holding out her staff, "and if you sink, I'll have this ready for you."

"It can make me fly?"

"No. You grab on for dear life while we pull with all our might."

"Oh." Arthur plopped his shell down on its back and stood upon the belly of it. He wobbled and smiled. "It seems steady enough, presently."

"Here." Parsifal handed Arthur one of his shells.

After all the shells were set into a path, and Arthur was all the way across to a sturdy interior field of grass and bushes, he called back, "Now hurry before our little bridge changes its mind."

Nimm hopped from one shell belly to another until she was across, then called back, "Careful they don't toss you off."

Mother Hubbard crossed, yelping a few times at the difficult balance. "It's indeed sinking," she called back to Parsifal and Abbot Babble Blaise. "Hurry!"

Parsifal pushed Abbot Babble Blaise so that he'd go on ahead, but the monk wouldn't go and gave Parsifal a push in return. "Nay, you go and I'll stay back and pray for you."

Parsifal was across in a flash. "Pray quickly. Hurry, the shells are laying very low in the mud by now."

When Abbot Babble Blaise took his turn, the shells sank fast, and before he could get all the way to the other side, he was sunk to his waist in muck. "I can't move!"

Mother Hubbard decided her staff wasn't enough where she stood and she threw herself onto her belly into the churning black mud, with both hands holding fast to her staff. She ordered Abbot Babble Blaise to grab the staff. Then she yelled behind her, "Grab my feet! Pull for the life of me! Even if it rips me in two! *Pull!*" With Mother Hubbard as a human chain, Abbot Babble Blaise was slowly pulled out with many loud suction noises until they were safely on firm ground. As they fought to catch their breath, they tried to shake some of the muck off their clothes.

Arthur praised Mother Hubbard, "You were fast and brave!"

"And a sorry sight." Mother Hubbard moaned looking up at the menacing tree. "I was getting too old for adventure ten years ago."

Abbot Babble Blaise joined in. "Evil, evil, evil! This mud is evil, I can *feel* it! O' Virgin!"

Quietly to Merlin, Arthur in his shadow self asked, "What good has it been for us to have the abbot along?"

"Why not?"

Arthur answered, "He warns us of evil in a manner no more helpful than if he were always warning us of air."

Merlin quietly answered, "Some only help with their guts."

"But he has no guts."

"What do you think is inside with his liver?"

That confused Arthur. "*What?*"

"What were you saying?" Abbot Babble Blaise asked them. "Were you speaking to Merlin?"

"Only in my imagination," Arthur assured them. "Don't get excited; he isn't really here."

"And what did you smell?" Mother Hubbard asked.

"Nothing."

"Good then. It was but an idle fancy."

Looking back at the sunken turtle shells, Nimm frowned, "how will we get back home? Our bridge didn't last very long."

Mother Hubbard dismissed it. "One horror at a time. We'll have to worry about that after surviving a wheedling Pict witch and her tree."

Parsifal reminded them, "There's many of us and one of her. She won't last a minute with my hunting skills."

Nimm said, "But she has tricks"

"I wish I had a squirrel," Arthur said. "Merlin told me that the warriors of old used to release one into the battlefield just before the charge and that would tell them how things were going to turn out. I'd like to know how things are going to turn out."

Nimm said, "How easy for us all if we always knew how things would turn out."

"*I* know what I should do before we take another step," Mother Hubbard proposed, bending over. "I should've done it before." She ripped grass up from the ground and knotted it until she'd skillfully crafted a doll in the shape of a human. "A poppet! Is it ugly enough? It's to be our wheedling Pict witch."

Nimm asked, "How do we make it work for us?"

"I'll not share my spell with you for you to steal and someday use against *me*." Mother Hubbard went ahead a few steps and whispered some spells over the poppet so the others couldn't hear, then she returned to them.

"What now?" Arthur asked her.

Mother Hubbard instructed them, "One at a time, take this ugly poppet, and place it standing upright on the top of that bush and then release it and let it fall within, as you say: *fall and die, break your hay for bone, land and break, slip from your tall throne. Fall and die, this bush for a tree, by oak, ash and thorn, so mote it be.*"

"I'll not participate in any witchcraft," Abbot Babble Blaise protested. "It sounds evil."

"Then step aside and do your thing on your knees, and do it *over there.*"

"And don't you, either," Abbot Babble Blaise warned Parsifal. "Remember you come from a house of the Christ and his Virgin!"

Parsifal grinned. "I really like the idea of pretending to tip the Pict witch off the tree. Let me go first."

"Nay! I go first," Mother Hubbard insisted. Then, one at a time, Mother Hubbard, Nimm, Parsifal, and Arthur acted out the dramatic spell of sympathetic magic.

After they'd all taken their turn toppling the poppet, Nimm asked Mother Hubbard, "Aren't you worried about the spell-as-curse coming back to you three-fold?"

"I'm too clever for that," Mother Hubbard assured her, walking to the tree. "It's part of my secret that I keep secret."

"The cart!" Arthur spotted behind a few bushes. "The Pict witch's cart! Certainly the one that carried the cauldron all the way from the village!"

"Aye," Mother Hubbard spotted it, impressed. "That's a nice fine magic cart to carry something so heavy. It could steal six cauldrons; it's such a fine thing."

Nimm frowned. "There's no black bog stuck to its wheels."

"It's evil! I can just feel it! O' Virgin!"

Mother Hubbard stomped her foot. "Hush about that!"

Chapter Eighteen

Arthur stepped directly under the giant tree and felt the bark, then carefully looked up into it, smelling dusty gamey moss. "It seems to be just a tree. No knives and hatchets for branches. That's odd fruit hanging from some of them."

Nimm asked, "What strikes the bell and makes it ring out?"

"I hope to never find out," Mother Hubbard said. "I'll cut it out of there before it ever rings again." She spotted the black withered fruit berries Arthur had seen hanging from the ends of some of the branches. "Eee-*ucht*! That's not fruit. The stolen eyes!"

"Can they see us?" Nimm asked.

Mother Hubbard grimaced. "They all look rotted. I hope the rotted ones are especially blind."

"Can rotted eyes see?" Arthur asked.

Mother Hubbard shrugged. "I've no idea how long the Pict witch gets them to last for her, to see for her, while she's somewhere else. Maybe now she's deep in the depths of this tree."

Arthur guessed, "I'm sure she has many ways of knowing we're here by now. So be it. We're here and there'll be a confrontation anyway, unless she's away trying to steal more goods. But her wagon's here so I guess she's home."

Parsifal said, "So let's go up and slay her."

"Slow down boy," Mother Hubbard warned him. "Keep your own eyes and wits about you. That wheedling Pict may really be an arrogant careless fool, or she may be like any wheedling Pict, a great tricky warrior who even the Romans couldn't conquer. So be careful!"

"I'm not afraid!" Arthur stated.

"That's why I warned you to be careful! Fearless squirrels fly out of trees and break their necks. Careful squirrels live until mating season."

"The Virgin will give us strength." Abbot Babble Blaise folded his hands. "I can just feel it. Good always wins over evil! If need be, the Virgin will make angels fly to us to protect us!"

"Thanks for the profound homily." Mother Hubbard firmly planted her staff into the earth and gazed up at the bright promenade of clouds. "I can see an angel coming at us too, or something coming at us with wings. Remember, I was a tree witch once, and I always saw wings more than anything, and squirrels."

Nimm asked her, "What happened to you when you were imprisoned in your tree. You're such a good person now. Most of the time. It must have really reformed you and good."

"The nature of trees is to make us good. That's why a bad witch goes in bad but comes out good, usually, to those of us capable of redemption."

"What happened?"

"In particular, a swarm of wasps moved in with me and after awhile I became impressed with their diligent work. One can't live in the center of such elaborate activity and not be influenced after a time."

Arthur said, "Enough talk to bide our fears, we're going to go get our cauldron back, so stop trying to scare us more than we're scared to death already."

They kicked out of their clogs. Arthur went to his knees to help Parsifal unlace his boots.

"Don't bow to *me*."

"I'm not bowing to you," Arthur assured him. "I'm bowing to your wonderful boots! The laces. They're stuck! What are these boots made of? They won't budge!"

"They're a good stiff leather and I always wear them, so leave them be. I've climbed in them before."

"You'll slide," Nimm warned him.

He tapped his fingertips on the heels. "They're metal but I'm surefooted."

"What's that mean?"

"I'm used to them."

"Oh. Then let's hurry." Nimm looked up in misgiving. "If you insist that we womenfolk shouldn't wait for you down here."

Mother Hubbard reached up to grab a branch. "We're all going up." She warned Nimm, "Don't trip up on your apron. Be careful."

"Let's tie these up," Nimm recommended. So the two women took off their aprons and pulled their skirts forward between their legs and knotted them to the front of their belts. "Don't look!" she scolded the boys.

"You have legs!" Parsifal blushed at Nimm.

"Don't look!"

"I'll go first, of course," Parsifal offered, reaching up to touch his fingertips to the lowest branch.

"Nay!" Mother Hubbard groaned, walking away. She grabbed the Pict witch's wagon by its handles and returned, slamming it tightly up against the base of the trunk and climbed up onto its bed, reaching for the lowest branch. "First give me a good push!"

They all pushed Mother Hubbard up, then followed, Parsifal going last, and once they were all within the tree and past the first branch, they found they were on a sequential ladder.

"What's ripping?" Nimm asked.

"The back of my trousers. Catapults!"

"What's attacking you?" Nimm asked.

"I'm not being attacked. My other pant leg is freeing itself from the stitching. I don't think the stitching was made for tree climbing. Everything I have is getting ruined."

"And I'm naked without my staff," Mother Hubbard moaned.

Arthur said, "Walking sticks are not for trees."

"Neither are goodly abbots of Christendom," Abbot Babble Blaise grumbled. "Climbing a tree seems so pagan. But I'll do anything for the holy grail! O' Virgin!"

Halfway up, they hit a ceiling of spider webs. As Parsifal chopped through them with his dagger, they began to vibrate and play a solemn note. "Careful!" Mother Hubbard alerted them, watching countless pale spiders race down the trunk toward them.

Nimm screamed, "I can't stand things in my hair!"

"Spiders aren't all that bad," Arthur assured her, thinking of Merlin's beard.

"O' Virgin. They're evil!"

"These might bite," Mother Hubbard warned him, "and I don't want a swollen face from that. Eee-*ucht*!" She turned to Nimm and slapped her hard. "I'll share a spell with you just this once. Repeat it just as I say it."

Nimm watched them scuttle closer. "Go! Hurry! The *spiders*!"

Mother Hubbard quickly flapped her hand through the air and screamed, "*Fire in hoops! Circle fire burn up straight!*"

Nimm paused a moment, bewildered at the contradiction in words, but then repeated the spell to double it. "*Fire in hoops! Circle fire burn up straight!*"

"Clever!" Arthur praised. "Flint on steel!" He pretended to hit together the contents of his long-gone tinderbox, to encourage the spell.

The women said together, "As above, so below, so mote it be!"

There was a bright crackle and smell of soot and sulfur. Two wobbling rings of orange fire rose up around the trunk of the tree, detaching at the branches but still burning so steadily that all the spiders were cooked. Their black bodies pelted down onto them. "*My Hair! They're falling in my hair!*"

Mother Hubbard reached out and grabbed Nimm. "Keep your nerves or you'll fall to your death before you even get a greeting from the Pict witch. Just be glad I shared a spell with you, you dizzy toad. I may never share a spell with you again."

"Don't worry, I already forgot it, I was so nervous." Then Nimm made herself become calm, shook out her hair one last time, and they continued up the tree. "And what good is such a spell if forgotten?"

Parsifal looked at the women in alarm. "The two of you have aged visibly from the last spell. It must have been a mighty thing to do."

Mother Hubbard moaned. "Aye, it was very taxing."

"Hush," Arthur chided him. "Don't point such a thing out to a vain sorceress!" Then he asked, "Have *I* grown older?"

"Nay," Abbot Babble Blaise answered. "Only the two spell casters. May the Virgin have tolerance with us."

Nimm looked like she'd cry. "My hair's full of dead spiders! I've croned! Look at my hands. They've shriveled. Magic isn't so fun when it sucks the marrow right out of your bones."

"Keep your nerves calm about you!" Mother Hubbard warned her again. "Or you'll fall out of this tree and you'll be dead before even a greeting from our Pict witch!"

Though her legs were stiff with her newfound advance in age, and having to groan indignantly, Mother Hubbard reached the cauldron first. She rubbed her hand across it. "It hasn't cracked from the ringing, and we're lucky for that."

"This should be easy to take down," Abbot Babble Blaise said, making the sign of the cross over it. "Just cut it and let it fall to the earth and we're back down after it."

"Can that crack it?" Nimm asked.

Mother Hubbard shrugged. "If it hasn't broken by now from being rung, it's a solid cauldron, a good iron casting. Methinks."

"Cut it down," Arthur ordered. Parsifal pulled his dagger from his belt and sawed and sawed until he cut two of the vines that held it. The cauldron flipped right side up. He moved to cut the last two vines, to release it completely, but was stopped by an odd voice.

"Fee faw fum fail, I smell the blood and blubber of a landlocked whale. Let him be alive or dead, off with his empty Roman head."

"What was that?" Mother Hubbard asked, questioning whether she'd heard anything at all. "Did anybody hear that?"

"Hear what?" Parsifal looked around.

"My ears are ringing," Nimm complained. "Can spiders get in your ears?"

Arthur ordered, "Cut the vines."

"Catapults! My arm won't move! What's happening?"

"Listen!" Mother Hubbard cautioned Parsifal.

"Snouk but and snouk ben bale, I smell the blood and blubber of a landlocked whale. Be he alive or dead, his heart this night will be my kitchen bread."

"There!" Abbot Babble Blaise pointed. "From inside the tree!"

A naked bald maiden, succulent, youthened and pink, slipped out of the trunk where there was a long scar in the bark. "Blessed be." Though a girl in appearance, her voice cackled as if she were a hundred years old. "Why have you come to visit? Have you come to nibble? Do you think I live in a house made of honey biscuits and almonds?"

"Blessed be," Mother Hubbard finally responded, trying to quickly recover from the shock of the sight of her.

"Blessed be," the Pict witch greeted. And then asked, "Have you come to steal my fine bell? Daft fools. Why not come inside my roomy tree and take all my fine jewels, instead. I have treasure of jewels. And a nice long jeweled sword for the bravest hunter."

"And don't look at me like that," Mother Hubbard threatened the Pict witch. "I'll not abide by the evil eye!"

The Pict witch assured her, "I wasn't giving you the evil eye. I was just shocked at how withered and old you appear, you poor unhappy dear. You splash through your magic like a child splashes through boiling acid."

"A sword?" Parsifal questioned. "Did you say *sword*?"

"Aye, I have a fine sword in here and it is sharp and covered in jewels and it is yours if you come for it."

"It's a trick," Mother Hubbard warned him. "Ignore her and her ugly eyes. She only has rotten bark for her pillow. Ignore her spell."

"Nay, I've many fine things inside this tree," the Pict witch enticed the boys. "I have honey biscuits and mead. Who'd like a fine treat to refresh them after such a long climb, this ladder to Heaven?"

Parsifal licked his dry lips. "I'd like to eat a good snack." The Pict witch licked her pink shiny lips and rubbed her hands over her youthful-looking nude body.

Mother Hubbard warned him, "That's only because you're a growing boy, but she can't help you. A honeybee would rather sting a wet boulder than visit this tree. Ignore her spell."

The Pict witch squeaked, "I have many fine things. I have many fine things. I have many fine things. Food and swords and my pretty, pretty things." She rubbed her hands across the tree bark. "I have many fine things. I have many fine things."

Nimm ordered Parsifal, "Finish cutting down the bell, *cauldron*! We don't have all day to ignore her spells!"

The Pict witch reached up and pulled down on a branch. When she released it, the branch sprang back up and flicked Parsifal's dagger away. It fell all the way to a branch far below, far from reach, and it punctured the bark. A stream of blood squirted out of it.

The Pict witch grabbed her shoulder in pain, as if she had been punctured, while Parsifal was left with nothing to complete cutting the last two ropes. "I've lost it! Everything I have is getting lost and ruined!"

"Where's the prince? He loses his liver first." The Pict witch looked about but didn't notice Arthur standing nearby. His invisibility spell was keeping him camouflaged as long as he didn't look directly at her or he didn't move a muscle.

"Ah!" the Pict witch marveled. "A well done spell! A spell done well! Well done! I feel it coming from… from… beneath my thumb!" As she held out her thumb and scanned the tree, her thumb paused just before Arthur's nose. While she felt his breath, Parsifal swung from a branch and solidly kicked the Pict witch on her bald pink head with one of his metal heels, making a loud crack. She screamed and fell against the trunk of the tree, then in a wild vibrating fit of panic and fear, she slipped between the bark and was gone.

"I've still got my *boots*, you *witch*!"

"She'll be back," Mother Hubbard warned him. "Let's hurry with the cauldron and be out of here." They all tugged on the last two vines that held it up, but they couldn't pull them away.

"I'll have to get my dagger," Parsifal decided.

"It's so far down," Nimm said.

"Only a blade will cut these away."

"We don't have the time," Nimm alerted him as the Pict witch came back out of the tree, her head already bandaged with a poultice of black moss.

"Blessed be," the Pict witch re-greeted them.

Mother Hubbard angrily replied, "Blessed be!"

"O' Virgin!" Abbot Babble Blaise trembled as he climbed higher up to be away from her.

"Fee figh, clumsy fundamental fumble, I fear you'll be afraid as you head-to-toe tumble!" The Pict witch spread her twig-thin fingers into claws and ripped Parsifal's lacings off both his boots.

He tried to kick her head again but she was too quick for him and he missed. His boot flung off his heel and it flipped out of the tree. "My boot!" She plunged at his other boot with her teeth flashing and when he tried to kick her in the face, he lost that boot too. "My boots!"

Now feeling invulnerable, the Pict witch stood tall and waved her arms wildly about and started to spin a violent spell into the air, "Shatter all bones, tear legs from arms, rip skin from muscle, tear testicles from torso, slice breasts from ribs, slice the ears from the head and the head from the heartbeat, blood pour into my veins, tree of eyes see souls depart, lose all." And then she was interrupted by a joyous hawk's call. "What?" She twitched as if shot with pain.

"Here!" Arthur called out, reaching high. "Do you see me here?" A glorious hawk flew down to Arthur, holding Excalibur in his talons, still dripping water as if just snatched out of Ys' strait.

Parsifal gasped at the grand sight of it. "What a sword! Magnificent!"

"Thank you Gwy!" Arthur said, taking Excalibur. "Blessed be." He swung the sword only once and the cauldron was completely freed, dropping a few feet to rest right side up on an intersection of branches.

Watching the sword in awe, Parsifal slipped. Nimm grabbed him quick enough to save him from falling. He said, "Look at that weapon!"

"We see it," Nimm continued, scolding. "Careful now!"

The bald pink Pict witch cackled. "Tricks, tricks about your leaves. Roots and trunk will spin a breeze. Blow into the depths to earth. Break to bits for my own mirth. *My own mirth!*"

"Rotten eggs on you," Mother Hubbard cursed her. "Your magic babblings have no power over any of us, and in fact, have come to bore us. We don't fear you. We're stubborn. We're mad. We hate your tree. So you have little power. Eee-*ucht!*"

"I've power enough to offer you a bargain. If I let you go with your lives and the cauldron, the cauldron will be forever cursed, for it's more than a bell but is a prison. If I lift the curse so the cauldron is again fit for cooking, you all fall and die in bits and broken pieces for the ravens to peck, and your blood will all be in my veins." She cackled.

Arthur said, "I only bargain with those who have honor." He swung the sword at her and it was as light and fast as a goose wing in his hand, but she was still too fast for it and stepped aside.

"Then you'll have neither," the Pict witch said. "I've more than spells." She climbed up several branches and stopped in front of Abbot Babble Blaise. She pointed her spike-sharp fingers together to make an arrow, and thrust her hand deep into the abbot's belly, ripping through his robe and into his guts. Before he could feel a thing she pulled out a handful of intestines. "I read your fortune like a druid who is clever. It says death comes in haste to a man whom I sever."

"O' Virgin! I'm dead! But... but... not altogether dead!" His eyes fixed in horror at the sight of himself so undone.

Nimm shrieked like a caught beast to distract the Pict witch, while at the same time, quicker and surer than a squirrel, Mother Hubbard leapt up to Abbot Babble Blaise, bravely grabbing a handful of the poor abbot's intestines and looping them tightly around the Pict witch's neck. "Round and round so mote it be," Mother Hubbard chanted quicker than a heartbeat. "Live and die at this great tree. Druid seer who'd see our death; see your spell uncross, sleep without breath."

"Oh stop it." The Pict witch impatiently put her hands to her neck to remove the guts but before she could loosen them, Mother Hubbard gave both the monk and the witch a deft push.

The force sent the Pict witch, Mother Hubbard, and the monk all falling to opposite sides of the forked branch. The tree witch expertly caught her balance, flapping her arms like chicken wings. Arthur swung Excalibur out at her and lopped off her feet. She still kept her balance, and angrily grabbed the sword away from him as quick as a snake strike. Arthur looked at his empty hands in astonishment. "My sword!"

"I'll kill you for this!" the Pict witch screamed. "Though you were to die anyway." She tried to swing Excalibur to cut away her hangman's noose but her face registered complete and utter incredulity. The great magic weight of the sword beset her and she slipped off her footless perch. Falling, the astonished Pict witch tried for any spell she could toss out, to save her black soul.

"How could the sword have been so heavy?" she asked Arthur, while she fell.

"I pulled it from the stone. It is only for my hands."

"How could you do this?" the Pict witch asked. Mother Hubbard, also falling, and falling out of time, leaving Arthur behind, with the hunter's arrow of time stopping and starting in manipulated confused fits and starts, the time warped so oddly that all was sideways and crawling to a dizzying widdershins.

"You arrogant little creature," Mother Hubbard replied, plummeting swiftly but as slow as cold honey. "I was once a tree witch, just like you are now, but not so vile and vampire like, and so I know a tree's tricks."

"Curses on you! How did you escape?"

"That's a long story and we're falling so very fast. How did *you* escape to steal the cauldron?"

"Curses on you!"

Mother Hubbard said, "Don't give me the evil eye, don't you dare, or I'll poke your eyes out right here!"

As the Pict witch fell faster and faster, unspooling all the monk's guts, branches hit both her arms and sliced them cleanly off. Excalibur fell to the ground and imbedded in a root of the tree releasing a long belch of blood. "Blight!" she screamed. Then all her stolen blood squirted out through her opened shoulders and in an instant she went from looking like a girl to being a dried old crone: wrinkled, brittle, and ash grey.

The withered Pict witch continued to fall until the monk was at the end of his rope and they both jerked to a violent stop. The Pict witch's dry grey neck snapped off in an explosion of dust, and her head continued falling without her body, her eyes wide with confusion and still grappling to plot victory.

Abbot Babble Blaise caught in a cradle of branches. "O' Virgin! I can feel it! I can feel it!" Then he breathed his last and the tree absorbed his blood.

Mother Hubbard stopped falling where she was able to grab onto a branch. She swung and screamed, "Nimm! Help!"

Nimm asked, "Are your fingers cut off?"

"Nay not yet. I'm blessed, but hanging like a sick squirrel. Help! Help! No wait! Don't move a muscle to come down to me! It'll get you killed."

"How?" Arthur asked. "The tree witch is dead."

"The branches will cut you like knives. Just stay where you are!"

"What'll you do?" Nimm asked.

"I'll try to get inside the tree and leave this earth in a manner that has me facing Merlin's sour face." Hand over hand along the branch, Mother Hubbard climbed close to the trunk and kicked at it. "Eee-*ucht*!"

"Is that possible?" Nimm called down. "You're a powerful witch, but is jumping through to the Realm of Dragons something so deliberate?"

"Nay, but Merlin did it. And *you* even did it, you wheedler. And I'm jealous. Besides, I was once a tree witch, and am now Merlin's wife. I'll get through this gate and find him and make him be my husband again, even if it has to be in the Realm of Dragons."

Nimm admitted, "But I don't know how I did it. If you're going to pass on into the tree, how? What is the deliberate spell? Do you know?"

"My memory spell has finally brought Merlin's words back to me."

Arthur cautioned her, "Merlin's spells were more than words, methinks."

Nimm said, "All spells are more than words. You also have to know the path along the great spider web."

"And you don't have your crystal staff."

She ignored him. "I've done powerful egg magic! I know the spider web. I've been a tree witch once, and know the insides of trees well."

"But you didn't imprison yourself within the tree," Nimm said. "You were put there as punishment by someone else. And I went to the Realm of Dragons through well water!"

"I saw Merlin go into a tree and I'll do the same!"

"But Merlin comes and goes all the time," Arthur warned her. "He's good at it and certainly didn't practice his walking into trees so high up in one, so far from the ground!"

"You could slip and fall!" Nimm added.

"I'm going to the Realm of Dragons! I have Merlin's spell!"

Arthur called down, "How will we know if you've made it safely?"

"You may never know."

"Careful!" Nimm cried down to her.

Mother Hubbard commanded with a great voice of authority, "To the Realm of Dragons, through the gates of Apple Island, Furious Host, Goddess Ceridwen awake and transform me with your great inspiration, an inspiration as great as the Greek muses of old. Transform me into art and poetry that I may breathe in the Realm of Dragons! Boibel to Jaichim, fith fath!"

Arthur repeated, "But you don't have your staff!"

Nimm added, "And Merlin may have made arrangements with the tree that we don't know about."

Mother Hubbard ignored them and swung with all her might into the tree and let go, surrendering with total abandon as if she were swinging off a rope into a deep pond. She crunched hard into the bark but didn't go through. She screamed in horror and regret and anger as she rebounded backwards, "Eeeeeeee-*ucht*!" Tumbling against the branches below, they cut her into dozens of pieces. The tree drank her stolen blood, while bits of her scattered across the ground.

"Catapults! I think we now know she didn't make it."

"Nay," Arthur agreed. "Not in one piece anyway."

Nimm said, "Nor did she really know a spell to get her through."

"Not done correctly, for sure," Arthur said.

"And *we* are doomed to her fate," Nimm said weeping. "We can't live up here in a cursed tree for eternity, and the tree won't let us back down alive. It's a one way tree!"

Chapter Nineteen

"Why don't we just climb back down?" Parsifal gazed sadly at his bare toes. "I want my boots. I've never gone without boots. I'm an inheritor."

Arthur said, "You can climb without boots if the rest of us can. You can fetch your boots again when we get to the bottom."

"Wait!" Nimm stopped him. "You can't climb down!"

"What?"

"I know it now to be true, without question. This is a one way tree."

Arthur said, "You keep saying that but how can you be sure?"

"A soul can only go *up* this tree. It's a one-way trip to Summerland. If you try to go down, the branches will cut you to shreds, we've seen it. It'll happen to us too!"

Parsifal argued, "I won't be cut to *anything*! We must be clever."

Nimm pushed at the cauldron to make it drop out of the tree, but began to lose her balance and quickly leaned against the trunk. "Falling stars, I'm so clumsy! I may be the tree's next repast. My common sense warns me that I'm not an eagle."

"The evil Pict witch is dead," Arthur spoke with reverence, hoping the tree itself would not seek out some revenge. "Certainly we can outsmart a tree."

Nimm nodded. "Aye. So mote it be. I'll never be a tree witch. The heights are dizzying."

Arthur asked her, "Why would you become a tree witch on any account?"

"Ooooh, Mother Hubbard once told me that many young witches think they'll only do good, happy with youth and hope. Then when a witch gets old and horrible as life leaves us all with disappointments, we become as bitter. And we end up stuck in our prison, in an unmoving tree. In a perverse way, after a time, you get used to getting stuck high up, removed and away from the bosom of Mother Earth. That's what she told me. Alas."

Arthur climbed over to the cauldron to push it out of the tree, but was also only able to make it rock on the branches. "Merlin would push this off with his evil eye."

Nimm whimpered, "We'll never make it out of here with the cauldron!"

"Then we must fall with it," Parsifal said.

"And give in to death so nonchalantly?"

Parsifal smiled. "Step into the cauldron."

"Aye!" Nimm smiled with him at the cleverness. "No knives or hatchets can cut a cauldron to ribbons. We'll fall to earth inside and be safe from the murderous branches!"

The three climbed inside the big black bowl. They sat facing each other, but their added weight didn't break it free from the branches it was cradled in. "Move your leg!" Arthur griped to Parsifal. "There's room for all of us."

He wriggled, loudly ripping his trousers some more. "I'm as small as I get."

"I wish I had Excalibur," Arthur grumbled. "Then I could cut us free so easily."

Parsifal asked, "Is there something else in here with us?"

"I pray not."

"Burn us free," Nimm suggested. "The fire spell!" Then she frowned. "But I can't remember what Mother Hubbard said when we burned up the spiders."

"I know a fire spell," Arthur offered. "Merlin has told me never to try it on my own, but I'm growing bored of sitting with you two like this and would very much like to get down from here."

"What is it?" Nimm asked.

"Wait," Arthur cautioned, "I can't burn down a fairy tree. Do you think one may live in here?"

"Not on your life," Nimm assured him. "That nasty Pict wouldn't have shared her tree with anybody, not even a brownie. I feel certain of that."

"Don't kick me!" Arthur scolded her.

"I didn't," she said.

"Something just kicked me too!" Parsifal said. "When you mentioned a brownie, I got kicked."

"Ouch!" Arthur yelped. "I just got kicked again."

"Something's in here with us!" Nimm warned. "A wild animal!"

"I see nothing," Parsifal assured her.

"I feel a wild animal, a badger, or a brownie, or a nasty imp!" Nimm warned. "What's that between your legs!" she alerted Parsifal. "What is that thing?"

"That's mine." He crossed his shins, clobbering Arthur with his knee. "My pants ripped."

"No it was hairy!"

"That's mine!"

"This makes no sense." Arthur spotted nothing in the cauldron but themselves. "Just the same, can we hurry out of here with a fire spell to burn us free."

"*Ouch*!" Nimm yelped. "I've been bit!"

"You're only kicking *me*," Parsifal hollered at her.

"I'm trying to kick the thing that's in this cauldron with us!"

"I see nothing but your foot kicking me!"

Arthur concentrated, pretended he had his tinderbox, and began, "Fire from rock, sky, and water, hit the dead fairyless tree." Then he invented, "Burn where we sit stuck and plea. Intuitively, by oak, ash, and thorn, so mote it be."

Nothing happened, so Arthur and Nimm did the spell again and again until Parsifal gasped, "*Arthur*! You're turning into a stunted wrinkled little dwarf!"

"I am? How? Oh my stars! The spell is sapping me!"

Nimm asked, "And am I growing even older?"

"Aye! You now look *just a bit* older," Parsifal said, instead of, *like a skull on a twig*, which was what he was thinking.

"*Naaaaay*!" She cried anyway, putting her corrugated hands to her head to catch locks of hair that were falling out. "I'm ruined!"

"*I* can't become king looking like this?" Arthur gasped in panic at his own shriveled hands. "I'll be laughed at! What'll I do?"

"And you can't be the king stuck up in a tree," Parsifal pointed out.

"Oh toad," Arthur moaned. "Nothing's working out. Before I even had a chance to grow up, I wither into a withered dwarf, oh what horrible fates! Where's Merlin to save me from everything I've done to myself!"

"I smell smoke!" Nimm interrupted him. "Smell!" Thin tongues of fire hesitantly sputtered up about the cauldron. Then the flames began to crackle the branches under them.

"I feel the cauldron growing warm under me," Parsifal finally complained. "Do you think we could be three cooked stews before it has burned through enough to release us?"

"Aye, it *is* growing hot," Nimm joined in, becoming jittery.

"What luck!" Arthur pouted. "Oh has O' Fortuna smiled upon me today! Look at me and what I've done to ruin myself for all time. I'm soon to be a cooked wrinkled dwarf high up in a cursed tree, instead of being King!"

Nimm wept. "And I was once so beautiful." Her fingernails fell off. She touched her withered nose and it broke inward.

"And I once had so many fine things," Parsifal said. "My boots and sleeves are gone. All the stitching in my pants have ripped out. I am but in rags!"

Just when they were about to jump out of the hot cauldron so they wouldn't cook, the branches below them turned to ash and crumbled. The cauldron plummeted down so fast, it sucked their breath from them. Their weight and speed crashed through the branches until they rode all the way down, with wood loudly splintering about their ears, until they collided on the bed of the Pict witch's magic cart. For awhile they were too stunned by the violence to even move. Then an avalanche of the tree's stolen blood poured down onto the tops of their heads, and filled the cauldron to the brim.

Nimm finally moaned, "We're sitting in a deep bath of tree blood. But it's so cold! We won't cook."

"Oh what luck." Parsifal smiled.

Nimm noticed her hands and arms filling out and her wrinkles washing away as the blood in the cauldron sucked into them. "We're absorbing it!" Her nose plumped anew and popped back out. Her fingernails grew out thick and long.

"Aye," Parsifal grinned from ear to ear, "and you look like a comely maiden, a lass of my age."

Nimm felt her face and it was tight and smooth, her cheeks plump again with youth. "I've been restored! Youthened! The blood! I'm a supple maiden. Forget what I said about men. I'll have to run from them all over again. And now I can run with the mighty speed of a girl."

"I just look red," Arthur moaned.

"Nay!" Nimm said. "You're young Arthur again and even more handsome!"

"I feel spent."

"You look beautiful," Nimm said to Arthur.

"*You* look so beautiful," Parsifal marveled again at Nimm, leaning close to her.

She smiled, flattered. "Aye, I feel like a lass in May. Come give me a holy Beltane kiss, you handsome young lad."

He did and then hopped out of the cauldron and swaggered over to Excalibur to retrieve it from the tree root. "I'm a man today," he crowed, but then he couldn't budge the sword. "It won't yield! I'm suddenly too weak to pull a sword out of wood? That's not likely."

"It's not you; it always does that," Arthur assured him and went over and retrieved the magic sword with ease for himself.

Parsifal eyed Excalibur in envy. "How much treasure would you sell that for?"

"It isn't mine to sell," Arthur told him.

"It isn't yours?"

Arthur shook his head.

Parsifal asked, "Whose is it?"

"The Lady of Lake's."

"Who is that?"

Arthur explained, "A powerful Water Spirit who made the sword from lightning when it struck her lake."

Parsifal marveled, "I'd like to have such a grand weapon." He went to look for his boots as Nimm sadly went over to Mother Hubbard's remains, scattering the ravens who had gathered to peck her up. She pulled at Mother Hubbard's clothes.

"What are you doing?" Arthur asked her.

Nimm said, "I'll have this mighty witch's buttons."

"For a remembrance?" Arthur asked. "Or a clever spell?"

"Nay! For my next warm jacket."

Parsifal asked, "Why would you think of stolen buttons at a time like this? Help me find my boots. I need them!"

"I don't see them anywhere," Arthur said.

"My boots! Aw, my boots! All they need are new lacings and they'll be the only thing I have that hasn't been ruined!"

Arthur helped him look awhile, and then finally asked, "Both of you come here and help me roll the cauldron back to town." Arthur climbed up on the cauldron and struck a victorious pose. "I wonder if Merlin somehow saw our adventure." He swung Excalibur so it sang out, cutting the air into invisible chiming ribbons that sounded like bells ringing.

"I wonder if he saw the death of his poor bride," Parsifal said, still sweeping his toes through the long grass until he saw a fleeing snake.

"I was his bride too. So I'll have to insist that I was the one who imprisoned him, it's only fair. I'll not be an abandoned wife or whatever it was that the Realm of Dragons tricked me into."

Parsifal asked her, "Is a story about what happened to Merlin something you can just make up?"

She nodded stubbornly. "I'm now a witch with experience, and I'm young and beautiful. I'll have great pride and insist it wasn't I who was abandoned."

Two tall pillars of fire blasted out of the ground as if from dragon's nostrils, jolting the earth, igniting the grass. Arthur pointed to the sky and they watched the green mist rise up and shake, then snap like a serpent's tail. Parsifal begged, "Hurry! My boots! I can't find them! Everybody help me before they burn up! Help me!"

"Nay! The sea!" Arthur warned.

The waters around the island bubbled violently until it rose in tall silvery waves to come crashing toward them so forcefully that the ground before it pounded up in a wave of dust. As foaming water gathered around them, Arthur screamed, "Onto the cart! We'll hope it can also be a boat!"

A very angry Parsifal tried to take advantage of the confusion and grabbed at Excalibur. "If it's not yours then I'll steal it from the Lady of the Lake!"

"Nay!"

"I want it! I want such a marvelous sword for myself!"

"You're greedy! You can't steal Excalibur. Now let go, it won't be taken. It won't let you use it!"

"Of course I'm greedy!" Parsifal admitted. "I'm tired of losing everything and I want a fine sword! If it's not yours, then it'll be mine and the Lady of the Lake can find more lightning!"

"You won't be able to swing it!"

"I'll learn!"

Arthur let go, so Parsifal flipped backwards from the unwieldiness of Excalibur and splashed into the rising waters. Arthur jumped after him and pulled him up. "The sword's gone!" Parsifal cried. "I couldn't keep my grip on it!" He tried to dive after the sword while Arthur pulled on him again.

"You can't hold onto it, you aren't to be a king. It's only a gift to legitimize a king." The water churned and boiled higher and turned into hot blood causing Parsifal to give up and climb back into the wagon.

"Hurry you fools!" Nimm watched a shimmering red wave as tall as a keep tower rolling toward them. The hot blood hit and washed them and the cauldron and the cart together all the way across the sinking bog and through the woven wall of yellow vines and clear off the island. They rode the wave all the way across the strait until they crashed to a rest in the dead thicket of the mainland. "We'll be crushed!" Nimm cried, staring in horror at the entire island tipping up on end towards them. "The entire underwater world of Lochlann is coming up at us!" After the island became a towering pillar, it shook loose thousands of boulders and trees until it finally split in half and then cleft into smaller pieces. While hiding behind a veil of thick dust, it slipped entirely beneath the sea of blood, and was gone. "Locklann is eating us all down!" Nimm cried, hugging a tree. But the rumbling stopped and the water turned blue and calm, smelling again of cold salt.

"Excalibur! It's gone again! Warts!" Arthur punched Parsifal in the face. "Your greed has lost it to the sea!"

Parsifal returned a good clobber to get Arthur back. "I wanted it and had every right to fight for it!"

Nimm threw herself between them and scolded. "Excalibur is over your heads this very minute!" They looked up to see Gwy the hawk flying away with it.

"Can I have it back?" Arthur yelled up to the bird.

"Bring it here!" Parsifal shouted. He picked up a stone and tried to take the bird down with it, but Gwy was too far away. "Come back! Bring the sword *here!*"

"It was in my hands." Arthur pouted. "Now I won't know when I'll see it again."

Parsifal threw more stones at the sky in anger. When he looked back down, he spotted the white stag washed by in the draining flood—dead—its antlers caught in a long branch.

"A great sacrifice from the forest gods," Nimm said in great reverence, and then turned to Parsifal and ordered, "You want to be the great hunter? Catch him before he washes away."

Arthur agreed, "Tonight, methinks we'll all be eating stag stew. And it was such a gift that we'd better bury the heart in the earth, to give it back, so our gift doesn't end up as some Spirit's insult."

Nimm chanted, "And nine maidens blew on the cauldron with their breath that will not boil the food of a coward."

"We're not cowards."

"I know that. It's just what's always said over the cauldron so the village stays brave."

Parsifal parceled the white stag into red cakes, and after burying the heart in the earth for good luck, they cooked the meat in the cauldron, but the stew came out tasting like the worst acrid dung ever. It made them retch. "What happened?" Arthur gasped, his eyes burning.

"Maybe the stag was poisoned or ill," Parsifal suggested, spitting. "Game should never taste so vile."

"We can't eat this," Nimm griped. "Try a new animal."

Parsifal went off and stoned a squirrel. They cooked the squirrel in the cauldron and it came out tasting just as unbearably putrid. "Why does it taste so horrible?" Parsifal asked. "How?"

"A curse!" Nimm moaned.

After he finished coughing, Arthur agreed, "The cauldron was a demon bell and so now is surely forever cursed against cooking."

"Cursed?" Parsifal asked, spitting again and again from the horror of the taste.

Nimm wiped a tear. "It's certainly held too many dead souls! I thought I felt the presence of something in here. This can't ever be used for cooking again! I bet Merlin or Mother Hubbard would know how to clean it, but I'm a witch with no experience in proper spells. Not even a cleaning spell."

Parsifal complained, "Must we abandon the cauldron? Is it so ruined that we had it for nothing?"

Nimm nodded. "We worked too hard for it. Did the Pict witch win, dead as she may be?"

"Nay," Arthur assured them. "Maybe it's cursed to ruin all food, but it's still our hard won cauldron, and maybe a spell can be found to clean it, someday, or at least I can use it to dump boiling oil from my Camelot walls. Who cares how bad tasting burning oil is to the Saxons. I certainly hope dumping burning oil is within the code of honor for a warrior, and doesn't anger the Goddess Victory. I *would* like to do that at least once someday."

Depressed, they began to push the wagon eastward, but were only a few steps off the beach when Arthur's foot crunched oddly into the ground. He bent down to wipe at the eroded mud and pulled up coins. "*Gold* coins!" Arthur dug deeper and kept parting layers of bright yellow coins. "A stash of hidden Roman coins! The great flood washed their cover off. Now they're mine!"

Nimm said, "I'll have as many for myself as I can carry."

Arthur chided her, "Now let's not let greed kill us before we even get started back."

Parsifal pulled a human skull up out of the coins. "Could this be stolen by the Pict witch? Is this bone from a Roman tax collector or noble?"

Arthur shrugged. "We won't know. Fill the cauldron with as many coins as it'll hold, and that'll be what it's good for, for the time being. Who cares if it makes the gold taste bad."

"Dig deep!" Parsifal said in excitement. "Maybe there are grand swords and shields and fine belts."

Arthur came to the bottom of the hole. "Weapons? Nay."

As they pulled their treasure away in the wagon, Nimm said, "I think we should all split the gold coins for our being lucky enough to survive the Pict witch and her tree."

Arthur argued, "I'd like it all so I can secure a strong army when I'm king."

"The coins won't do you any good," Parsifal reminded Nimm. "No one takes coins anymore. The Roman days are over and I bet the fashion of coins will be gone forever."

"Why? They're so pretty."

"You can't eat, sleep under, or wear a coin," Parsifal told her. "It's just common sense that something so impractical can't last."

Nimm said, "I thought that with your greed, you'd love all this gold."

"My greed is for a big sword," Parsifal corrected her. "If a Saxon comes at me, I can't stop him by throwing coins at him. And I can't even melt the coins into a sword. Gold is a terrible metal. Too soft. I need a sword of great sharpness!"

Nimm asked Arthur, "Then what would a king do with such folly as a pile of gold coins?"

Arthur stated, "Spain and France are still in a time of folly and they'll trade me real things for gold coins such as these. I'll trade for arms made of sharp metal and I'll have a strong army."

"And I'll have a real sword!"

Nimm nodded. "And we'll have a coin to spare to pay the toll at the bridge since the men there are fools and think highly of coins."

Arthur maintained, "If the bridge doesn't collapse from under the great weight of our load, they can have a button, one of Mother Hubbard's buttons."

"Why not one of *his* fine buttons?" Nimm complained, pointing at Parsifal.

"Parsifal's buttons are too worthy. Mother Hubbard's buttons are too worthy also. They'll have to return a few lesser buttons for her fine one."

Nimm pouted. "But I took the buttons and they're mine."

"You'll get change in buttons and end up with more," Parsifal corrected her. "And to a woman of your stature, more is better than fine. Be glad Arthur is so clever."

"Sage and water!" Nimm suddenly announced. "I remember an uncrossing washing spell Mother Hubbard used on the bridge to remove its stink. It was washed with water and sage as she spoke a spell."

"Do you remember the uncrossing spell that she spoke?"

"Nay. She was stingy with her spells. But I've my own intuitive power, I'm sure of it. I've great feeling. I can make my own spell."

They scrubbed the cauldron with sage, and Nimm made all sorts of clever rhymes and danced many circles around the cauldron. "Stink so bright, stink day and night, come clean with sage, make calm from rage. Cauldron of plenty that never runs dry until the town all eats so no one may die, come clean as new for a bottomless stew that bubbles time and again for both egg and the hen."

They fished some squashed eels from the water, cooked them and it still tasted terrible and stank worse. "*Toads!*" they all cursed.

"How pathetic for us," Parsifal said. "We have seized the cauldron of plenty, the holy grail against the wasteland, and it now can't cook for us. It's a bottomless stink!"

"The grail has been ruined," Arthur agreed.

Chapter Twenty

Pushing the wagon east, they heard a beautiful chime. "That's from the abbey," Arthur marveled. "They finally have a bell."

"How?" Parsifal asked. "Who'd have brought them one?"

"Rome?" Nimm guessed. "Do they hand out bells?"

"If they do," Arthur stated, "it's at great expense. But how could a church be so rich?"

Nimm said, "Let's go to it. We'll see if it really is as big as it sounds."

At the abbey, the young monks saw them, ran to them, and asked, "Where's Abbot Babble Blaise?"

Arthur began to weep to have to break such horrible news to them. "Your poor master perished in the grail quest."

"That's not possible," the monks protested. "A servant of his named Gabriel was just here delivering a grand bell for the tower and said the abbot had sent the bell and then had gone on ahead."

"Gone on ahead to Heaven," Parsifal said. "He has no servant named Gabriel."

"But how could he have sent us such a fine bell?" the monks asked.

Nimm looked up into the clouds. "Blessed be."

"What do you see?" Arthur asked her.

She answered, "Do you feel his breath? Do you smell it?"

"Nay." Parsifal winced.

"He's here?" Arthur asked. "His ghost?"

Nimm stated, "Abbot Babble Blaise won't rest until every monk here is no longer in need of him. That's his promise. Do you hear it?"

Parsifal asked, "How does a ghost arrange a real bell to be delivered?"

"Is the bell even real?" Nimm questioned. The three looked at each other in dismay, then climbed the tight winding wooden stairs inside the bell tower. They found that there was no bell at the top.

"Where is it?" Parsifal asked. "Has the bell already been stolen by a new monster witch?"

"Nothing!" Arthur sat on the stone ledge in despair.

"But we heard it!" Parsifal was puzzled.

Nimm told him, "There was never a real bell. We know that for a real bell to have been delivered by a phantom would have been too fantastic to be true."

Parsifal reminded her, "But we've experienced so many fantastic things. I've grown accustomed to them."

"Magic can only be so much," Nimm maintained. "It needs a web to travel on or it can't exist. A real bell would have just been too much to expect."

Arthur said, "As we climbed the stairs, I had just come up with an idea to switch the bell with the cauldron! I thought that would be clever."

Parsifal asked, "What would that have done?"

"For the welfare of this village, I thought it might work out to take the bell and turn it into our cauldron, and take the cauldron and turn it into a bell."

"A brilliant idea!" Nimm exclaimed. "If perchance one was as real as the other."

Parsifal pointed out, "But how sour would the cursed bell have sounded to our ears? Would we have just restarted the same old demon bell problem?"

Nimm agreed. "It'd be too risky to have done just what the Pict witch had done, in spite of our wholesome intentions. Be glad we now aren't tempted."

"Your poor town has no cauldron yet," Arthur said. "I was hoping to have been a clever enough prince to leave everyone happy."

Parsifal smiled. "You still have something to dump burning oil on the Saxons."

Arthur, Nimm, and Parsifal returned from the bell tower and saw that all the monks had become so hysterical about losing Abbot Babble Blaise that they had grabbed their birching branch bundles and were wildly whipping each other as they screamed and bawled in unison, "Purge the devil! Purge the devil!"

"From what?" Arthur asked them all. "Purge from where?"

"Purge the devil! Purge the devil!"

Nimm pointed to the cauldron and ordered them, "This is the devil that needs purging! Birch the stinking cauldron!"

They paused to look at it, nonplussed. "Huh?"

"There's no bell in your tower; it's a ghost sound," Arthur sadly informed them.

"Monk Babble Blaise died to bring this cauldron back from the clutches of a Pict witch," Nimm told the sad young monks. "This is the cause of his death!"

The monks crowded around the cauldron and violently birched it, screaming at it, "Purge the devil! Purge the devil!"

"That's kind of you," Arthur said to her, "to have them birch their anger out on something that can't bleed."

"Aye." She nodded. "And it'll break their birching whips so they no longer have such implements of self abuse."

"Purge the cauldron! Purge the cauldron!"

"*Aaaar-ag!*" a brown shaggy creature leapt up out of the cauldron, screaming. "Stop beating me, so!"

"A bear!" they gasped.

"A *brownie!*" Nimm pointed. "What are you doing here? Why have you been ruining our goodly cauldron with your stink?"

The brownie only screamed some more and spun about, his spindly little arms punching out of his long fur in a rage, "Don't ever hit me again!"

"You're suppose to do good in the domestic realm," Nimm yelled right back at him, growing angry. "You're supposed to be a *helper*, not a curse!"

The brownie stopped jumping to glare at her directly. "I was cursed, so I am a curse! A nasty Pict witch imprisoned me here, within, bound round and round by all black bell, and she said that if I leapt out to escape to find a proper hearth, she'd take a rusty sheep sheers to my belly and cut without care!" The creature then looked at the monks in fear and asked them, "Where's the witch?" The brownie screamed and jumped back into the cauldron and was gone from all mortal sight.

"Where'd he go?" Parsifal asked. "I don't see a thing!"

Nimm ordered the monks, "Birch that stupid fur back out of there."

The monks birched the cauldron again. "Purge the brownie! Purge the brownie!"

"Stop it!" the brownie screamed, jumping back out into the open. "I can't abide by this abuse! Stop it I beg you! Never before in the history of feather, fur, or fin has a brownie ever been whipped! *Ever!*"

"The witch is dead!" Nimm quickly said before the creature could slip away again.

The brownie paused, smoothed the fur over its belly, and doubted, "Dead?"

"Aye."

The brownie argued, "But that was a mighty witch! The mightiest witch I'd ever known and she had such power that it drove her mad!"

Nimm asked, "What made her more powerful than any other witch?"

"She had a long piece of a dragon's tail hiding in the darkness in her tree. It was deep inside, out of the light of the sun, so it kept and it fed her its magic in this world."

Nimm assured the brownie, "The witch who tricked you into ruining our cauldron is dead. Very dead and in pieces."

"In pieces?"

"Many. All over the ground under her cursed tree. She can no longer threaten to cut the hair off your belly. You can be helpful again, without threat."

The brownie asked, "How do you know? Did you see her dead?"

"We did it!" Parsifal bragged.

"Prove it."

Arthur stated, "Would we have this cauldron back from her clutches if she were still alive? Nay, she'd never gladly part with it."

"Aye," the brownie had to agree. "She was cruel." Then feeling safe, the furry creature ran off and was gone.

"What was that?" Parsifal asked.

"Is the cauldron clean now?" Arthur asked. "Was the brownie making our stews so rotten? Is his fur like a billy goat's hinder?"

Nimm shrugged, wondering, "How come we can boil the creature's fur with no effect on its feelings, but it won't be whipped?"

Arthur guessed, "Maybe because the brownie is such a secretive helper and hides during the day within the hearth? That's as hot as anything I can think of."

"Perhaps," Nimm said, "And leave it to that vile Pict witch to make a brownie into a curse, as she made everything else in this world so topsy-turvy."

Parsifal said, "The cauldron has been saved! Now we can finally say that the holy grail's been found! I'll forever be known as Parsifal the Grail Hunter!"

Arthur reminded him, "Baron Bearloin would *not* be pleased with that. That title doesn't remind everyone of where you came from and your father wants to be remembered too, remembered through you."

"I want to be remembered for *me*!" He sat down and rubbed his sore bare feet. "Oh who am I jesting? Nobody's remembered for long."

"Not even kings," Arthur agreed. "Merlin once said that kings are only remembered if something really bad happened. I'll surely be forgotten for all time the day after I'm dead, and the next king claims the land as his."

Chapter Twenty-one

Growing impatient in his mansion, Baron Bearloin traveled to the village to learn of the fate of his son, and in the greensward yelled at Rafe, "Where's my son! Where's Parsifal! He's to inherit! What kind of a village is only filled with children? And where's my son?"

"They haven't come back yet." Rafe shrugged. "You were just impatient and came to us before they could return."

Baron Bearloin admitted to Rafe, "I had to come. I had such a terrible visitation by a banshee. I fear for my son. I fear the banshee had forewarned me of his death!"

Rafe asked, "Are you sure it was a banshee that visited you? What's a banshee, really?"

"A creature from the highlands. A frightful creature. The highland place is from afar, up north, but the creature has wings and can travel. It can travel to my window."

Rafe looked around nervously. "Oh, there are frights anywhere."

"Nay, this was the worse I've ever seen. This is worse than when I was in the Roman battle and the dogs of hell came out at us and Mithra saved us with a midnight sun!"

"Huh?" At that comment, Rafe's eyes grew wide.

"Aye. This banshee is worse. I'll never sleep again."

Rafe questioned, "I don't know if I want to hear about it, if it's terrible?"

Baron Bearloin explained anyway, "It was a dark and windy night, when an odd *whooooshing* sound grew louder and louder until all the furniture rattled, and the servants ran to and fro but that didn't stop it, and then a horrible little woman creature flapped and scratched at the shutters. After she'd broken them away I saw her! She was horrible! I saw a bird with a deformed childlike body. She had long wild raven black hair, black cold eyes, and fangs coming down like two black bird beaks."

"That's horrible!" Rafe shuddered, hugging himself. "No one's seen anything like that around here, I'm sure."

"Because she's from the highlands, and she only visits important families to tell of an impending death. I was in the highlands for a while as a Roman Officer. My son was conceived there and he was born of a Scot, a new tribe that had just come over from Ireland and was pushing out the Picts better than we were. Every night, we'd hear a banshee cry and sure enough, a son or daughter of an important family would be dead within weeks."

Rafe asked, "Why does the banshee bother folks, so? How does she tell of impending death?"

"By making much noise," Baron Bearloin answered. "And last night I was shocked awake by a terrible screech and wail as the banshee attacked all the windows, and when she'd visited each and every window and scratched at them as if she'd tear them all out, she flew off in the night and all was silent. Even the wind died away and was gone."

"Why do you tell me such stories to frighten the wits out of me?"

"It's true. The banshee is a true thing."

Rafe said, "But she must have visited the wrong house, then."

"I hope. Not only is my son Parsifal brave, but he's fast to leap away from danger when he has the squirrel sense to be scared."

Rafe asked, "Is there any charm you can put on such a terrible creature to keep her away?"

Baron Bearloin grandly took out his claymore. "The only curse I know of is my sword."

Rafe nodded, impressed by the man's grand sword. "Aye. That would slay anything."

"The claymore is used by the Scottish Highlanders. When one once lopped my thin Roman sword in half, I was most impressed and decided I must have one for myself."

"How did you survive having your sword broken?"

"A good punch in the face with the pommel knob at the end of the hilt. That'll never break. And this is that very claymore that broke my old sword."

Most impressed, Rafe said, "You're so clever. You'll *never* be cut down!"

* * * * *

Traveling on to the abbey to seek word of his son, Baron Bearloin spotted a deformed little girl by the roadside. Her face was obscured under a shock of wild raven black hair, and she was washing blood out of his cape from a red puddle. First fearing he'd lost his cape, he reached behind him but he found that it was still on him, clean and dry. So then he had to wonder where the little creature got a cape exactly like his. "Ho there, wee one," he bellowed out. "Why are you washing blood out of a cape that's just like the one I have on?"

She replied in a squeaky little voice, "I'm washing blood from your cape because it's sad that you died."

"My cape is on my back. Why are you washing out that one?"

"Your blood stains it so, I can't get it out."

Baron Bearloin insisted, "I'm not bleeding and my cape is on my back."

"It's your cape," she answered. "And it's your blood."

"How can it be mine if I'm wearing it? And I'm not bleeding, I assure you, I'd know this!"

"I'm washing the blood from your cape a few moments from now; what you see is a vision of what will be."

Baron Bearloin asked, "How does my cape get blood on it?"

"Your stomach and liver are cut in two."

"That'd kill me, and I've made arrangements from the northern Gods that I'll live all the way my whole life long!"

"The northern Gods have sent you a banshee all the way from the highlands to take care of that worn out promise."

"Show me your face. I want to see who'd dare defy the Gods with blasphemy!" She lifted her head and pulled her hair away from her face and he saw that it was the crumpled face of a little old lady, but she had cold black eyes like a bird. Then she opened her mouth and he saw two fangs like bird beaks. A terrible sound came out of her mouth, shrieking and squealing loud enough to burn the hairs inside his ears.

"I'll not die!" Baron Bearloin yelled, pulling out his sword. "I'll chop off your hideous head and that'll be the end of you! And I'll display your head at the fair. How's that? To view such an ugly banshee head should fetch me many gold coins."

She shrieked louder, so violently that her hair shot up like a black bird's wings flapping in a quick fit to rearrange its feathers.

"Quiet, you meddlesome whelp!" He stomped toward her and swung his sword with perfect aim at her white candle-thin neck, but she was gone and there was nothing to strike, so he slipped on the edge of the puddle and fell on his sword, cutting this liver and stomach in two.

When he rolled over in agony, he saw that Opie the raven was where the banshee had been. "Opie? *You*? But my son loved you so!"

Opie walked up close to his face and hungrily cawed. As Baron Bearloin blacked-out he noticed how the banshee and the raven had the very same eyes. Before his breath had stilled, Opie hopped up on top of the old man, and with her fierce beak, she began to dine on the hot meat inside his splayed wound.

* * * * *

As soon as Arthur ceremoniously reinstated the cauldron to the town's greensward, and he finished telling the tale of its complicated rescue, a dozen armed Celtic soldiers and Roman centurions majestically rode large horses up to them. "We seek Arthur! We seek the new King!" They looked to Parsifal in hope.

"It's not me you seek," he corrected and pointed to Arthur. Then the warriors regarded Arthur with a bit of discontentment.

"The new King? Vortigern is dead?" Arthur asked, trying to make his shoulders seem wider. "And, aye, I'm Arthur, Vortigern's grandson."

"*You* drew the sword from the Coronation Stone?"

"Aye. It doesn't take strong arms to weld Excalibur, one just has to be in the great favor of Merlin and the Lady of the Lake." Arthur looked at his empty hands and badly wished he had the sword presently to show off.

The soldiers looked to each other in a moment of confusion, then adjusted their expectations and dutifully proclaimed, "Arthur is now King and must return to Gwynedd for the coronation. That'll assure great patriotism."

"What's patriotism?" Rafe asked Arthur.

"Merlin told me it was an odd feeling people get where they feel that their nation is best because they were born in it."

"Aye," Rafe agreed with a knowing smile. "I always felt in my heart that where I lived was best. It's all I know."

"We'll stay the night," the soldiers said, "and set off to escort Arthur to court first thing tomorrow at daybreak." Then they proceeded to take up a lot of space in their elaborate activities with their horses, tackle, and banners as they expropriated the barn.

Watching the soldiers and horses, off to the side, out of the way, with Arthur, Rafe, and Parsifal on a low fieldstone wall, Nimm asked Arthur, "How does one coronate a King? It sounds so thrilling."

"Aye, it is," Arthur said. "I'll be drunk and raced round about, carried high on a seat of shields, and all the lords of the land will shout out my name in affirmation, and a diadem of fine linen is to be tied about my head. And now that it's the nowtimes of Christendom, the new fashion is to pour sacred oil on the diadem, poured from a seashell. And we'll all shout out that Rome and Christendom and Druidom will unite in a holy trinity against the thieving Saxons and their vile northern ilk!"

"That sounds dreadful." Nimm made a ghastly face. "If you want to feel like the King of this land then you should first have a proper *traditional* coronation—druid only. Otherwise you'll end up a very confused king. We'll do it tonight!"

Arthur said, "You just want another party."

"Aye. A party. Before you get lost in the bog of a castle's court, its awful diplomacy, and before you mix all rituals together to make too many different people happy, you should celebrate your humble druid roots."

"Let *us* be the first to call you king." Parsifal nodded. "Aye? We're your true friends."

"Aye," Arthur smiled. "I'd value that more than any pompous show of royal shields of arms. And I'd like this party to be a long one. And the more parties, the better."

"And it's Samhain in a few days," Nimm reminded them. "Celtic New Year, forget the Roman calendar, I can't follow it anyway!"

"But, Mum," Rake said, "but we have no harvest of food to celebrate with."

"We have a new king for the land," Parsifal said. "And that's harvest enough!"

"Aye," Nimm agreed. "A fresh King and cauldron of plenty to bring back fertility. And just in time, because at this time of year the veil between the living and the dead is the thinnest."

Arthur asked, "So that all the dead people will watch us? I'd feel even more important then, to have such an ancient audience."

"Nay! Don't be silly," Nimm scolded him. "It has nothing to do with those who died before us. They're not watching us. They're happy and getting plump in Summerland. They're only thinking of themselves. The veil between the living and the dead is for us, alone, and we're very alone at this perilous time."

Arthur asked, "Dead people aren't watching us?"

"Nay. It's only about us. It's about seeing into the veil as far as we can, on this side if it, into our own coming death. At this time in the year we contemplate our own starvation. The seasons have been cruel. We adults will all be dead by Mayday, that's certain since we've had such a drought for so long now, but if O' Fortuna smiles on this village then all of our children will have health enough to be able to carry on with a new planting. And the oldest ones will frolic in the spring fields and beget new children. New life will rise."

Rafe wept. "Mum, you'll live!"

"One must eat to live," Nimm said. "And I'll not eat another bite, to save those shares of the seeds for the next spring planting."

"Nay, Mum!"

"Aye, and promise me that come spring you do what you must to make new babies grow so the village will live on."

"Nay, Mum!"

Arthur promised her, "As King, I'll order the Horned God to make it rain geese!"

Nimm looked up, put her hands guardedly out, and then chuckled, "My hair!"

"You won't die!" Rafe repeated. "Not ever!"

"We won't talk about it then," Nimm told him. "We'll only talk about heroic things because Arthur will be King."

"As the King," Parsifal asked Arthur, "can your first order be to change my name, to be corrected, to be *Parsifal the Grail Hunter*?"

"Aye, that's a name of action," Arthur agreed. "And someday you'll be a mighty knight."

Parsifal frowned. "But knights are thieving scoundrels that take all bounty from the land. I hate knights."

"That'll be my second order," Arthur decided, looking at the grand horses at the barn. "I'll get what we have, the new Church of nowtimes, and the growing number of lords, both as higgly-piggly as they all are, to conspire a new order of knighthood that does the opposite of what knights are now. I'll create an order of knights that aids in providing security for the land instead of such selfish land grabbing."

"Why?" Nimm asked.

"Why should the men with horses be such a nuisance when they could use such a mighty thing for the commonwealth."

Parsifal argued, "I've no idea how one would take on such brutes and make them kind. That's like asking the fox to share his meal with the wolf. It doesn't happen."

Arthur asked, "Are we all but mere foxes and wolves?"

Nimm nodded. "Aye!"

"Well," Arthur fumed, "I'll have to try *something* and desperately. It's far too savage out there to make a King prosperous. You're a few years older than me and you're clever. When I'll be the King,

I'll order you to help me think on it, and you'll be one of my first knights for right, I'm sure. That's it! Knights For Right!"

"Thanks for the warning," Parsifal said.

Arthur smiled. "What luck for me, O' Fortuna. A new kingdom of clever subjects to bring order like the Romans had it."

"*Better* than the Romans," Nimm stated. "It'll be the land of Camelot."

* * * * *

In the eventide greensward, Samhain fires were lit in tall pillars and the children of the proud village were all marched through the smoke, along with the cauldron, for another season's blessing. The smell reminded Arthur of marrying Merlin to Mother Hubbard while a town burned around them and he felt oddly comforted by that, making him feel passionate and powerful. Slipping into his shadow self for a moment, he said to Merlin, "I'm to be King and you'll be there to see it, even if you are only looking through my eyes."

When the first tower of sticks collapsed into a heap of coals, shimmering sparks swirled up like a tall roaring animal. The crowd shouted to Arthur, "Jump through the wall of creation as prince, come out of the wall of damnation as King!"

Nimm added, "Prince be nimble, prince be quick, prince come clean from the fire stick. Transform from boy to King, Fath-fith! Fath-fith transform, change form, forthwith!"

Arthur asked, "And what if my clothes set aflame?"

"That'd be considered a sign of bad luck," Nimm agreed, wincing to show that he'd better not catch on fire for the kingdom's sake.

Arthur pulled his raggedy tunic off and said, "I don't tempt O' Fortuna." He soaked it in a trough. With great effort he fought to put the dripping cloth back over him. Deliriously cold and shivering in the autumn bite, he raced at the fire and jumped through it, landing solidly on his feet on the other side. A wool blanket was wrapped around his shoulders. He cheered, "I'm King!"

"*Apples!*" Nimm exclaimed so loud it was easily heard above the cheering, "The cauldron is filled to the brim with apples!"

"Who put them there?" Rafe asked. "Did you do it Arthur? Thanks for the feast!"

"Nay, I've no apples to offer."

"It's a blessing!" Nimm wept with joy.

"Now you can eat," Rafe told his Mum.

"Nay," she cautioned. "It must be saved for the children to get them through the winter."

"Nay!" Arthur hollered. "It's the cauldron of plenty! No one will go hungry this winter!" He gave the cauldron a mighty push and tipped all the apples out onto the ground. When he set the cauldron back upright again, it was refilled to the brim with plump red apples anew.

"A miracle!" They all shouted.

All but Nimm. She didn't seem convinced that one apple pile was enough to get them all through the winter, so Arthur tipped the cauldron and spilled its contents yet again, and when he set the cauldron back upright, it was filled to the top for a third time.

The spilled apples were picked up from the ground and carefully stored away in barn barrels, and then everyone lined up in their order and took one apple from the cauldron, and then lined up again to take two, and then lined up again to take three, and the cauldron was bottomless and they had apples unending until spring, with apples to spare, and not a soul—man, woman, bird or squirrel—perished in that village that entire winter.

Visit
StoneGarden.net Publishing Online!

You can find us at: www.stonegarden.net.

News and Upcoming Titles
New titles and reader favorites are featured each month, along with information on our upcoming titles.

Author Info
Author bios, blogs and links to their personal websites.

Contests and Other Fun Stuff
A forum to keep in touch with your favorite authors, autographed copies and more!

LaVergne, TN USA
11 August 2010
192944LV00001B/18/P